THE SAND CASTLE

THE SAND CASTLE

K. S. HOLLENBECK

FIVE STAR
A part of Gale, a Cengage Company

GALE
A Cengage Company

LIBRARY OF CONGRESS CATALOGING-IN-PUBLICATION DATA

Names: Hollenbeck, K. S., author.
Title: The sand castle / K. S. Hollenbeck.
Description: First edition. | Farmington Hills, Mich: Five Star, a
    part of Gale, a Cengage Company 2020.
Identifiers: LCCN 2019049257 | ISBN 9781432868543 (hardcover)
Classification: LCC PS3608.O484568 S26 2020 | DDC 813/.6—
    dc23
LC record available at https://lccn.loc.gov/2019049257

First Edition. First Printing: June 2020
Find us on Facebook—https://www.facebook.com/FiveStarCengage
Visit our website—http://www.gale.cengage.com/fivestar
Contact Five Star Publishing at FiveStar@cengage.com

Printed in Mexico
Print Number: 01   Print Year: 2020

THE SAND CASTLE

CHAPTER ONE

Flossie Abbot, the once celebrated Flame of San Francisco, resisted the urge to climb into the barrel of water behind the mess hall. Tempting as it might be, it was most certainly against the rules. And she'd rather be mercilessly hot than risk a visit to the Snake Den.

Instead, she lifted the rusted ladle and spooned the murky liquid into a tin cup that was chained to the lip of the large barrel. Lukewarm and gritty with sand, the water nevertheless eased the red rash that was her throat. Thirstier than she thought, for she was always thirstier than she first believed, she didn't stop to breathe and gulped the water until she couldn't swallow any more, and it pooled in her mouth and streamed down her dusty chin.

She always waited too long to drink from the barrel, and she supposed it was because the relief brought a brief moment of pleasure in an otherwise steady inlet of dread. That this pleasure had to be prefaced with the suffering of thirst didn't dissuade her.

The landscape, earlier a blur with her thirst having such grip, cleared. And she watched the few guards pacing on the catwalk fifty or so yards to her right from her place in the women's bullpen. To her left was the men's, separated from her own by a twenty-foot rock wall topped with barbed wire. Gila Territorial was one of the first prisons to figure out that the wire could stop more than cattle.

Yet that's what she'd become. If she considered it, she was less than livestock. She was nothing here. Nothing but a number. With that thought, Flossie scooped more water into the cup and poured it over her head. But with her thick, ginger hair so matted, the dampness failed to reach her scalp, and the tangled locks absorbed the water as quickly and efficiently as the cacti sopped up the rare rain.

The water served to wake her in that startled way a nightmare or nightmarish reality did. The realization that here she would be, and here she would stay. Unlike the days spent in jail before her trial, she had no more decisions to make, no more thoughts or plans on how justice could be served, no idea what might happen after she completed her sentence, or if she'd even live long enough to worry about life beyond Gila. She didn't know which was better. The nightmare of the here and now. The dust. The heat. The thirst. The work. The filth. The confinement. The shame and utter lack of dignity. Or before, when she had some hope left. Her hope had started strong and large as a forest. Judson Horner couldn't do this to her. Impossible. He was a treacherous and brutal murderer, and the judge and jury would surely come to understand the truth. As the trial went on, this hope withered. She was a harlot, an *adulteress*. A woman who had everything and tossed it all, including a loving husband, in the trash.

Before Flossie could pity herself further, she heard the unmistakable timbre of Emma's sing-song voice. "I'm out."

Flossie swung from her thoughts and squinted at the sun hovering swollen and sickly behind her cellmate, who was thinner and more bedraggled than she'd been before being tossed into the den.

"Five days up already?" Flossie asked.

"Snake Den can't snuff out a ray of sunshine like me." Emma twirled her filthy, brown skirt around one bony wrist. " 'Sides, I was a very good girl. Slept, mostly. Guards thought I deserved to be pulled on out cuz of my good behavior." She held one finger up to her lips, as if telling a secret.

Flossie felt torn at the sight of her cellmate. Having the space to herself was far better than sharing with the garrulous Emma. But the Snake Den had killed many. Though she could only guess at what Emma meant by saying she slept *mostly*, she was pleased Emma had at least survived.

Flossie ladled and poured more water over her head.

"That water ain't gonna help that weedy hair of yours," Emma said, all rabbity.

Flossie held out a clump of her strands for inspection. That her once lustrous hair had become so knotted vexed her almost as much as the heat.

"Could just clip it," Emma suggested. "Ask the dentist. He's savage as a meat axe. Likes to chop things off."

"Well, he won't be allowed to chop on my hair."

"Won't be cutting on mine, neither. Need it to measure my time in here. I figure it grows about six inches a year, and I don't plan on letting it get past the middle of my back."

Emma started coughing and leaping around, a cold film gleaming on her head.

"You feeling well enough to dance?" Flossie asked.

Emma licked her lips and spoke the next words as if she were eating them. "White dragon. Can't stop the cravings. If I get to moving around, that prickly feeling goes away."

"Then you mustn't let Mr. Crandall visit. He gives you any more, you will surely have the devil as a cellmate instead of me."

"Wasn't careful, is all. Crandall slipped me the little pouch, and I should've stashed it right off, saved it for bad times. Plumb daft to smoke it the very day Crandall had his visit. What with the guards watching and expecting such things." Emma waved her arms toward the catwalk and almost fell to the ground. "Hot day like this would've been just right if I'd held onto it. Just a little smoke on a day like this, I wouldn't even be noticing the heat. This air here, this dang hateful sun, would become a warm glow of fairy dust stretching into my limbs, turning me into a cool, twinkling star. And I mean the kind in the sky, Flossie, not folks like you."

"Gets hotter," Jo said, approaching the pair.

The older woman snatched the ladle up and scooped just enough water to quench her thirst, not a drop more or less. In her life before Gila, Flossie had been called theatrical. Jo Brown was clearly the opposite. Unlike her own mind's meanderings, Jo didn't affect hand movements to emphasize her point, didn't seem to worry about elocution and pronunciation, and did not spare a minute on her appearance. Her small frame was topped with a brown face piped with wrinkles. Flossie didn't know if Jo was Mexican or Indian or African or White. Nor did she know her real age, only that Jo had been at Gila Territorial Prison for the past seven years.

"Give it another week or two," Jo said. "That's when the big heat settles down hard. Save your gripes for the big heat. You'll be needing them."

"I reckon I got enough gripes for now and later," Emma said.

Jo grunted her disapproval, and Flossie let her gaze wander toward the great Colorado, moving past the prison as swiftly as it could. She envied those travelers on the barges and steamboats but envied the river more. Half a mile wide, she longed for its cool ripples and fierce currents. Being a current in the river would be preferable to this life of heat and boredom, of nothing to wake for or gladly anticipate. Just dread day after day, and sometimes not even that. Just no feeling at all.

Appearing gray and clammy, Emma grasped Flossie's sleeve and held on. "Sorry," she said. "It's the goddamn heat. Can't hardly bear it today."

"That's cause you been down in the Snake Den," Jo said. "Sun's gonna bother anyone who been down there."

"How'd you know?" Emma said. "You ain't never been."

"Can't be good living in the dark, else the good Lord would've had us seeing colors at night instead of the day."

Emma glanced around vacantly, as if for a moment she'd forgotten where she was.

"You got the eyes of a mole," Jo said. "Gotta work your way back to the living."

Emma, pale and swoopy, drifted away toward the women's cellblock, not bothering to hear the last of Jo's sentence.

"Sand Castle ain't too terrible," Jo said. "I'm thinking there's places out there that would make hell look like a cool stream. I sure am."

Flossie heard picks chipping away at granite. "I imagine it *is* hell for those men."

"Don't be fretting about those in the quarries," Jo said, then scowled.

"One of them died last week." Flossie swallowed, noticing how thirsty she still was. "Dropped his pick and collapsed, toppled to the earth like a felled tree. Wilhelmina told me."

"Wilhelmina said that part about the tree?"

"That's just how I imagined it."

Jo nodded, as if approving of the description. "How'd she hear?"

"The prisoner with the white teeth and clean uniform sneaks letters to her."

"That convict is going to land himself in the den or worse," Jo said. "He know what Wilhelmina did to land herself at Gila?"

"Wilhelmina swears she didn't do it how they said. Says it was an accident."

Jo scooped up another cup of water and gulped it down.

11

"Can't be cutting out your lover's heart and throwing the mess in his dead face and calling it an accident. That don't happen by accident."

Jo's logic was sound. Still, the details of Wilhelmina's manslaughter case seemed exaggerated.

"Did she tell you anything else about the man in the quarries?"

"No."

"She didn't say nothing about the teeth chattering or the drooling and wetting on himself?"

Flossie winced as Jo cracked her leathery knuckles.

"Don't be getting yourself full on pity for that man, Flossie. That fellow who got the heat sickness did his business with the young daughter of his new wife."

Her stomach turned. "That why he's here?"

"All I know is that the good Lord saw to it that the fiend who was her husband got his comeuppance."

Flossie reached to scratch her scalp. Jo didn't believe in much, but she believed in her good Lord's justice. It was always the good Lord, as if there were another Lord, a bad one, who might be causing all the trouble.

"You might have the nits," Jo advised. "You should visit the infirmary."

"I wouldn't want them to cut my hair."

"Get Armando Madrigal to rub in some of that potion he's got for such things."

"What's in it?"

"Don't know. Said to be best for killing nits." Jo's tongue, the size of an apricot pit, shifted around behind her cheek.

Flossie wiped her brow and looked away. It pained her that Armando Madrigal, a Mexican doctor turned revolutionary, was wasting away at Gila. As she saw it, an entertainer like herself didn't add much value to the world. A doctor, however, was needed. Especially a good doctor like Armando.

"Time to start supper," Jo announced, glancing down at the barrel's shadow. With their footsteps stirring up clouds of red dust, Flossie trailed Jo down a worn path to the side door of the mess hall, which was broad and painted a dark yellow, where the guard, Christ H., was waiting for them. Flossie had heard he was called Christ H. due to a former guard with the same first name. No one remembered what the H stood for. After crushing his hand-rolled cigarette with the heel of his black book, he used a key from his fat ring to let them inside.

Jo squinted disapprovingly at the colossal cast-iron stove before laying a palm on it. "Why ain't my stove lit?"

"Ramon's been released," Christ H. said, yawning.

Jo pursed her wrinkled lips and scowled. "Who'll be lighting our stove, then? Fetching our wood? Plucking my chickens?"

"You got Flossie, here," Christ H. mumbled.

"Flossie's got her hands full already," Jo snapped.

Flossie tied an apron over her dress. Though male prisoners were outfitted in the traditional black and whites, women were allowed to bring along one dress, which is what they wore day after day as a prison uniform, washing it only once per week when they also got to bathe. Hence, the brown cotton of her skirts was so utterly soiled, the apron was not meant as a buffer against splatters of food; instead, it protected the food from the filthy garment.

Every night, she and Emma shook the dust from their threadbare clothes and then climbed onto their thin, straw-stuffed mattresses. These were provided for the women but not the men, who slept on a blanket atop a narrow metal bunk. Flossie knew she should feel as grateful as Emma was for the mattress, but prior to being arrested and jailed, she'd only ever slept on goose down. Though this fact wasn't something she'd ever share with Emma.

It took her months to adjust to the straw, but the dust was worse. Pervasive. Constant. Every surface powdered with filth within seconds of being wiped clean. Despite her and Emma's crusade against it, dust clung to their skin and clouded their hair. Flossie would find it in her food, eyes, nose, and mouth. Her first few days at Gila, Flossie thought she might go mad from the dust. Now it was part of her, almost like another, albeit grittier, layer of skin.

"How did a soft man like Ramon land himself at the Sand Castle?" Flossie asked.

"Mayhem," Christ H. answered.

Flossie questioned this because Ramon rarely spoke, nor did he ever make sudden movements. He was the antithesis of mayhem, far as Flossie could tell.

"Once," Jo said, "he asked me what that word meant. Wondered why he'd be asking such a thing." Jo opened the stove, inspecting it for even half-burnt logs. "Empty," she huffed.

Christ H. wandered over and peeked inside.

Jo looked up at him, hands on board-straight hips. "Mr. Christ H.," she said, "we'll be needing someone to keep our stove lit. Else the prisoners will be supping on cold stew."

"Perhaps," Flossie said, "our Ramon in his absence will finally be guilty of mayhem."

As he fiddled with his shaggy muttonchops, Christ H. seemed to consider Jo's request. Regardless, the lame guard did nothing to salve the precarious situation. With his left leg nearly useless, Christ H. wasn't quick to help with anything, except to feed or pet the three prison hounds that seemed like Christ H.'s closest companions.

Within weeks of Flossie's arrival, Emma had delighted in telling her how the superintendent's wife, Agnes, had accidentally shot up the guard's leg. A few years before, four convicts had managed to swipe one guard's rifle and were headed out the sally port when Mrs. Samuels decided to stop all the nonsense by climbing the tower and manning the multi-barreled Gatling. She shot to death all the escapees, becoming a hero in the Arizona Territory. Unfortunately, she also killed a twenty-one-year-old guard and shot four prisoners who hadn't been involved in hatching the plot. They all lived but with egregious injuries, including disfiguring burns and amputated limbs. She'd also crippled the startled Christ H., who had simply been trying to ease the suffering of the gunned-down guard.

Now Christ H. wore the look of perpetual exhaustion, eyes that retreated like shadows over barren and gaunt cheekbones the shape of aging headstones. He apathetically watched as the women stirred last night's stew, hoping to break down some of its fat. With his bad leg, Christ H. had become a guard in the true sense of the word. He hunkered here or there, watching and guarding, but did little else except care for and have long conversations with the dogs. Whether due to his misery or not, Flossie knew that Christ H. believed wholeheartedly in the institution's novel philosophy of autonomy. For here at Gila Territorial Prison, prisoners did every scrap of work, from repairing the gates that kept them inside to burying their own dead.

It wasn't merely Christ H. who believed in this philosophy; so did the territory of Arizona. Gila's first convicts built the prison with their own hands. As some murderers forced victims to dig their own graves, those unlucky first prisoners were ordered to carve out their own granite cells and erect adobe walls that would keep them from all they loved and yearned for. In this spirit of self-reliance, the facility hired no outside help besides the superintendent and the guards, so every inmate was assigned work details. Flossie's assignment, upon her arrival six months prior, had been the mess hall. Since her first days at the penitentiary, she'd been helping Jo prepare the meals and then serving those same meals to the convicts.

Today was no different. Within an hour, Flossie was wordlessly spooning dollops of stringy chicken stew, which was both cold and laced with hardened lard, into the prisoners' wooden bowls. A line of bone-tired men in baggy black and whites stretched and coiled out the door like an odd caterpillar. The few women housed at the facility were to wait in their cells until the men finished eating. Emma often griped about how hungry the wait was and wondered why they couldn't eat together and whined that it wasn't fair and nagged the guards considerably about being starved and having to eat cold doings and rattled on about how she wouldn't mind talking to a few men now and then.

Flossie did mind. She considered Emma fortunate to be separated from the men on nearly all occasions. Barring the occasional visitor, Flossie, Jo, and the superintendent's wife, Agnes, were the only women with direct exposure to the male prisoners. This put the men in a dangerous mind. Men needed women, Flossie knew, for the men she fed day after day soaked her up with their eyes, leaving her dry as dirt.

Despite the stares, most inmates, done in from working the quarries, meekly shuffled past her. Even tonight, what with the food so unappetizing, they held out their bowls and gratefully accepted their ration without complaint, eventually moving toward one of the dozen or so long tables. But there were those few who stopped long enough to leer, licking their lips, hungry for something else. Their eyes were slippery fingers pinching her underneath her dress, and Flossie felt violated by the time she'd filled their bowls.

Flossie had sung, acted, and danced in front of at least ten thousand miners and cowboys before she'd arrived at Gila Territorial, so this type of ogling wasn't a novelty. But these men differed. They weren't merely separated from the fairer sex by distance; these men were separated by law.

Even so, each had his turn to stand directly across from her, a butcher-block table the only barrier, her only weapon a wooden ladle.

When one prisoner stopped to complain, Jo stepped in with her blunt advice: "Could be air! Or you could be eatin' dirt, mind you."

The prisoner moved along, for most wouldn't sass Jo. She fed them, and, though she'd been advised by the superintendent to coat all the prisoners' meals with saltpeter to prevent sodomites from carrying out their "nefarious activities," she'd refused.

"Few sodomites is better than a few stabbings," she proclaimed. " 'Sides, they'll be up to that business with or without the saltpeter. Might as well make the fixings tasty."

She did, too. Jo made the most of the meager ingredients, almost all of which were grown or raised by Jo, herself. The prisoners—and the guards—acknowledged and appreciated her for it. If there was one woman who could coast safely through most sections of the prison, it was Jo. The meals she prepared, most downright delicious, offered the only moments of pleasure in the inmates' largely unbearable lives.

The other female prisoners cleaned and mended and washed. Some knit doilies, which were then sold for profit in the nearby town of Ocotillo. On her first day in Gila, Flossie confessed to the superintendent that she had not one iota of experience when it came to domestic chores. She didn't knit, mend, wash, nor cook. Because her father had been one of the wealthiest bankers in San Francisco, she'd always been sheltered from such things. Even the New England boarding school she'd attended failed to teach her anything practical. She and the other privileged students learned world history, Latin, French, and music. Whereas other girls her age studied sewing and embroidery, laying the foundation for their lives as wives and mothers, she was reading Homer and Ovid and studying Ptolemy. Her later life as a stage star only augmented the level of pampering to which she'd become accustomed.

After her parents' deaths—her father's heart attack and her mother's subsequent suicide—Flossie moved back to San Francisco from New England. Her parents had always been inseparable, their only daughter more of an impediment to their great affair than an extension of their love. Their deaths brought a dull obligation of grief, more as if distant relatives had died.

Returning to the city, however, had its benefits. With its thriving theatre, Flossie set out to become San Francisco's greatest actress. That she could sing anything from opera to ballads eased her passage onto the stage. Her mother, in one of their rare conversations, had insisted that Flossie's social status prevented her from mingling with such riff-raff. "A life in the theatre is for girls from a lower station," her mother had said after Flossie had expressed an early interest. With their deaths, however, she changed her name from Florence (named after the city where her parents had honeymooned) to Flossie. Already somewhat well known as an heiress, landing plumb roles and securing venues in which to sing was easier for her than it was for other aspiring actresses. And the profound fame that followed offered comforts and advantages that even Flossie had not previously experienced.

Comforts she'd likely never experience again.

The superintendent had stared at the ceiling after Flossie announced her utter ignorance of all possible "jobs" at the prison. He seemed at a loss. So was she. She prided herself on being prepared for work, always insisting her costumes be custommade by the best designers and seamstresses. As if it were a small helpless child, she mollycoddled her voice. Too, she studied her roles and memorized her lines weeks before the other cast members. But she certainly hadn't prepared herself for life at Gila Territorial Prison.

"We'll give you to old Jo," Samuels had finally decided. "She'll straighten you out."

Thus, Flossie had come to Jo, who had complained under her breath when Flossie informed her that she'd never used a knife or even boiled water. But she quickly earned the woman's respect through hard work and persistence. She did all her chores in the kitchen with care and vigor, not for the prison or the other inmates, but for Jo, who had been the first person in months to treat her like a human being. Best of all, Jo was the only person who had no interest in her fame or scandalous fall from grace.

It turned out that Jo was the only advantage to the kitchen assignment, for the actual work was excruciating. The outdated cast-iron stove put forth a formidable and suffocating heat, and the two women took turns stepping out for fresh air, lest they faint. At least tonight, without the stove lit, the heat had dissipated, but Flossie could feel a different sort of fever generated by the prisoners.

Eyes downcast, she scooped and poured the gelatinous stew, rationing just enough for each inmate.

"Gracias," Roberto, the next in line, said. He palmed his bowl and inched toward a long table to eat. The squat, black-eyed Roberto always thanked Flossie before sitting and bowing over his food to say grace. Before every meal, Roberto prayed for a good five minutes or more. These prayers took so long, the others were typically finished before Roberto had even begun eating.

Flossie spotted Kane two men down behind Edmund Townsend. Edmund had a kind, handsome face and bright eyes. He was the only convict she'd make eye contact with on a regular basis. His smile rivaled some of the leading men she'd worked with before Gila. She didn't know why the polite and quick-to-laugh Edmund was here, but his sentence kept being drawn out due to escape attempts. He held the record for trying to escape. He'd climbed the wall, went missing from the quarries, tried to swim the Colorado, and once feigned insanity and was shipped off to a Phoenix asylum for a month before being pronounced sane and promptly returned to Gila.

Kane was as rancorous as Edmund was affable, and she dreaded having to serve him the cold meal. He was finicky about the best of Jo's creations, and nearly every night he had to be placated for one reason or another. His many stints in the Dark Hole, though he'd been at the prison a shorter time than Flossie, did little to quench his wickedness. She hadn't been told what Kane's crime or crimes had been, but Flossie was certain they were bad enough to lock Kane in Gila for the rest of his days. Kane behaved as if he had nothing left to lose.

Now Kane stood across her, his features as pink and shiny as a freshly skinned animal. His hair, coal black and the consistency of catgut, nearly dunked into the stew with its length. Flossie delicately pulled the pot toward her to avoid this contamination.

After she'd ladled the correct portion into his dish, he sniffed around. "No biscuits?"

Flossie didn't answer. And it wasn't because she wasn't allowed to speak to the male prisoners.

"I'll be having my biscuits."

Flossie looked to Christ H. for help, but he was occupied with two inmates—one Chinese, the other Mexican—who were heatedly arguing over a place to sit. One shouted in Mandarin, the other in Spanish. Christ H. looked baffled and simply started shouting back in English.

Three other guards were strategically positioned around the mess hall: Philip Rodgers, gruff and likely to club any inmate who moved from line; Oliver Muldoon, hardly an authoritarian but fair; and Breen Dwyer, a lanky young rookie who'd been hired shortly after Flossie's internment.

The rules stated that prisoners were to move swiftly past Flossie, so it didn't take but a few moments for the long-legged Dwyer to notice Kane holding up the line. With gratitude, Flossie watched the guard cross the breadth of the room.

"That'll be all, Kane," Dwyer said.

"I'll have my goddamn biscuits," Kane growled.

Jo had been ignoring the unpleasant exchange, concentrating on preparing the batter for tomorrow's breakfast of corn bread.

"You got my biscuits, old woman?" Kane shouted to her back.

Measuring and pouring corn meal, Jo didn't bother turning around. "Just take your stew and set on down. You ain't the only one who'll be missing out on my biscuits. This ain't no country club."

"Find yourself a table," Dwyer said, his jaw clenched and grinding.

"This cunt will give me a biscuit." He jabbed a short, fatty finger at Flossie. "Or I might have to bite off one of her fingers to dip in my stew. I like to have something to dip. Might be a biscuit or might be something off this bitch." He smiled, showing a bottom row of abnormally sharp teeth.

Flossie saw Breen Dwyer's eyes glint his ire and harden to silver coins. Plunging toward Kane with an agile swoop, the guard twisted the convict's arm and bent Kane's fingers backwards. One swift knee to the scrotum, and Kane was down, the contents of his wooden bowl crisscrossing the black and white vertical stripes on his shirt, the bowl broken in half at his feet.

A sliver of chicken skin dangled from Kane's hair while Dwyer lifted the scruff of the convict's shirt, dragged him to a table, and roughly shoved him onto a bench.

21

Flossie could make out Dwyer's threat about the Snake Den and saw that Kane had relented and stilled. Another inmate, sure to be one of Kane's underlings, quickly offered up his own helping. Dwyer shook his head, slid the bowl back down the table, and returned to Flossie.

Dwyer knelt and with a bare hand scooped chunks of spilled stew from the floor, tossing what he could into one half of the broken bowl, along with bits of dirt, dust, and sandy pebbles that the prisoners had tracked in. He strode back to Kane's table and jammed the concoction under Kane's chin.

"Thank the lady," the guard demanded.

Kane offered only a slight grin.

Dwyer gritted his teeth. "Reckon you have less than a second to show your good manners."

Dwyer waited several seconds before hooking a long arm around Kane's neck and squeezing. "You *will* thank her," he growled.

At this suggestion, Kane dug his teeth into Dwyer's arm, which caused the young guard to flinch, releasing Kane's neck. In an instant, Kane clutched the edges of the long table in front of him and upended it. Stew now streamed down countless faces and necks, and several prisoners began cursing Kane while wiping chunks of white fat and cold cooked carrots from their uniforms.

"Next time, they'll light my stove," Jo said to Flossie. "Remember the last fit Kane threw?"

Flossie shook her head.

"Next day, the fella who done the angering was found choked to death on his own unmentionables. A man doesn't choke on his own britches. They was stuffed halfway down his throat."

Flossie paled as she watched all four guards, even the ordinarily indifferent Christ H., wrestle Kane to the ground.

"That man's always had the devil," Jo said above the noise.

"The good Lord don't want nothing to do with him. He done let him be."

With that, she returned to her batter, cracking an egg on the edge of the counter before stirring faster than the wind. Meanwhile, Christ H. and Rodgers hauled the writhing Kane out of the mess hall, dragging him off for yet another stay in the Snake Den.

With Dwyer having his bite checked in the infirmary, Superintendent Thaddeus Samuels joined Muldoon in the task of guarding the other prisoners. Both gripped their government-issued Marlin rifles, while Flossie, hands trembling, continued dishing up the cold supper.

Jo came from behind the counters and tables to approach the superintendent. She'd need her stove lit by tomorrow morning, she said, so he'd best send her a new helper, and she wouldn't have anything to do with a fellow like Kane. Give her Roberto, she said. Nice polite fella who didn't hold up the line with his swearing and demands. A God-fearing man like Roberto would do.

The superintendent agreed, conceding that the grief of cold food would be coming from more than Jo if he didn't acquiesce.

Flossie scraped the remaining chunks of stew into bowls for the women. And, eventually, after the last man left the mess hall, the hungry and irritable women—six in total—tromped in. Emma, Wilhelmina, Rosa, Berthalea, Mabel, and sixteen-year-old Jesus-Marie, who shot and killed her brother because, as she put it, she was tired of him telling her what to do. Berthalea, who helped hide some outlaws in her house, had been pregnant when sent to the prison. She'd had her baby boy, George, inside. Now George was two years old and officially the youngest inmate. Most the women doted on little George, all but Mable, who had no interest in children and claimed to be

23

as tough and wicked as any man and much better on a horse. Mable's job at Gila, in fact, was to care for the horses in the stable.

Rosa was either always complaining, laughing, or singing. The only time the boisterous woman was quiet was when she slept. Still, she talked so much, they'd eventually given her a cell to herself. This didn't stop her, though. Rosa would shout out objections and observations to the cell next door, or even to the guards, and wouldn't stop until someone responded. Now she was complaining about the cold stew. Flossie didn't mind. She would have been shocked if Rosa hadn't carped and moaned. Still, it didn't do any good. Her own elbow stung from feeding so many, but she wouldn't mention it to Rosa, Jo, or even Emma.

She was glad the women ate so quickly. After the last woman finally left, a half hour or so after they'd entered, Flossie lifted the heavy, cast-iron pot and heaved it toward the two washtub-sized basins attached to the back wall.

Jo helped her ease it into the basin, and the two wiped their food-caked hands on their stiff aprons.

"Sure went fast, heated or not," Jo reached into a cupboard and pulled out two pork chops. "From two nights ago." She grinned mischievously.

Ravenous, Flossie took a chop and started gnawing.

Jo, too, bit down and began chewing with the few molars she'd managed to keep.

Between bites, Flossie said, "Delicious. No wonder they won't let you out of here. The prisoners and guards would undoubtedly starve."

"Wouldn't have no place to go, no how."

"Why sure you would." Flossie wished she could tell Jo that she could come and live with her, that they could travel together from town to town, and that it would be a life to love, how she would meet so many people and hear so many stories, and all the while the earth would keep moving, but they'd be moving faster than the earth, so Jo wouldn't even notice it spinning.

Along with her reverie, Flossie tossed her bone into the giant bin of trash.

"You're wasting the marrow. Best part of the chop, I'm thinking. Just cut it in two." She swung her meat cleaver into the center of the bone. "Now suck it on out."

Jo made a big production of sucking out the marrow, as if all day she'd been looking forward to this one amusement.

Flossie stared at the meat cleaver. "Why is it they trust us with that?"

"I got no plan on cutting anyone's head open, and you don't either."

True. Flossie wouldn't be killing anyone with any sort of weapon. But Samuels didn't know this. After all, a man had died because of her. That's what the prosecution kept claiming at her trial. The jury was convinced he'd be alive if it wasn't for her behavior. And they were right, Flossie decided. Matty's death was her fault. No matter that Judson Horner had pulled the trigger.

As if reading Flossie's thoughts, Jo said, "It's true we're both killers."

"I'm not a killer. I am an adulteress. And adultery, according to many, is worse than murder. Still, I might be able to kill now. There is one man in particular I would like to see meet his maker in the grisliest of manners."

"That man Kane? The guards will handle him."

"I'm not talking about Kane."

Jo raised her brows. "Well, I am a killer. Didn't have time or energy for the business you got up to. One man was enough to handle. I did kill one man. And I'd do it again. But the man who died by my hands went softly toward the good Lord. I didn't rush at him with knives and cleavers and such."

Flossie had turned away and begun to scrub the kettle when Oliver Muldoon poked his rather large baby face into the kitchen.

"What you need, Muldoon?" Jo asked.

Flossie remained astonished at the dictatorial way Jo spoke to the guards and even the superintendent.

"Was just wondering if you had any of them chops to spare." Muldoon was from the deepest part of South Carolina, his drawl so thick that Flossie often couldn't understand what the young guard was saying.

"You think I'd part with an extra chop if I had one?" Jo asked.

"I think you might, ma'am, knowin' how much I love them chops of yours."

Jo's lined face sprang into a smile. She pulled a chop from the cupboard and handed it over to the rosy-cheeked man. "Saved it just for you." She patted his cheek, and Muldoon thanked her before returning to the dining area satisfied.

"I suppose they don't have much to fear from you, Jo," Flossie said.

"Muldoon's different," she said. "He's young and too tender to be doing this kind of work. I gotta watch out for him."

Jo, with no children of her own, treated Muldoon as if he were her son. And Muldoon reciprocated. It was one of the stranger relationships Flossie had observed at the penitentiary, but also one of the purest.

"We'll need this kettle for tomorrow's eggs." Flossie vigorously scrubbed the residual clumps of stew sticking to the bottom of the pot like horse glue.

"Sure will," Jo said. "The good Lord willing."

CHAPTER TWO

It took all Breen Dwyer's will to keep from slamming his rifle butt on the louse-ridden heads of the three convicts lined up in the yard. He'd caught them trying to scale an adobe wall near the mess hall. All he'd gotten out of the men so far was that Abe Kane had used Rodgers's keys to open their cell, and that's how they'd gotten out.

Rodgers was the meanest of the Gila Territorial guards. Still, he wasn't mean enough to have his head cut nearly clean off. The other guard who'd been escorting Kane to the Dark Hole was still with the living despite an egg-sized knot on his head. Dwyer was glad for that. Christ H. was lazier than most guards, but the man had welcomed him like family when he first hired on.

It rankled Dwyer that the superintendent had ordered most guards to hunt for Kane outside the prison but charged him and Muldoon to stay behind. He'd rather be out with the others but was stuck in here with this scraggly bunch and the hounds. As the guards charged out the sally port, the dogs hung back and seemed more interested in nipping each other's necks. To Dwyer, they didn't seem worth their feed. They were supposed to be sniffing out the escapee. So far, they'd only succeeded in rooting out a baby rabbit who'd attempted to dive into its warren under the guard shack before the mangiest of the three caught, thrashed, and ate it whole.

With Muldoon training his Marlin rifle on the three in the

27

yard, Dwyer went to fetch J. J. Ferguson. Ferguson was just a kid but had the sense to stay in the cell after Kane opened it. In for burglary, the boy was smart enough not to waste his work credits.

"Where would Kane get to?" Dwyer asked them. "That's the only question you men have to answer. Answer that, and you might be spending fewer days than all eternity in the Snake Den."

Jacob Hoddle spoke first. "Just came and freed us, then pulled foot. That's all we know. I was sound asleep, first time in a week. Can't sleep much with Kane's snores. When the gate opened, thought I might as well make a run for it. Thought it might be God setting us free. Far be it for me to ignore an answered prayer."

The yard reeked of kerosene from the lamp he'd lit, the shadows of the men tangling. "Would've been smarter to stay in your cell where you belong."

The men kept quiet.

"Listen good," he kept on. "If one of you is roaming free as a roadrunner, the rest of you will suffer for it. Kane will be living the high life, and you all, one by one, will be chained in the pit. If you survive, you'll find a few more years tacked onto your stay at the Sand Castle. Don't seem right, does it?"

"No sir," Jacob said.

Jacob Hoddle wasn't the worst of them, far as Dwyer could tell. Wasn't the best but wasn't the worst. Besides, Jacob had something broken in his brain. One day, he'd be weeping like a baby goat, sobbing and threatening to kill himself with a spoon at supper; the next, he'd be bounding all over the bullpen like a jackrabbit, tussling with the other prisoners, talking fast as fire. Jacob wouldn't sleep when those moods struck. And when Jacob didn't sleep, Dwyer had learned that cell eleven would be up for trouble. The man would take to yakking until morning. It didn't surprise him that Kane had twice tried to strangle the old coot.

"It's a curiosity," Dwyer said.

"What is?" Jacob asked.

"That you'd risk more time at Gila and all your work credits forfeited to protect a man who tried two times to kill you."

"Three times. Once wasn't reported."

"Why'd you protect such a man?"

"Not protecting nobody," Jacob swore. "Kane just up and left."

Dwyer approached the old man and held his lamp up to Jacob's lined and whiskered face. Then he shifted his attention, considering that Jacob likely wasn't smart enough to cover up Kane's escape. Jacob had tried to rob two stagecoaches and got nothing but a busted nose and four years in Gila for his efforts. Christ H. had told him the story about how the first coach was empty, save for an echo and the driver. Jacob had tried to swipe the driver's beef jerky and had his nose broken for his efforts. His next attempt as a highwayman was an even bigger failure. This time, the two travelers refused Jacob their watches and coins. And Jacob, in a desperate move, fired the one bullet he could afford into the air, intending to scare the men out of their valuables. They'd only laughed at him before wrestling him to the ground and tying him up with butcher's twine. Embarrassing enough to be tied up with rope, but they'd been able to contain Jacob Hoddle with string.

He paced down the line, past Pike and Quanto, two men with less conscience between them than a common housefly. He eased past the stuttering J.J. and felt the pain of pity for the boy.

"Stars sure are pretty tonight," Jacob said. "Might be worth getting punished to be able to see all these stars. Can't see stars from the cell."

"Not the stars I'm thinking on. It's Kane," Dwyer said. "We got a murderer wandering around while the four of you are

29

about to be holed up in the Snake Den, where you'll forget
stars exist. Shame, really. Guards won't take kindly to one of
their own being cut up and killed. Likely to drop a few scorpions
into the pit."

Dwyer stared at them, but they weren't talking. Either they
didn't know where Kane had gone, or they didn't fear the Snake
Den. If he were the prisoner and not the guard, he'd be plenty
afraid of the den, also called the Dark Hole. If an inmate broke
the rules, he or she would be stripped to their undergarments
and then dropped into an underground crypt-like space that
had been hammered out of solid rock. Six by six feet and
cramped with darkness, the only light came in through tiny
holes that had been drilled out so air could get in. But this light
only came in the middle of the day when the sun hung directly
overhead. Dwyer didn't care for the dark and understood why it
worked quelling the inmates' spite. Too, if the offense was severe
enough, the inmate would be shackled down there, unable to
get away from the rattlers, stink bugs, and scorpions.

Most scorpions in the area were not of the fatal variety. All
but one. The guillotine. He'd learned that the guillotine could
kill a man bigger than Quanto, who was as tall as Dwyer but
twice as thick. It was good that guillotines accounted for only
about one in twenty scorpions. But the others caused aches and
puking. And the pain from the guillotine's sting, he'd heard,
was like having a spike driven through your bone.

But snakes were the real killers. Rattlers, at least. When he
hired on, the superintendent told him that rattlers had killed
thirteen inmates. Later, Christ H. gossiped that at least half
those deaths should've been square on the shoulders of a few
overzealous guards.

"One at a time, you'll be chained and left in the dark to rot,"
Dwyer threatened. "I heard they spotted a Mojave Green near
the Hole last week. Greens don't back down. No sir, that snake

will come after you same as it would a field mouse."

His threats were met with silence.

"Easy way to avoid time down there. Just tell me how Kane got out and which way he went."

"He just disappeared. Honest," Jacob said. "One second he was there. Next he wasn't."

"He just vanish like a cloud?" Dwyer asked.

"That's it," Jacob agreed. "That's right."

Dwyer tried to keep his voice good and steady but couldn't avoid shouting at the group. "If you don't know how he got out, then tell me how, how in the hell, he came to possess a weapon sharp enough to take off Rodgers's head?"

That's when he heard Pike giggling. It took him only two strides to reach the stubby man. Face to face with Dwyer, Pike stopped laughing and looked away. The only noise now was Agnes Samuels's piano issuing from the superintendent's cottage on the hill. Mrs. Samuels, the super's wife, often played her piano at unusual hours. Tonight was no different despite the events that had surely addled her husband.

Dwyer gritted his teeth and looked down on Pike, the top of his head looking like a dying cactus. "You think something's funny?"

Pike grinned, his breath a foul mingle of tooth rot and something that smelled like mulch.

"Maybe they'll blame you for it, Pike," Dwyer said. "Maybe you and your buddy Quanto, here, will be strung up as accomplices. You seem to know something. Something you're finding awful entertaining."

"Don't know nothing. Was just pondering how amazing it was to pull off."

"You think murder's amazing?"

"Didn't say that."

"Where'd he get to Pike?" Dwyer asked. "You think he just

walked through these walls? Walked through like some sort of ghost?"

The man didn't answer. All Dwyer heard now was Muldoon yawning and the river water moving past. Even Mrs. Samuels's piano had stopped.

"So, he just up and vanished? Rode off on a star? He some sort of witch?"

J.J. nodded. And Jacob Hoddle joined him, lifting and lowering his head slowly, as if it were too heavy for his body. "He did witchy things," Jacob said. "Once, I seen him bring back a bug with a blue back. Stuck a long bone sliver through one of its purdy wings. Said he was seeing how long it took the bug to die."

Pike asked how long it took.

"A week I think before it stopped its squirming and flapping," Jacob said. "Ain't that so, J.J.?"

The boy nodded again.

Dwyer shivered at the thought of Kane breaking free from Gila under such unnatural circumstances. He thought the mystical was a load of bull, but the idea of it still made his palms sweat. He didn't believe in anything he couldn't see or touch and wanted nothing to do with strange ideas, especially after a Sioux squaw told him he had the soul of a dog. Then, a week later, a Chinese whore told him he'd been born in the year of the dog. After that he started seeing dogs everywhere.

Dwyer tried not to think on the dogs. He avoided all that bull, though it was treated like a parlor game in the big cities back east. He avoided church, too. He wasn't sure if there were a God or Devil, but the idea of either made him jittery. Traveling revivals were as peculiar as the Navajo warriors who painted snakes on the soles of their moccasins to better sneak up on their enemies. As bad as hell seemed, heaven didn't seem any better. An eternal afterlife of sitting around on gold-paved streets, listening to a herd of gauzy angels singing, didn't appeal to him. He didn't much care for hymns here on earth and didn't think his taste would change once he crossed the pearly gates.

"No man can will himself out of the Sand Castle," Dwyer told them.

Jacob was still looking at the stars. "Pardon me for saying, sir, but Kane's in cahoots with the devil."

Muldoon sounded fearful when he asked what Jacob meant. The softest of Gila's guards, usually left to look after the prison's few female inmates, Dwyer couldn't afford his weakness and hoped the man would just shut up. He didn't need any more talk that led him nowhere. He needed to know where Kane went.

He swung toward Pike and Quanto again, hoping to get something real, something that would lead him straight to the missing convict. The two stayed behind the others, kicking and shifting their feet in the hard dirt. Quanto had filthy boot marks on his shoulders from where Pike had stood to try and get over the wall.

"What you two hiding?" he asked the pair.

Pike spat hard and fast, wiping the spit off his chin with his hand. "Got nothing to hide."

"I'm letting you know that if you or Quanto had a hand in this, I'll see to it you're strung up on either side of Kane."

"Can't hang us," Pike said. "We don't know nothing."

Towering over all the men but Quanto, Dwyer circled the group. "I want to know, and I want to know now, which way Kane left. Did he climb a wall? Were you three going after him? Did he just up and leave somehow through the sally port? You tell me which way he went, and I'll see to it that the den stays vacant."

Though Jacob, Pike, and Quanto remained silent, J.J. pointed toward the women's cellblock.

33

Dwyer stiffened his grip on his rifle.

That an escapee would linger within the prison walls never crossed his mind. But it should have. Kane wasn't a normal prisoner. He'd never done what was expected, so no reason to think he would now. Like everyone else, Dwyer had pictured Kane roaming the Sonoran desert or attempting to swim the Colorado.

Leaving the men with Muldoon, Dwyer headed toward the western corner of the penitentiary—readying his rifle before launching into a sprint. Soon, he was at the bulky iron gate separating the men from the women. The padlock was in place. Nothing out of order. Didn't matter. Kane had Rodgers's keys. That he might relock the gate after stealing inside seemed possible.

A precious minute slid by while he thumbed through the key ring's batch. Finally, he recognized the right key, jabbed it into the lock, and then shoved the gate open with his shoulder. Fast at first and then more slowly. Collecting a heavy rim of dirt as it slid across the earth.

The lamp swayed as he raced down the two hundred yards between the actual cells. Now he extinguished it and gripped his rifle. If the convict were here, Dwyer could guess which cell Kane had headed for. Based on what had happened earlier in the mess hall, Kane had his eye on only one woman.

Hunching down, he crept toward the middle row of cells. Hers was located in the center of the row. Moving as quietly as he could to avoid waking the other female prisoners, he eased toward the cell holding Flossie Abbot. Creeping from cell to cell, he swore that if he were too late, he'd find and torture Kane.

But he didn't want this revenge. Instead, he wanted to find her alone in her cell, sleeping soundly. He started to imagine this, which helped ease his nerves. Why had he wasted all that time with the worn-out good-for-nothings in the yard?

And that was when his worst fear pricked his skin. He heard him. Kane. Heard him as he used to hear coyotes in the middle of the night back when he ran cattle.

Kane was with her, and the noises from inside were animal.

Burning his fingers, Dwyer struck a wooden matchstick and re-lit his lamp. He knew it'd let Kane know he was there. But if Dwyer couldn't see, he wouldn't be able to take aim at Kane's head.

The noises paused as he raised his rifle to his shoulder. Placing the lantern on the ground, he lunged forward, kicking wide open the already unlocked iron lattice. He kicked it with so much force, he was sure it would never close right again.

CHAPTER THREE

Emma, shaky and feverish, couldn't hold down her meal and was sent for the night to the women's infirmary, really just a vacant cell, the bunks replaced with gurneys.

Flossie regretted Emma didn't feel well, but coping with the nights was easier when given time apart from the others. Only in these quiet moments could she imagine her life before Gila, the one that included Shakespeare, sleek, black carriages, silk skirts, and auburn curls all the women envied.

She was grateful she had just the one cell mate. As a woman, she only had to share these cramped quarters, barely nine by eight feet, with one other. Because merely eight women currently resided at the prison, they weren't forced to stack themselves six to a cell like the men, who were crammed inside like salted fish.

Scratching her incessantly itchy head, Flossie lay on her bunk facing the solid granite wall. To sleep at all, she had to block out the iron lattice bars that kept her from leaving. She couldn't stare at those bars all night, wishing she could walk through them like a ghost in an old hotel, drifting through the prison toward a life that had died the day Horner pulled the trigger and killed her lover. Even if the gates swung wide open, as if a mad wind had grabbed a hold of them, she knew she'd never survive an escape attempt. Few could. Fact was, most of the escapes happened while the prisoners were on work duty and away from the compound, its sole architectural motive to keep inmates like herself inside. Certainly, there was the Gatling, positioned like a gargoyle at the top of prison hill. The greater obstacle, however, was nature. Two rivers—the Colorado and Gila—flowed on opposite sides, the prison between, as if squeezed between two torrential moats. The Colorado, a swirling vat of mud, had treacherous currents and shifting quicksand along the banks. A half mile wide, twice that in a flood, the Colorado was nearly impossible to swim. The Gila, especially during floods, was just as turbulent and unpredictable. If by the grace of God a prisoner made it past either river, then he or she would have to contend with the Sonoran desert. The road connecting the nearby town of Ocotillo to the prison was also an impossible route, what with the guards watching it with hawk-persistence.

In order to sleep, Flossie had to turn away, had to allow the prison and all that had led to its insurmountable walls to fall from her. Every night was the same. Flossie would stare at the textured granite and dream of San Francisco. Soon, her breathing would ease, and she'd float off, becoming the cool fog of the city she loved.

Her mind in its musings didn't hear the unmistakable scratching of footsteps on the dusty path outside those lattice bars. Didn't hear until the lattice had already opened, the rusty hinge howling for oil.

Flossie couldn't sit up straight due to the bunk overhead, but she flipped around and would have screamed if the man now in her dark cell had not slammed a large, fleshy palm over her mouth and nose. The intruder's other hand bore a weapon, as she could feel some sort of cold metal pressing against her left jaw. Yet, with the cell so steeped in darkness, Flossie couldn't make out what the weapon was or who was in her cell. Not even moonlight had fingered its way inside.

The man slowly lifted his hand off her mouth. Relief came,

her head tingling with the rush of oxygen. A scream, too, began to burst from her throat as she exhaled. Before it was audible, the man pressed the weapon into her face, opening a moist gash on her cheek.

Flossie fretted that it would scar and then puzzled that she'd consider such vanities the moment her very life was at stake.

She didn't dare scream now as the man hovered over her, reeking of body odor. Gripping a fistful of her hair, he yanked her to the hard, clay floor. Smacking her tailbone, Flossie couldn't help but call out in pain, and the cold weapon came at her again. This time she flung her hand up in an attempt to shield her face, but the sharp edge slashed at the soft, white flesh on her arm.

Instinctively, Flossie shut her eyes. She didn't want to witness her own death. But the darkness so overwhelmed the small cell, shutting her eyes made no difference. The darkness and horror were the same as the man savagely ripped her cotton shift. Snorting, his hot, rotting breath intolerable, he gripped her ankle to keep her from kicking out, as his other hand crept up her bare leg. "We'll taste those fingers afterwards," the man spat, now astride her.

Flossie couldn't breathe, but she knew now who the foul-smelling man was and couldn't understand how Kane had broken through the gates to the women's section and entered her secured cell.

Oddly, her tailbone ached more than the stab wounds on her face or arm. At least, she justified, he'd only cut her twice. Only two scars. If she were dead, scars would no longer matter. But death did matter. And Flossie began to imagine the theatrical version of herself laid out in a satin-lined coffin, black-clothed mourners weeping near her grave.

But there would be no mourners here at Gila. Maybe Jo would cry for her. Maybe she wouldn't.

Wrought by this vision, Flossie again started to scream. Kane slapped his hand over her mouth, inflaming the wound on her jaw. With the other, he groped at her thighs and pried them apart. But Flossie had no intention of just lying on her cell floor in a prison she didn't belong in only to be violated and killed by this animal.

She shoved and kicked at him, the wound on her arm bursting wider and stinging. She managed to lift her leg around his weight and slam it into the small of his back. His rage invigorated, Kane locked her neck in his two rough hands and squeezed.

Not being able to breathe, she choked and scratched at his face, reaching and stretching for his small eyes. Her lungs burned, as if her chest were full of thick smoke. The dark now darker, something not possible moments before—

Inexplicably, Kane seemed undeterred when Breen Dwyer plunged inside swinging the butt of his Marlin and connecting with Kane's torso, knocking him off the lifeless woman. Kane merely scrambled up and flashed the head of a pickax—the type used in the quarries—that had been fastened with strips of blanket to a smooth wedge of whitened driftwood.

Dwyer had raised the rifle to strike the man when Kane charged and brought the ax head down toward Dwyer's arm. Dwyer instinctively withdrew, the weapon barely grazing his hand.

Kane shifted to the left, and Dwyer swung the rifle as he would a club down towards Kane's skull. But Kane had dropped to the right and avoided the blow. While doing this, the convict managed to swing upwards with his makeshift ax. Dwyer leaned back like a skilled boxer, and the uppercut harmlessly sailed by.

He longed to stand to his full height, but the cell's low ceiling prevented this. So, crouching down, he wheeled around, knocking the now fleeing Kane off his feet with a swing of his rifle. Lit by the shadowy lantern light, Kane's expression was little more than a fleshy wad.

Shoving one of his boots on the man's neck, Dwyer could barely resist the urge to shoot him dead with a close-range blast. He thirsted for the bullet to shatter Kane's ribs and organs and could picture the destroyed man in pieces on the floor. He pressed the barrel into the man's chest, creasing Kane's black and white uniform. If he had a pistol, the man would already be dead. It was the rifle that kept him from pulling the trigger. Shooting a rifle in this small space would make them all deaf for weeks if not forever. One guard had quit due to firing his rifle in a cell like this. He'd never regained his hearing, and the ricochet had nearly destroyed the cell. All that, and the guard had missed his target.

In the dusty mist of the lantern light, Dwyer watched Kane's plump lips lifting off his teeth in a sneer. His urge to kill Kane intensified. More so when the son of a bitch started laughing. "Why don't you shoot me, cowboy?"

Dwyer clenched his jaw, steadied his hands, trying without result to cool the gut-anger boiling inside.

Kane, with unexpected strength, shoved Dwyer's boot off his neck, nearly knocking him down. Then Kane rolled to the left and crawled spider-like toward the tier of three bunks that were permanently attached to the wall.

In the dim light, Dwyer attempted to keep the rifle trained on the man while blocking the cell's arched entrance.

Several voices sparked the air. Dwyer couldn't tell how far away the other guards were, but Kane was cornered. All Dwyer had to do was hold the rifle on him until they arrived. Kane seemed resigned, crouching down near the bunks, shifting the ax head from one hand to the other.

Again, he had the craving to shoot. Flossie Abbot hadn't

moved since he'd entered the cell. He didn't know if she was dead or not. Even if she wasn't, Kane should die now for hurting her. Dwyer's finger warmed against the trigger, and his urge to kill Kane flared. It took all his will to keep from firing the gun.

Then Kane moved. He shifted toward Flossie, the ax head in hand.

In a rage, Dwyer lunged toward the man with the intention of swinging the rifle into Kane's head so hard, the man would never wake. Instead, Kane turned and bull-rushed him, knocking him down, Dwyer's head meeting sharply with the metal of the lowest bunk.

He tried to right himself and the rifle, but the cell was shrinking and closing up on him. Addled, he struggled to open his now half-shut eyes. In this new dimming world, with Kane only inches from him, Dwyer chilled when he realized he'd dropped his rifle. The cell shoved up against him, a musky animal's cramped and dangerous den. Thoughts of death, both his and Flossie Abbot's, collected and pooled in his mind like rotten water.

The murky voices echoed outside the cell. Though blurry eyed, Dwyer spotted the rifle and reached for it. When Kane raised the ax toward his hand, Dwyer pulled it back. But he hadn't been fast enough, for the blade met with his right index finger and came down hard. He reached again without knowing that Kane had already scooped up the rifle. When the convict smashed him in the side of the head with his own rifle, Dwyer lost his fight with consciousness.

The prison's head guard, Cornelius Hammond, known to most as Corn, knelt in front of Dwyer, thinking the young guard was dead and blaming himself.

"Neck broken?" Superintendent Thaddeus Samuels asked.

"Ain't all twisted up. But he ain't moving neither." Corn checked the guard's breathing and was relieved the man was still with the living.

"Get a few inmates to move him to the infirmary," Samuels ordered. "Her, too."

"She alive?"

"Looks like it."

"She been violated?"

"Can't rightly tell," Samuels said. "She ever wakes, she'll let us know."

Corn shook his head in disgust at a man like Kane or any man who thought women were just for the taking. He'd had to woo his wife for four years before she'd even look his way. And then it took two more years to convince her to marry him.

"I want every damn guard hunting for Kane," Samuels ordered. "Every crevice. Every corner. Don't let that son of a bitch leave these grounds."

Corn agreed with the superintendent that they should all be looking for Kane. Problem was, all the guards but a few had been sent out the sally port to hunt for the son of a bitch outside of the Sand Castle. Getting the lot back in time was impossible. "Sir, not sure how to corral the guards back inside in time."

"You best find a way, Corn. We cannot have that bastard escape for good."

Corn passed on the order to Muldoon. Both understood the task impossible, but they'd feign compliance, which would ease the superintendent's temper.

Two trustees now arrived to lug Dwyer over to the men's infirmary. The men weren't gentle—one roughly grasped his arms, the other, his legs. They carried him as if he were already dead. Corn followed. Samuels had ordered that Dwyer be treated by the inmate Armando Madrigal, the only political prisoner at Gila. Corn had seen his paperwork and didn't know what violating U.S. neutrality laws meant. What he did know was that Madrigal was a real doctor in Mexico, so they put him to use at the prison, as the doctor Gila employed couldn't be trusted to pop a blister.

Now he watched as Madrigal examined the man, lifting the closed eyelids and looking into the pupils for response.

"He all right?" Corn asked.

"May wake. May not." Madrigal gathered his thread and medicines to treat the bleeding wound, and Corn watched with fascination as the man began to sew up what was left of Dwyer's finger. The tip was missing, and Corn thought the man was lucky for only that.

Two stitches in, and Breen Dwyer opened his eyes and didn't cry out loud as most would. The needle Madrigal was using on the end of Dwyer's open finger was likely causing a pain most couldn't stand. But the young guard only flinched. Madrigal quickly dosed the man up with morphine, which made Dwyer's eyes roll to the side, though he remained awake. Ten minutes passed before Breen Dwyer began to babble.

"How you feeling, Señor Dwyer?" Madrigal asked.

"I had one job," Dwyer mumbled. "Should've shot him. Shot him dead."

Corn stepped up and looked down at the injured guard. "You both lived through it. And we'll catch him. Mind you—we'll scrub the desert looking for that scum."

"*Presagio?* An omen, Señor. You not work at Gila?"

"My mama believed in signs from God," Dwyer rambled. "Could be a bird flying inside the house or a sudden burst of rain, but my mama always saw a message in such things. I always thought that God had to be mighty weak if he could only talk to his subjects through finches or clouds. And a God that weak wouldn't be able to help much when it came down to it."

Madrigal shrugged and just kept stitching. Corn was hoping

Dwyer would just fall on back to sleep. He didn't like complicated talk like this.

"If I have to die, I'd like it to be quick. Am I dying?"

Madrigal didn't use any words of comfort. "The blow to
head could cause death. The brain swells. *Tu entiendes?*"

"No one ever goes without a fight in my family," Dwyer
slurred. "Mama suffered a good year before the consumption
finally took her. I tell you about that, Corn? And my daddy,
Duncan Dwyer, after trying to save a foal from drowning on a
drive to Wyoming, succumbed to currents before I yanked him
from the river. Daddy clung to the living for days, not
remembering the skills it took to swallow. Breathing's the only
thing he could remember. Didn't help much when the thirst set
in."

"If you live, finger should heal. *Bien, si?*"

Corn glanced down at the guard's finger sewn up as neatly as
a laced boot. If he'd been the one beaten and set on with an ax,
he'd make sure Madrigal did the doctoring. The gal Flossie
wasn't so lucky. The doctor the prison employed had been
brought in from town to work on her wounds in the women's
infirmary. And Corn, if he were a betting man, which he was,
would have put all his money down on the quack killing or
maiming the songbird in the process.

CHAPTER FOUR

Thaddeus Samuels slipped inside, heedful not to put much pressure on the cottage door's rusty hinges. He'd even removed his boots, at the slight chance his wife might be sleeping.

He guessed his efforts would be in vain, because sleep for Agnes was as rare as the rain in these parts. Fact was, Agnes wouldn't sleep unless the prison doctor dosed her up with a potent elixir. She rarely took this particular medicine, however, preferring to sample an entirely different narcotic, one that kept Agnes up for days, nullified her appetite, and caused her heart to beat faster than a jackrabbit's.

Stepping into the parlor, Samuels saw that she was indeed awake. As if expecting the governor's wife, she, fully adorned in her satin skirt, sat poised on the edge of the chaise. A pot of tea steamed on the mahogany table in front of her. Agnes looked primed to drink every drop.

"Did you catch and kill the gentleman?" Agnes said in her squeaky yet tidy little voice.

"No, ma'am," Samuels said, easing into the kitchen for a glass of buttermilk. He was hungry from the search and stress, and nothing did a better job quelling hunger than buttermilk. "But I'd hardly call Kane a gentleman."

"We need more ice," Agnes said, as she followed him in.

"Ice man should arrive Tuesday. We'll have to make do." Samuels guzzled the buttermilk, a few drops ticking his gray beard, then he set the cup down on the spotless gas oven. Much

45

to the consternation of Samuels, Agnes had insisted on this major expense. A gas oven in the mess hall would've been a practical choice, but Agnes had raised a fuss, harping that she needed the oven more than those "dirty men."

Samuels wasn't thinking on the men. He was thinking of the women who cooked for them, Jo in particular. He'd never tell the old woman how much they depended on her to keep the peace at Gila with her tasty fare, but he knew it. They all knew it. Even Agnes knew it.

What made him bristle even more about the gas oven was the plain fact that Agnes didn't cook. Ever. In her rare hungers, she had her meals brought over from town or nibbled on the pricey canned cookies she'd order from various cities across the nation. Her husband was always left to fend for himself. If Agnes was in the kitchen, it was usually to polish away the dust that had drifted in through the windows. The only thing his wife prepared was tea. She was famed for brewing the perfect pot, importing only the finest leaves from England, India, and China. And she sure as hell didn't need a gas oven for her damned tea.

"I take it you did as I asked?" Samuels said.

"I despise that crank phone."

"I don't ask much of you."

Agnes didn't respond.

"Did you do it?" he pressed.

"Yes."

"You spoke to the sheriff?"

"I spoke to the operator," Agnes said, "who in turn spoke to the sheriff. He, too, is searching with his deputies. I have faith that Mr. Dobbs will locate your mistake."

Samuels walked back into the main room, what Agnes called her parlor. The night's events flipped around in his head. He recalled the ax head abandoned in Abbot's cell. How in tarnation Kane managed to smuggle it from the quarries still baffled the superintendent. He'd taken every precaution with the picks by chaining each handle to unmovable, prehistoric stones. Never in the history of the prison had an inmate been able to remove the pick's head during work duty.

"Will Mr. Dwyer live?" The two scowl marks between Agnes's dark-blue eyes deepened.

"Can't say. Kane chopped off the tip of his finger and beat his head in, from the looks of it."

"So he'll likely die," Agnes said.

"Don't know yet."

"When will you know?"

"Madrigal is watching him. He's got cures and stitching for such things."

"Why isn't Dr. Adair tending to Dwyer? Surely, Dr. Adair could release some of the pressure on his skull. He has drills for matters like these." Her eyes blazed.

Samuels didn't tell her that Madrigal was the young guard's only shot at living. Telling his wife that the prison doctor, Adair, was a ham-fisted ninny would only rile her. The fact that Adair had killed more convicts than he'd healed couldn't persuade her, either. If it hadn't been for Agnes and her cravings, Samuels would have fired the no-account man long ago. "Adair's got his hands full with Flossie Abbot," he said. "Stabbed twice. Kane missed her organs, though. Knife got to her arm and face, near the jaw."

Agnes clenched her teeth. She'd told him on several occasions that Flossie should be hanged. Women like Flossie Abbot, born with beauty and grace, shouldn't be allowed to live after spoiling their souls with the rot of adultery. A man died, after all. And a true lady should know how to control her lascivious impulses, Agnes had said. Men can be overcome by the devil's desires, but a woman cannot.

Samuels knew it was unbearable to Agnes that none of the

women at the prison would be hanged. Not even Wilhelmina Yeoman or Jesus-Marie. Though both in for manslaughter, Samuels held the belief that the women were stone-cold killers. But women weren't executed in any of the territories, and Agnes had written to Governor Zulick on multiple occasions in an attempt to change this unwritten law.

"She's fortunate to have Adair to sew her wounds rather than that dirty convict, Madrigal."

"Lucky indeed." Samuels slugged back the rest of his buttermilk.

"If you capture Kane, you think we'll have a hanging?" Her eyes lit up like a child's. "It's been so long."

He wouldn't answer his wife's question, though he wanted to hang Kane himself, either that or kill the cretin with his bare hands. Still, Samuels didn't understand how his wife had come to consider hangings the pinnacle of entertainment. He shuddered, knowing how she particularly relished seeing Mexicans, Indians, and Negroes on the gallows, especially if the rope didn't do its job breaking the neck, and the condemned suffered. At every execution, Agnes had set up her folding chair and snack as she watched the condemned choke and writhe. It was on these occasions when she ate the most. Typically, she wouldn't consume a pound of food in seven whole days. But, during a hanging, Agnes would eat and eat, devouring nearly two pounds of pork cracklings in one sitting. Then, once the death was complete, she would applaud, slapping together her white-gloved hands stained brown.

"Kane is free," she now said. "You might lose your position, Thaddeus."

"I could."

"That won't do," Agnes said. "It most certainly won't do."

Samuels rose from the chair and veered toward the bedroom. His wife had ordered the finest feather bed from New York, the one expense he relished. As soon as his head hit those gentle slopes, the sound of Agnes would retreat along with the rest of the world.

"Did you hear me, Thaddeus?"

He paused on the other side of the bedroom door. "I heard you, woman. I heard you. And yes, you are correct. I will most definitely shoulder the blame for this travesty."

"We will be ruined."

Her high, childlike voice reverberated like tiny needles.

"Are you listening?" she screeched.

"I'm turning in. Won't have more than a few hours' sleep, but I plan on sleeping hard, so don't bother me."

Before he shut the door and sank down into the bed, he saw Agnes fluffing her skirts before sitting down and pouring herself another cup of tea.

Against a backdrop of carved rock blackened from kerosene smoke and dried blood, Adair attempted to stitch the long gash on the woman's arm. Though unconscious, she flinched each time his overly thick needle passed from one side of the trench-deep wound to the other.

Before long, Madrigal eased into the cell to assist the prison doctor.

Adair paused to wipe the perspiration from his hands and clean the fog from his glasses. "Aren't you supposed to be working on the guard?"

"He will live, or he will not."

"Where's Corn? Super knows I detest being left alone with prisoners."

"Just outside. Guarding door."

Adair didn't believe a word the man said so left the woman in order to peek out the cell. Corn was standing nearby, and Adair was glad for that. Though the Flame was unconscious, she was likely full of female ire from her ordeal. Such women could be as dangerous as feral fear-biting dogs. And the other patient, Emma Something-or-Other, though sleeping soundly on a bunk, could wake and join her cell mate in a murderous rage. Worse than them, however, was Madrigal. Adair didn't trust Mexicans. He doubted the man was a real doctor . . . doubted Mexico even had real doctors.

"Not fond of being crowded, Doc," Corn said from outside. "Won't be enough room for the five of us in there."

Adair snorted before returning to his stitches, which were as large and awkward as a schoolgirl's first sampler. As Adair saw it, the only reason Madrigal had landed the job as infirmary trustee was because of the publicity surrounding his imprisonment. If it had been up to Adair, Madrigal would have been extradited back to Mexico, where he could hang by his own stethoscope, if he even owned one.

But, for some unbeknownst reason, the super considered Madrigal's doctoring skills invaluable and seemed to prefer Madrigal's treatments to Adair's own or the half-blind Maguire's, a sadistic dentist who came once a month to pull teeth. Adair understood Samuels not using Maguire, but he considered himself the finest doctor in the territory.

He seethed whenever Madrigal was near, telling him that he should be working the quarries with the rest of the Mexicans. Yet, his disdain for Madrigal was nothing compared to the loathing he felt for the adulterous Flossie Abbot. Though the woman remained unconscious, Adair knew from experience how quickly she could wake, her eyes jolting open like the fiend she was. If she did wake, he imagined how she would snatch up his needle, burrowing it into his neck before he could cry out to Corn for help.

"You want," Madrigal said, "I finish."

Adair ignored the man. His hot breath and the perspiration

50

on his forehead kept clouding up his spectacles, but he forged on, stitch after stitch. The results would be worth it—scars that bubbled red hot off her skin like patches of lava.

"Won't trouble me to finish, Señor." Madrigal pressed.

Adair dismissed the offer, though he was having difficulty being in the same cell with all these prisoners. His knees trembled, and his breathing labored. He'd had similar experiences at the prison. With a few prayers, however, he had usually been able to summon the strength to complete the task. Good pay and the fact that no one complained when a patient died were his motivations. Certainly, if Madrigal wasn't such an amateur, he would have allowed the criminal to finish, for all Adair wanted right now was to go home and sip on his laudanum and read his King James until the squishy dreams that lovely liquid brought billowed around him.

"It's a very deep cut," he said to Madrigal, scrutinizing Flossie's arm. "Takes expertise to repair a wound like this."

"*Si.*"

Adair kept on with the zigzag of black stitches. If and when the cut healed, the pattern he'd created would resemble an animal bite. The doctor grinned as he stepped back, massaging one sore hand with the other. His eyes watered, and he yawned. When they'd called him in, it had been frightfully late. This yawn was followed by another, and he fought the exhaustion, returning to the stitches after a drink of water.

Now desperately wanting to leave, to go home, he felt obligated to continue. He was determined to avenge her cuckold of a husband. To his way of thinking, it would be fortuitous if the woman simply died, either of blood loss now or infection later. If she didn't die, he wanted her to be so profoundly disfigured that she'd never again send a heart fluttering the way his own had when he'd seen her perform, a mere year before her dreadful crime.

That night, her voice had seemed truly Biblical, and Adair had been moved enough to send her a box of chocolates, accompanied by a note of admiration. A full day passed without response. And then another. Frustrated, Adair eventually approached her Irish piano player, the poor fellow who'd ended up dead, to ask if she'd received his generous gift. Adair was brusquely informed that Miss Abbot had many chocolates and flowers and other gifts every night. Each one with a special note. She simply didn't have time to personally reply to them all.

This scar, his newest gift to her, might put an end to some of those irritating gifts. And, if he could persist and finish the job soon enough to sew the facial stab wound, he would ensure that the Flame never again received any pesky notes of admiration.

Perspiration soaked his armpits and back. He'd just had his coat cleaned and was irked that he would have to take it again to the Chinese laundry. His hands fluttered as he finished up, tying a knot and crimping the woman's flesh in the process.

Just as he yanked hard on a string of black thread, she opened her copper-hued eyes, her pupils convulsing with pain and shrinking to seeds under the lamplight.

Stunned, Adair pushed himself as far from the woman as he could, nearly falling onto the sleeping Emma.

"You appear ill," Madrigal said to him. "I finish this. Would not be done good, but will I try?"

Having dampened a cloth in the basin, Adair patted his forehead. "I wouldn't be pleased if those stitches became infected. If you say you're not much good, this could very well occur."

Madrigal shrugged.

"An infection might result. I really shouldn't allow you to complete such a difficult procedure."

"May hurt her, but I take time."

Flossie moaned and tried to sit up.

"Yes, yes," Adair said, backing away. "You take your time. Take as long as you want." He clambered out of the cell, knocking his head on the granite in the process. Rubbing his scalp, he assured Corn he was fine before dashing toward the stables.

Dr. Madrigal adjusted the lantern and sidled up to Flossie, examining the damage Adair had inflicted. "You have lived through worse, *meja*. Do not move the mouth. Keep face still. Understand?

She nodded, and he could feel her breathing ease.

He brushed aside Adair's instruments and wiped his hands on a clean cloth. Early on, he'd discovered that allowing others to underrate his abilities and intelligence worked well in the hierarchy of the prison. People had individual ways of coping, a personal folklore to help them make sense of a world tipping on invisible whims. And this, he convinced himself, was why so many in his country turned their backs on Porfirio Diaz's atrocities. After so much land was stolen by Diaz's friends and fellow capitalists, and those who protested either killed or sold as slaves to plantations, he, unlike so many others, could not idly go about his days as a physician. He'd seen too many starve. Too much oppression, which then begot illness. As an educated man, he and several other radicals had begun publishing a newspaper in an attempt to organize like-minded thinkers to revolt against the government.

A year ago, his dear friend, a school teacher named Ricardo Rivera, had been writing, publishing, and distributing the paper *Los Trabajadores Superaran la Tiranía*. For Rivera's work, Diaz's rural police, the *Rurales*, murdered him. With Rivera's death, Armando Madrigal fled Mexico and came to Texas, where he believed he could continue his work on the paper, ensuring the truth lived, as the free press and the freedom it brought had been eliminated in Mexico. He managed for several months to print the paper in Texas and ride back over the border to distribute. Then on one afternoon in June, eight months ago, he rode into the states and was met by rangers. They could have extradited him, which would have meant certain death; instead, he was convicted of violating United States neutrality laws.

With his eyes having already adjusted to the dim light, he easily threaded the needle from a spool of thin, yet firm, thread. He slipped a dropper of sleeping herbs into the corner of Flossie's pale, cracked lips. Then he waited for her eyes to close. When they did, he scooped two fingerfuls of a paste from a blue jar he'd brought over from the men's infirmary. The paste was a strong anesthesia made from the saguaro root. He smoothed the mixture on Flossie's arm and face and waited for it to take effect before he began stitching.

Flossie twitched in her unconscious state, but Dr. Madrigal took his time, just as he had told Adair he would. He worked slowly, not out of ineptitude, but because anything other than the smallest possible seam would scar.

After finishing, he applied a different liniment to ensure the gash didn't pucker or swell. Flossie Abbot would only have a sliver of a line—thinner than a hummingbird's beak—to the left side of her mouth. No one would even notice, save for those in kissing distance.

Flossie remained asleep while he dabbed a special salve to the not-so-delicate pattern, courtesy of Adair, on her arm. The potent solution should annihilate any germs Adair left behind, but it would do little to repair what was certain to scar.

"This scar be forever," he said to the sleeping woman. "But a scar is a story. Friends will ask about, and you have something to talk of over coffee."

Emma Partridge made a noise behind him, letting out a crispy grunt before sitting up on the gurney.

"Who you talking to, Doc?" she asked, waking with a long yawn.

Dr. Madrigal explained the night's events to her, the details he knew at least. And the story seemed to make Emma giddy. Maybe someone else's bad luck had enlivened her spirits. She must have been sorry about Flossie's misfortune, but, now that it had already happened, he saw that she felt better that she was, at least for the moment, the luckier of the two. Before he could stop her, she swung both legs over the gurney and started to get up before dizziness overcame her.

"Take care." He caught her before she fell to the floor.

She lay back down. "Nice of you to say, Doc. Most don't care whether I take care or not. Most don't think about me at all and would laugh if I fell down. Might laugh myself."

"May want to sit up slowly."

She did as instructed and managed to rise again. This time, it seemed as though her head felt right, because she was able to walk the few steps to Flossie's gurney to observe the wounds.

"I'm guessing Adair got to that cut on her arm."

He nodded.

Emma leaned over to examine the thin ray of stitches directly above her jaw line. "Did some nice work here, Doc. Won't be nothing but a laugh line. You be welcome in any quilting bee where I come from."

"Where is Emma Partridge from?"

"Where I'm from and where I am don't have no roads between them."

He began to clean the blood from the walls.

"Think Kane would have sliced me up the way he did her?"

"Maybe."

"I think I just won my first hand at God's poker table. Maybe he's beginning to like me. What do you think? Think God's starting to like me again? All the trouble I've caused?"

"God is used to trouble, Senorita. He wrote an entire book about it."

CHAPTER FIVE

That first night, Kane had watched a few guards and deputies ride off toward Ocotillo. They were looking for him, which is what he'd been counting on. None would believe he would stay as close to Gila as he could without being noticed, for few could survive in such a landscape. But he had only one reason for being there, and she was still inside.

For the past several weeks, Kane had eaten anything he could catch: jackrabbits, kangaroo rats, roadrunners, lizards, rattlesnakes, insects, and a few chewy scorpions. To quench his thirst, he'd sliced the saguaro for its juice. On the twelfth day, game grew scarce. On the thirteenth, he went without. The fourteenth, he considered slaughtering the palomino Giannahtah had left him but decided he would need the mount after the deed was done.

Giannahtah had already returned to his small band of dog soldiers, a mangy group of displaced Apache, Comanche, Mexicans, and a few filthy outlaws who robbed, killed, and mutilated with delight. Kane was not welcome. Nor would he have gone. His old gang wouldn't stand for the attention his presence as a wanted man could bring.

Giannahtah had been thirteen and orphaned when he'd joined the group. Kane took a shine to the boy, nursing the boy's hatred, stacking kindling on a campfire of hate birthed after the murder of the boy's entire family. Giannahtah loved to kill. As did Kane. Someone screaming in agony was the pair's favorite music.

They'd been separated four months ago, after he'd signed the contract, collected the first half of his payment, and broken away from the gang. Within days, he held up a wheelwright, then allowed himself to be caught and incarcerated. Even with his hunger pains, it made him laugh to think of breaking *into* prison, rather than out. That day, Kane had the desire, just to see the look on his face, to tell the wheelwright how lucky he was, that ordinarily he'd kill him dead just for the fun of it.

Giannahtah had known this action was deliberate but had never asked Kane his reasons. It wasn't the sort of conversation they had. They talked of killing. They talked of death. How taking a life made them feel like gods. The way they saw it, if it were a god who granted life, then they, too, must be gods since they had power to grant death.

Kane crouched in the mealy sand and waited. He'd have to eat one way or the other. Dipping his two left fingers in an anthill, he drew up a black army. After quickly shoving the creatures into his mouth, he crushed the rest with the heel of his boot. Then Kane glanced behind him at the palomino he'd tied to a cottonwood. His mouth watered thinking on all that horsemeat.

"He's worthless," Jo complained. "I give him three tasks, he can't complete one before dropping to his knees for prayer. The good Lord enjoys a proper thanks for the supper now and again but stops listening when a man won't do his work on earth. Wouldn't have been born with two hands if the good Lord didn't plan on a man working hard with them."

"Maybe God gave Roberto two hands to pray with," said Christ H., who'd fully recovered from his concussion. Flossie suspected that Christ H. knew himself well enough to realize he worked less than most men at the Sand Castle, including the devoted Roberto. "Besides," the guard said, "you asked for Roberto. Superintendent just granting your wish."

"Made a mistake, I admit that much. I'm a woman who claims her mistakes and makes them right. Unlike some around these parts. I want this one fixed." Jo impatiently pointed out Roberto behind a flour bag, his eyes shut tight, his lips moving for the third time that hour. "Nope, the good Lord won't stand for someone pestering him night and day. No sir. Roberto is like company who won't leave you be, sitting on your porch past sundown while you ache for shuteye."

"Sorry, Jo," Christ H. said, "Roberto will have to do until Samuels can consider practical matters again."

"Kane's long gone, and I got folks to feed in the here and now. Super wants another incident like the one that got to Flossie here, then he can go on shutting his eyes to my needs. I don't ask for much, but I need someone to bring in enough wood to light a proper fire. I hand Roberto a match, and he looks at it a spell before trying to swipe the flint. You'd think he ain't never seen fire before. It takes him a good four or five of my good wooden matches before he can get a flame. I don't like waste in my kitchen. You know how I hate waste. And the men are getting restless, tired of the lukewarm eats."

Not having a good answer for Jo, Christ H. turned his attention to Flossie. "Glad to see you're healing up, Miss Abbot."

She offered a cursory nod in response and continued chopping carrots on the butcher block. For fear of ripping the stitches, Dr. Madrigal had yet to give her permission to speak. She could talk without opening her mouth, but the muffled words were barely audible, and only Jo seemed to understand her.

"If Adair had his way," Jo continued, "she'd be one armed right now. Then I'd really be in a fix. Super should rid himself of Adair, too. That's what I think. Prison doctor shouldn't have a streak of meanness. Meanness and healing don't mix. It's like baking a cake with salt 'stead of sugar."

"Guess he's the only doc who'll work in such a hell hole."

Flossie knew Christ H. had no use for Adair, either, since he was the one who'd botched up his leg.

"Could be," Jo said.

"He's got it in for you," Christ H. said, "Adair, that is."

Flossie continued with her carrots, her arm throbbing enough to make her wince.

The guard lit a cigarette. "Adair's full of religion. Doesn't cotton to a woman who can't stick to one man, I suppose."

"You don't know nothing about it," Jo snapped. "And get out of my kitchen with that. You know I don't allow smoking in my kitchen, dang it."

Christ H. shrugged and drifted away while Jo began to shuck corn. Jo had twice the load with Roberto on her hands. He barely did a lick of work, and the work he did do had to be done over. Half-peeled potatoes and plates with globs of sticky food still attached, though they'd supposedly been washed and dried by Roberto, had become the norm.

Fourth day on the job, and Roberto had been sent to the yard to kill, parboil, and pluck a chicken. An hour or so later, he brought the chicken back inside. The chicken was only half-dead, and the poor bird was offering up a few weak clucks. Roberto strolled in, plucking the feathers off the pathetic fowl, as if he were plucking petals off a daisy.

"You even know how to kill a chicken?" Jo had asked.

Roberto had stared blankly before laying the suffering bird on the table. He'd taken to praying over it before Jo swept him aside and with one flip of her wrist broke the fowl's neck.

Now a sharp pain caused Flossie to drop the knife, and it clanged to the floor.

"You all right?" Jo asked.

Flossie nodded before picking up the blade and continuing to work despite the pain.

"Breen Dwyer's back on the job today," Jo said. "Came in earlier to ask on you."

Flossie was glad when she heard the guard who'd saved her had lived. That happiness was later tainted with fear when she'd found out about Kane's escape. But her fear of Kane dulled the more she thought on it. Surely, he wouldn't risk returning to the prison to kill her.

When she was a very young child, her father had beaten the side of the house with a stick whenever something roped his ire. After he'd swung the stick for a while, he'd come back inside with the eyes of a calm lake. Thinking on it, she was almost certain she was no more significant to Kane than the side of that house her father beat. Her father had beaten the house because it was there, because it had resisted the force of the stick. Same with Kane, she supposed. It helped some when she thought like that, helped her sleep and eat again. At night, it had helped her heart to stop racing whenever she heard a creature or anything else moving outside her cell.

But if she succeeded in quelling her fears over Kane, no matter how hard she tried, thoughts of Adair still terrified her. Dr. Madrigal kept the infection at bay with his ointments, but Adair seemed intent on increasing her suffering. Just yesterday, he'd roughly examined her arm and face, smearing a burning oil on both. Today, they were on fire, the work in the kitchen aggravating the pain.

With Roberto mumbling again, flattened to the floor as if in front of the pope rather than the stove, Jo walked over, an abnormally large yellow squash in her hand.

"That man's draining the virtue from me, Flossie. He's draining it right out."

The hot winds had chapped Dwyer's lips and dried out his eyes. If he hadn't already drained his water canister, he'd take another swig, even though he was only a block from his room above the dry-goods store. He considered whether or not to head over to the Golden Bead to drown and sink the clutter in his head. But it was solitude he craved more than whiskey, and none could be found at the Bead, for someone was always around, wanting to strike up a windy conversation with him.

He led his mare, an Arabian he called Gabby, to the stall behind the store. He brushed her down and watered her. After he'd moved to the desert, he'd discovered that Arabians were best for the sandy geography. And for the first time in his life, he'd had plenty of money to choose whichever mount suited him.

Her white mane nearly brown with the dust, Gabby shook off the brush and backed up in the stall the second he removed, with some effort, her saddle. He'd only returned to Gila Territorial this week, as it had taken too long for his head to stop aching, and he still wasn't used to missing part of his finger. All the tasks that he'd taken for granted had to be done differently. Like saddling his horse or removing a saddle. Tying his boots. Taking his money clip from his pocket. But he was finally feeling himself and had a job to do. So he'd returned to the prison as soon as the superintendent had allowed it.

He gave the mare a few tender words before trudging up the back steps toward his room and locking himself inside.

As he pried off his boots, someone knocked on the door. One boot on, one boot off, Dwyer limped over to answer it.

"Who's there?"

"Jenkins."

Jenkins owned the store below and had rented the room to him for five dollars a month. Dwyer eased open the door to

Jenkins's sun-wrinkled, freckled face and sparse, yellow hair.

"You got another package," Jenkins said, his voice higher than a woman's. Jenkins handed Dwyer a brown box, no bigger than saddle soap. "Same queer fella dropped it off."

Dwyer nodded.

"I find his manner unnerving." Jenkins swatted at a fat horsefly that had landed on his lip. "Man made me promise to pass the package right to you. Hand to hand. Paid me ten silver dollars to do it."

"Ten?"

Jenkins blushed, as if taking the money went against the grain of his moral character. "Hard not to listen to a man when he goes and gives you a sum like that. And he bought all my horehounds and paid double the price! Paid for the horehounds and gave me the ten silver dollars without as much as a blink. It's good candy, but—"

"Don't know a soul with that kind of money lying around," Dwyer said, "especially for sweets."

"Made me swear on a Bible I'd give you the package. Got the Good Book out of his satchel and heaved it on the counter like he was buying it along with the candy."

"He does sound queer."

"Haven't seen many queerer," Jenkins said. "But I'm here. Man made me promise. I keep my word."

"Yes," Dwyer said. "You do. You always have."

"And you've been a good tenant. Haven't given me trouble like some of them other guards in the past." Jenkins again batted at the fly, clapping his hands in front of his face. "Sorry. Dang flies."

"I've got the window open."

"It's that time of year," Jenkins said. "Big heat coming and all."

Feigning patience, Dwyer was waiting for the man to leave.

"Think he's some sort of outlaw?" Jenkins stalled. "You know any outlaws?"

"I'm a prison guard, Mr. Jenkins. I know plenty."

Jenkins nodded. "Well, he was a strange fella. Don't know many with that kind of cash lying around for horehounds."

Dwyer agreed but didn't add anything else.

After Jenkins was gone, Dwyer shut the door, locked it, and sat down on the edge of the horsehair mattress. After slicing the package wrapper with his pocketknife, he tore it open. The paper money and coins dropped into his lap. Neither the money, nor the amount—one hundred U.S. dollars—shocked him. He already knew the money would be there, as it always was. Dwyer was more interested in the letter that accompanied the payment. He read and re-read the neat script until memorized. Then he took a match from his satchel and lit the parchment on fire. He let it burn out, ashes skittering across the room, before stomping out the flames with his remaining boot.

He'd been expecting that this day would come. Fact was, he'd been waiting for it. Still, the stump of his finger began to tingle. Phantom pains, Dr. Madrigal had called it. People get them when they have anything amputated, be it a leg or the tip of a finger.

He pulled his left boot back on. The letter had changed his mind about having a drink. He'd head over to the Golden Bead and guzzle enough whiskey for two men. He'd need the courage. And he'd need to figure out how in the world he was going to accomplish the task laid out in the letter. He regretted taking on the job at all. Even so, he'd follow through on his promise. Like his father before him, he'd rather die than break his word.

CHAPTER SIX

The next day, with the letter and its instructions in mind, Dwyer headed to the superintendent's office.

"What do you need, Dwyer?" Samuels asked from behind a wide cherry-wood desk, smothered with papers.

"I'm here to ask for a reassignment." Dwyer's face was flushed from last night's whiskey and the shame of deception. Never one to tell tales, this occasion called for Dwyer to bend the truth. "I'm still feeling somewhat poorly, and I'd like to guard the women for a time until I've got my full strength back."

Samuels peered at him with hazel eyes, which were hooded by brows as long as the hair on some of the guards' heads. Then he rose and rounded his desk without answering. After slipping a file back in a drawer, he started out of the room. With no choice, Dwyer followed. They passed under an open archway and entered the adjacent sitting area, where Agnes Samuels was perched on the edge of a chair onto which birds and leaves had been ornately carved. Her violet skirts spread around her like upholstery, and, at the skirts' hem, her feet were soaking in a bucket of ice. As she vigorously fanned herself with a paper fan, her black hair blew wildly in all directions.

"You will not be allowed to guard the women," she quipped.

"For the love of God, Agnes," Samuels said. "You shouldn't be listening to private conversations."

Agnes lifted her slender legs from the bucket, splashing wedges of ice and cupfuls of chilled water to the planked floor.

She kicked the ice aside and straightened her skirts.

Dwyer watched as the ice shrank, melting and disappearing between the floor's cracks. Most prisoners would have traded their favorite food for a sliver of ice, especially on a sweltering day like this. Agnes Samuels had wasted the treat on her child-sized feet.

"I would like to know how you got the backbone asking my husband any favors." Her voice was chipper and sing-song.

"Now, Agnes, I don't see how any of this is your concern. Mr. Dwyer merely wants to heal after being nearly killed. Can't blame him for that, can we?"

"Risk is part of the job. What I care about is that Kane got away. It's dreadful, Thaddeus. Only two years into your service, and you've already had an escape! And you, good sir, are certainly responsible."

Dwyer was already crouching in the cramped room due to its low ceiling and chunky beams. Now he bowed his head farther.

"This isn't your fault," Samuels said. "Fact is, if you hadn't intervened, Kane would have killed Flossie Abbot. My book says you're the hero in the story. It's me who's in charge of this prison. I can only blame myself; can only take responsibility like any good leader would. That much I learned in the war."

"Thaddeus, do not tire us with your war stories. It is simply too hot to hear one of those boorish tales."

Agnes rose and walked out of the room barefoot, leaving little prints as she went.

"Not that my wife has any say-so," Samuels said, clearing his throat, "but she's right in that I cannot spare you for the women. I've got Muldoon and Christ H. for that."

Dwyer didn't argue.

"Those two can handle the whole lot on their own. I have other uses for a young guard such as yourself."

"Yes, sir."

Now Samuels stared, as if he were measuring Dwyer for a new suit.

"If that will be all." Dwyer headed for the cottage door.

"One moment, son. I'm actually pleased you came by." Samuels twirled the end of a dark muskrat-sized moustache and rocked back on his heels. "Something I wanted to ask of you."

"Go on and ask, sir."

"This is a very delicate matter, but it must be attended to."

"Of course."

"I need you to talk something over with Miss Abbot. Something crucial to the survival of this institution."

"I'm not much of a talker," Dwyer said. "You want me to escort her to your office?"

"No, no. I'd like *you* to discuss this matter with her. Think it'd be best if you asked her. I really do. We might have better results."

"Asked her what?"

"I need her to sing," Samuels said.

"Sing?"

"Yes. You saved her life, and she'll likely do what you suggest. If I broached the subject, it wouldn't go as smooth. A person, man, woman, or dog, doesn't matter, has a natural debt to anyone who's given them a few more days on earth."

"You want her singing for the men?" Dwyer asked. "I don't know if she'd—"

"That's not it. That'd just serve to rile them up. No, that'd be like waving a piece of bacon in front of a hungry man, then snatching it away, leaving only the smell behind. Can't have desire for a woman running through the cells like the smallpox. That wouldn't do. Wouldn't do at all."

"No, sir."

"My idea is entirely different," Samuels said. "And much more profitable."

"Profitable?"

Samuels's eyes twinkled. "As you know, this prison is almost entirely self-sufficient. Only paid workers are those like yourself, the guards, and that's because we can't have prisoners guarding themselves."

"That's true."

"I like to think of Gila Territorial as a small town."

Dwyer wouldn't want to settle in a town like this, and he was guessing the prisoners felt the same.

"A small town, yes," Samuels continued. "That's how I see it. And every citizen of a town must do his or her part. I believe Miss Abbot's God-given abilities are being wasted serving up slop and pulling turnips from Jo's garden. I believe we'd profit more if we let her do what she was born to do."

"We that low on funds?"

"That is certainly not your business, Mr. Dwyer." Agnes had re-entered the room. She didn't carry refreshments or lemonade, as Dwyer remembered his mother doing for his father's guests. She carried nothing but herself. Only thing different was that she now wore a pair of expensive leather boots.

"Funds are low," the superintendent said. "But even if they were high, I tend to believe she'll be happier singing and performing again. Doing what she was born to do. And I believe folks will pay to see her sing. I believe they'll pay a great deal. The audience would be happy, and she'd be happy."

"And we," Agnes said, "will be happy."

"The good news," Samuels said, "is the prison would get to keep seventy-five percent of the proceeds."

Dwyer scuffed a boot against the floor and stared at his feet. "They won't be lining up just to hear her songs, Mr. Samuels."

"I recently polished that floor, Mr. Dwyer." Agnes folded her arms over her ample chest. "If you would like to polish it again, please continue to scrape your dirty shoes on it."

Dwyer straightened, and Samuels shot his wife a scowl.

"I suppose," Samuels said, "that Flossie Abbot would be something of an oddity."

"A curiosity," Agnes said. "She rightly deserves to be paraded around as such."

Samuels continued. "I'm trusting you to ask her about this matter. Tell her she must, or the prisoners will do without."

"Don't they make plenty from the quarries and crafts? Seems like they're working hard as they can."

"They aren't making enough," Agnes said.

"Enough for what?" The minute the words slipped from his mouth, Dwyer regretted them. He'd have to learn to control his tongue if he wanted to keep his job. And he wanted to keep it— *needed* to keep it. He knew damn well it was Agnes Samuels running up debt. One look around the cottage told him that.

"Why are you asking this guard anything, Thaddeus? He is your employee and shall carry out your orders or lose his position."

"Agnes," Samuels sighed, "this is none of your concern. Please leave us be."

Agnes narrowed her eyes, thrust her pointy chin into the air, and sat hard on her piano bench with clearly no inkling to depart.

Dwyer flushed and looked away. He would have felt more comfortable had he been bareback on a twenty-mile ride over rocks.

"Not sure I feel right about this, sir." Dwyer didn't feel right, but he knew this might benefit him as well.

"I need her to agree to this," Samuels said. "Tell Flossie Abbot she must do this, or things might get hard for her. She must, or the prisoners will do without."

"Without what?"

"Meat, winter blankets, medicine, lye, matches . . . everything."

"Let them suffer," Agnes said. "A man perished because of that harlot. That man will be doing *without* for eternity. That man will never experience the pleasures of meat, nor will he have blankets to warm his bones. That man has nothing but the dark."

"Agnes," Samuels said, "for the love of God!"

"I most certainly will not be quiet," she snapped. "If I didn't have my say, Thaddeus Samuels, you'd run this penitentiary into the ground!"

Agnes found a feather duster and began to noisily swipe at the keys of her upright piano.

Samuels cracked his knuckles, his expression one of glazed resignation. Then he stomped out onto the porch. Dwyer trailed, shutting the cottage door carefully behind him. The two stood outside, the dry heat buckling around them.

"See here," Samuels said. "I am well aware of how humiliating this experience might be for Miss Abbot. But she *is* a convict. She was found guilty of causing a young man's death and of being an adulterer. And she'll be at Gila likely for the next five years or so. Might as well make the most of her life, because *this* is her life."

Dwyer observed the heat radiating off the hard dirt in the yard below the cottage.

"Don't go mute on me," Samuels continued. "I am in charge, here. And I'm only doing what I must."

"I'll ask her," Dwyer said. "I'll ask, but you'll be the one telling if she says no."

"Perhaps if you ask nice enough, it won't come to that."

"Where will she be singing?"

"A saloon called the Golden Bead . . . sits on the edge of Ocotillo. It's got a piano player who knows her songs, and a stage. That's all she'll need."

"She'll need some finery. Can't take to the stage wearing her prison frock."

"I've already looked into it."

"And some thick skin, too."

"Can't buy her that," Samuels said.

Dwyer started for the bull pen. Turning before the superintendent headed inside, he asked, "What about her injury? Dr. Madrigal said she couldn't move her mouth, not even to smile, let alone sing."

"The doc gave her permission to talk this morning. Two weeks and she'll be good as new, and she'll be able to hide the scar with face paint. Maybe she'll heal faster with something like this to look forward to."

"I don't think she'll see it that way, sir."

"See it or not, she's going to sing. Let her know."

"Can't make a bird sing."

"If she'd rather moan in the Dark Hole, then she'll refuse my offer of the Golden Bead. I think she'll choose singing over moaning, don't you?"

Dwyer trudged off toward the prisoners, who were milling hot and tired in the yard. Though he felt like he'd been given a gift, he didn't look forward to approaching Flossie Abbot about her newest assignment, one she'd surely reject. But he'd talk her into it. And not because Samuels needed the money for his spoiled wife.

The day felt hotter than any so far at Gila. Already, two prisoners had collapsed in the quarries. Flossie had watched as the two inert men were lugged toward the infirmary.

She staggered over to the shade cast by a row of unoccupied cells on the woman's side of the prison and shut her eyes, but the sun kept on. How long, she wondered, would it hang in her

71

head, all white, burning and itching behind her eyelids, striking at her like a life lived too long?

Leaning against the iron grate, she didn't care that it dug into her back and shoulders. She never could she have imagined a world where every day was the same, where the mornings of despair opened to hopeless afternoons . . . the nights, purple and splitting with regret, each a rotting plum.

Now the gorilla-like guard, Primm, and the tall Dwyer were plodding toward her. What were they even doing on this side of the prison? Flossie stood from her squatting position, brushing the dirt from the hems of her brown skirts.

"I reckon you're holding up this wall again, Miss Abbot," Primm said, "when it's likely to hold up itself."

"Simply relishing the shade."

"Just as hot in the shade," Primm said.

Flossie disagreed, casting her whole body in the wall's shadow, even her black boots. She slid one heel across the fine, caramel-colored soil, a tiny gulch materializing.

"I should offer my gratitude, Mr. Dwyer," she said. "I would have thanked you much earlier, but I couldn't speak. Was ordered mum after our ordeal."

He appeared to be staring at her healing wound as she ran a finger across it.

"Have you fully recovered?" Flossie asked him. "Christ H. mentioned you lost some of your finger."

Dwyer held his forefinger up. "Tip's gone forever. But my hands are working fine."

"Sorry," she said. "I truly am."

"He's got nine others," Primm said.

Flossie wished Primm wasn't there.

"Against the rules for you to be out here," Primm grunted. "Scampering off by your lonesome to sit in the shade of the cells ain't allowed."

Flossie decided to ignore Primm. "Mr. Dwyer, I really cannot go into the yard today. I'm feeling unwell."

"You're not a star at Gila," Primm said, smiling, as if trying to show off for the taller guard. "Ain't no special privileges for you or anyone else."

"Am I not still the epitome of beauty? This matted hair? This patina of sweat and dust on my skin?"

"What's *patina*?" Primm asked.

"Don't misunderstand me," she said, "I am tickled to look as though I've been stomped or dragged behind a draft horse." She lifted a handful of sand and rubbed it into her hair. "I'll never comb it again. Maybe each lock will become a live snake. Would you come this close to me if I were Medusa? I bet not."

"Medusa?" Primm asked. "She's gone crazy."

"Did you know that gentlemen who looked upon Medusa turned to stone?"

"It's the heat," Primm said.

"Maybe these walls here aren't walls at all." She tapped on the wall behind her. "Perhaps the men who looked upon the great Medusa are all around us, just like those Chinese who died building the Great Wall. Perhaps the guards tried to keep Medusa inside, but she turned them all to stone and then swam across the river, using her snaky hair for oars, making it to the other side before those who shut their eyes could stop her."

"Your fancy words don't carry much weight with me," Primm huffed. "All I know is that you need to get your tail back to the women's bull pen."

Resigned, Flossie trailed the two guards to where they'd ordered her to stay. In her tired state, it was difficult to keep up with the tall Dwyer, whose stride was so broad, she and Primm were both half running.

"Medusa is a close friend of mine," Flossie said to Primm. "Works in one of the finest playhouses in San Francisco. Fastens snakes to her head, and her hair comes alive, jutting and hissing from her scalp like lightning. I'll write her a letter and tell her all about you."

"Just stay over here," Primm snapped. "And stop your wandering. Or you'll be in the Snake—Hell, you know what'll happen!"

With that, the guard stalked off, his back as wide as two men.

"I am not fond of him," Flossie said, wobbling in place.

"You're looking mighty peaked."

Flossie licked her brittle lips, Dwyer's long face blurring.

"When's the last time you took some water?"

Not remembering the answer to this question, she shook her head and coughed.

"You forget to drink water out here, at least during the big heat, you'll die. Corn says he's seen it happen."

The mere mention of water caused a metallic swelling to crowd her mouth. She'd been thirsty for a while.

Dwyer guided her to the water barrel and scooped a cup for her. "Here," he said.

"Thank you."

"Just trying to keep you from knocking yourself out. Ground here don't bend much, not for a shovel and not for you."

She finished the cup and dipped another.

"Now," he said, clearing his throat. "I did have my reasons for fetching you from your hiding spot."

Flossie drank the second cup and wiped her mouth.

"It wasn't to scold you, Miss Abbot, though you do have to stay where we ask."

She peered at him over the rim of the tin cup. "Primm's a fool, but you don't seem to be. What do you want from me?"

"Mr. Samuels is the one who sent me over. It's important to him, this favor I'm about to ask."

"Favor?" Flossie said. "What favor could I possibly do for him?"

Dwyer had decided prior to finding her that he'd tell her straight off what she'd be required to do. "He wants you to sing again. Arranged for you to head to town. Place called the Golden Bead."

Flossie tossed the cup back into the barrel, whirled around on her dusty heel, and started off. She didn't make it three steps before collapsing.

Dwyer reached for her, but she knocked his hands away. "Get away from me."

"Just trying to help."

"I don't need your help. Leave me be."

"All right." Dwyer looked down at her on the dirt. "But you've got to sing again."

"No."

"What possible reason have you got not to?"

"I'll give you a reason," Flossie said. "I refuse to make a spectacle of myself. I will not take to the stage looking like . . . like . . . like *this*!"

Dwyer bit his lip and kicked up some dust. "You're still the Flame . . . despite the . . . I mean you're still her . . . the Flame."

"I'm hardly the Flame. I'm not even a flicker." She laughed madly, laughed until she cried.

"Flicker, flame, or ashes, folks at the Golden Bead will line up to see you."

"To look upon my scars?"

"The folks at the Bead might buy a ticket to see something curious, but they'll leave feeling different."

"I refuse. If you've been great once, great at one thing, then to do that thing again as only a shadow of yourself is painful, more painful than simply being extinguished."

"I don't think Samuels will be giving you much choice.

There's the Snake Den if you don't follow through."

Flossie gritted her teeth and closed her eyes. She could still hear the rivers. But down in the Snake Den, she wouldn't be able to hear the water rushing, that beautiful ring of freedom. She couldn't survive without that sound.

"He's arranged the whole shebang for two weeks from Saturday. They've already started hanging the broadsides."

"Then he and the others shall be disappointed."

The tall guard crouched down and whispered harshly into her ear. "Listen, and listen good. If you don't do it, it's going to be more than you who'll suffer. I don't want it to be this way, but it's the way it is. The super and his wife, mainly his wife, ain't gonna take your stubborn guff. They're going to work on you and anyone you care a lick about until you and your acquaintances are nothing more than rubble. And then they're going to stomp on you some more until the heat and sand look like heaven compared to the pain you and the others are in."

Flossie's breath quickened.

"I mean it," Dwyer said. "You have to do it."

Flossie imagined what they might do to Jo. Or even to Emma.

"The broads are up?"

Dwyer softened. "Sure are."

"If ticket buyers are looking upon pictures that display my earlier visage, they shall be in for quite a stir when the new me steps out from behind the curtains."

"Ain't no curtains at the Bead, ma'am." He pulled the cup from the barrel, filled it to the brim, and watched to make sure she drank every drop. "You're still just as pretty as you were before."

"Then God has struck you blind."

"Guess you've had your share of water." He tossed the cup into the barrel. "I'll tell the superintendent you've agreed." He started off toward Samuels's cottage.

76

When she was good and sure he could no longer see her, Flossie curled up in the dirt like an old dog and cried.

Emma hung her head over the edge of her top bunk and nibbled at her fingernail. "Man alive, that'll be something. Getting clear of here for a whole night. Think they'd let me come with? I can do up your hair real nice and paint your face."

"I could ask." Dread fixed Flossie to her mattress.

"Just tell them you won't sing without your sweet cellmate. Say you can't bear to do it without me. Will you? Will you ask them if I can go with you?"

Emma could keep this up all night. Of course, she wouldn't have this kind of stubborn energy if she worked the mess hall. Emma dusted. She flitted about with a few chicken feathers tied to a stick and whipped up offending dust particles into little sparkly clouds.

"You gonna ask?" Emma piped.

"I'll ask, Emma. Now, please allow me to rest."

"I'll let you, sure I will, Flossie-pie. If it's Mr. Dwyer doing the guarding, he'll let me come along. He's sweet on you and should be willing to do your bidding."

"Sweet on me?"

"Ask Jo. She knows all about it. Christ H. told her. All the guards think Breen Dwyer's sweet on you. And Jo don't lie. You know she poisoned her husband? Spiced up his food with the arsenic for months. And he ate it, yes he did. No one can turn down Jo's cooking. She started with the spicing after he attacked her with a boot spur. Said the good Lord recommended she send the man on to be judged. That it was time. Her husband wouldn't work. Jo sold pies so they could live. She told me that she'd fill the wagon with her pies before the sun rose. Then she'd drop him off at the saloon in town before making her rounds."

"He drank?"

"All day while Jo slaved away. After all them pies were sold, she'd swing back on by to pick his sorry ass up. Now, ordinarily, he'd let old Jo keep the reins. But one night he shoved her aside and whipped the dang horses through the town and over the skinniest bridge you ever saw. It was pitch black, Floss, and Jo swears the sot nearly killed them both. That night, she scolded her man as any man should be scolded for doing such a foolhardy thing. And you know what he did? He beat her blue for it. Beat her 'till her arm broke clean in two. Her cooking arm. Couldn't make her pies for a month. They lost their home, forced to shack up in a lean-to by the river."

"Then Mr. Brown certainly received his comeuppance."

A few cells down, Berthalea was singing a hymn to her baby, George. "That's a nice song, isn't it?" Emma said. "I wish I'd had a momma who'd sung to me like that."

Flossie was surprised to find herself agreeing. She recalled her parents singing at the piano. They'd play the instrument together and harmonize. But her mother had never sung to her. Not once.

"What poison did Jo use?" she asked Emma.

"Jo said she found the arsenic in the cellar before they moved. She'd used it to kill a couple of cat-sized rats the winter before at Christmas time. She thought hard about dumping half the box into her husband's blackstrap but figured slow was best for the son of a bitch."

"Less chance of being caught?"

"She didn't care about that. Planned on confessing once the bastard was pushing up daisies. She poisoned him slow because there's less pain that way."

"Why'd she care about his pain?"

"Said her husband had a soft side, one that leaked out after the beatings. After he broke her arm all up, and she'd bitten

78

down on a swath of gingham, yanking the bone back in place all by her lonesome, the pain so fierce she fainted and nearly fell into the crackling fire, her husband came in all flowers and milk. Cradled her head, calling her baby, gently stroking her chin and cheek."

"She told you this?"

"Parts. I'm just adding details as I see fit."

"You're making up details."

"Story's true," Emma said. "Cross my heart."

"Oaths like that are impossible in the dark."

"You know, Flossie, you gotta spit up some of that venom you swallowed."

Howling coyotes echoed in the distance.

"You want to hear the rest of Jo's story or not?"

"I know you'll be proceeding with the story whether or not it fits my fancy."

"Well, that night her husband told her he was nothing without her. He said, 'I love you, Jo, you know that? You're listening, right?' "

"I can hear you, clear as day," Flossie said.

"No, that's what he said to her. Asked her if she was listening. Jo told me she didn't dare not listen to her husband. And hearing the man out took energy. Took looking him square in the eyes and not blinking. One blink could set the damn fool off. When she was looking straight at him, he said, 'I'm happier than I've ever been.' Said he had the best wife in the world."

"You're making this up."

"No, I ain't. I ain't. See, this is what tuckered Jo out. She wanted that son of a bitch one way or the other, as mean as French pox or sweet as syrup. That's what she told me. That's why she had to go and kill him. That and the boot spur he started whacking her with after he'd used up all his love words."

"You shouldn't be spreading Jo's secrets."

"Not a secret. Jo don't keep secrets."

"She never told me."

"You never asked on it."

"She doesn't deserve to be here." Flossie felt teary over Jo's story. "I'm tired. Please let me sleep."

Emma finally stopped the chatter, but Flossie lay awake thinking on Jo. Her childhood offered no lessons on what women were expected to endure as a result of men. Jo's decision was to ration what was left of her life. Jo understood what lay ahead and decided a life behind bars would be preferable to a life with a violent husband. Sadly, Flossie thought, Jo was decidedly right. Jo was certainly the most sensible woman at the Sand Castle, if not the most sensible and practical woman Flossie had ever met. Certainly, Jo was more sensible than Flossie had been.

The others had made choices, too. Emma, a prostitute by trade, refused to engage in relations with a miner afflicted with syphilis. When she saw the sores, she handed the money back. Then he tried to force himself on her, and she broke a whiskey bottle over his head, leading to her conviction for attempted manslaughter. Rosa's story was simpler. Since her only crime was selling alcohol to an Indian, her stay would have been shorter if she hadn't been caught exchanging love letters with another prisoner. They'd both spent time in the Dark Hole because of it. For all her tough and mean speeches, Mabel was also harmless. Flossie had witnessed her sweet-talking to the horses. Like Flossie, Mable was in for adultery. She'd run off with a pair of vaudevillian jugglers, and her older husband hadn't appreciated the infidelity. The youngest of them, Jesus-Marie, seemed like the only real criminal of the lot besides maybe Wilhelmina. Jesus-Marie had told them all about shooting her brother. Flossie remembered listening to the story while the girl embroidered a sampler. She'd described the shooting just as someone else would talk about a picnic on a spring day. Flossie was convinced Jesus-Marie had something wrong with her head and belonged in an asylum. Wilhelmina, convicted of the most heinous crime, seemed to have another story lying under the surface. A story she'd never tell. Sometimes murder is less shameful than other facts a woman or girl child endures at the hands of men. And Flossie suspected that might be true of Wilhelmina. She didn't think the woman had ripped out a man's heart and thrown the "mess" in his face. No. She could never believe that about the dark-eyed, soft-spoken young woman.

Flossie didn't know how long she had left to sleep, but Emma's gentle snores wouldn't keep her awake. In truth, she'd become used to the noise of her cellmate's sleeping. And she concentrated on the sound until she too drifted off to a wet, ashy world, one in which the air and fire were too thick for even the phoenix to rise.

CHAPTER SEVEN

The prison's head guard, Corn, stood on the porch and looked fit to be tied. He had just explained how, when the head count came up wrong, he'd counted again but couldn't figure out who was missing until Jo solved the mystery by reporting that Roberto had never lit her stove.

"She told me it didn't matter much because he never built a fire big enough to cook a cricket turd," Corn said. "Still, she figured I should know he wasn't in the kitchen. I told Jo he was missing from more than her kitchen, but she said it didn't make sense on account of the man barely moving a foot before dropping to his knees for a long prayer."

Knowing two escapes in one month were enough to end any superintendent's career, Samuels felt a pain in his chest. "Who was stationed at the cell block last night?"

"Muldoon," Corn told him. "I came on duty an hour ago for morning roll call."

"Muldoon still around?"

"Hanging up his rifle, sir."

"Bring him to me."

Corn rushed off toward the guard's shack.

Meanwhile, Samuels headed into his office and dredged up Roberto's file from the bottom of a wooden cabinet. Convicted and sentenced to Gila in late '84. Horse thief. Looked like Roberto had less than a year before his release. Didn't make sense that the man would try to escape after fourteen months of work credits and good behavior.

Agnes, holding a steaming cup on a saucer, sauntered into the room. She'd actually slept the night before, and her eyes looked like wide fields of bright-blue cornflowers cleaned by rain. He hadn't recognized his wife in a good while, but, looking at her this morning, he could almost recall the girl he'd once courted in St. Louis.

"Husband."

"Agnes." He nodded, still reading the details of the horse theft. Evidently, Roberto had confused another fella's horse for his own. His own black-tailed bay was tied up next to another black-tailed bay, and he'd accidentally ridden off on the wrong mount. How the man had ended up with three years in Gila for such a blunder, Samuels didn't know.

"What is ever the wrong now?" Agnes asked.

"We've some news."

"They find Kane?"

"Nope." He folded the paperwork on Roberto and stored it in his drawer. "Roberto Mendez has fled."

Agnes's cup trembled noisily against the saucer. "Another escape?"

"Calm down."

"Do not tell me to *calm down*, Thaddeus Samuels. Do you realize what this could mean?"

"We'll find him."

"You said that about Kane," she said.

"Roberto's different. We'll find this one."

"Which one is Roberto anyway?"

"Fella who's been assisting Jo in the kitchen. Surely, you've seen him."

"I do not frequent the convict mess hall. And if you were as intelligent as you believed, you would avoid it as well. That you allow a woman who poisoned her own husband to feed you is beyond the pale."

"I might not have to eat like a convict if my wife cooked once in a blue moon."

"You married me, Thaddeus," she said, "and I didn't hear you complaining then. Maybe you should take up with that old cook of yours. Perhaps she'll kill you."

Samuels heard boots on their porch. Agnes clutched her teacup, as he brushed past her.

Corn and Muldoon stood at the door, rifles at the ready.

"He was in his cell the whole night, sir," Muldoon reported.

"You saw him inside?"

"Made four passes. Didn't see nothin' out of the ordinary."

"You see him go into the cell?" Samuels asked.

"He was there helpin' Jo last night, but she'd take offense to me sayin' that. Man don't help all that much."

"You see him return to his cell?" Samuels pressed.

"Did head count 'fore curfew," Muldoon said. "Roberto was there, right on his bunk."

"Question his cellmates," Samuels ordered. "That's all, Muldoon." Muldoon hurriedly left, and Samuels turned to Corn. "This is serious."

"Yes, sir."

"If we don't find Roberto, we'll have hell to pay from the governor."

"Roberto ain't no Kane, sir. Don't think the governor will have to worry on the current quandary as much."

"Regardless, it looks bad."

"Sure does," Corn agreed.

Agnes, now gripping a tiny parasol and fan, joined them on the porch. "My, my, it *is* warm today. Only eight thirty, and the heat's already stashed itself like a poisonous spider under these eaves."

"Yes, ma'am," Corn said. "It's the big heat. Came early this year."

"Would you gentlemen like a refreshment? Some lemonade or sweetened iced tea?"

"Some iced tea would be good," Corn said. "Thank you, ma'am."

"Iced tea would indeed refresh, would it not? I'm sure Jo has some. Run along and retrieve a pitcher."

"Corn isn't going anywhere," Samuels said. "We've got a problem, and we need to fix it."

Agnes twirled her parasol. "Standing around on the porch like a couple of country boys should help."

"He must've tried to swim the river," Samuels said. "All I can figure."

"Oh," Agnes said, "if that's all you can figure, then it must be so."

"Swimming wasn't Roberto's strong suit," Corn said. "Could hardly get the man to bathe."

Muldoon, his face drained to paste, sprinted up the porch.

"What?" Samuels asked.

"I found Roberto."

"Thank goodness!" Samuels said.

"Looks like your job's safe for another day or so," Agnes said.

"Where was he?" Samuels asked.

"Behind the mess hall."

"I want to speak with him immediately!"

"Can't," Muldoon said. "Throat's slit ear to ear. Ground's soaked all the way to China."

Samuels clutched the porch balustrade to keep from strangling Muldoon. "So someone must have killed him before he reached his cell."

"Yessir."

"So he couldn't have been in his cell!" Samuels shouted.

"Thought he was," the guard muttered. "Took a head count, but it was dark, sir. And that cell never gave me no problem before. Roberto, well, he was ordinarily under his blanket prayin' by the time I passed. Thought he was prayin', sir . . . jest thought he was prayin'."

"If he was," Corn said, "it didn't do him much good."

"You leave him where he fell?" Samuels asked Muldoon.

"Didn't touch him."

"Agnes," Samuels said with dread, "call up the sheriff."

Samuels took the six porch steps two at a time with Muldoon and Corn following suit. The three men sped across the bullpen and around the back of the mess hall, slowing only as they approached the body.

Muldoon swiped at a fly. "Not fittin' to end up out here. Don't matter who you are or what you done."

Roberto, face up, had one worn boot jutting up like a gravestone. So soaked with blood was the earth, Roberto's head had sunk into a skull-shaped cradle.

"Don't think he saw it comin'," Muldoon said. "The only brush that's flat is right here where he fell. Took him from behind, I'm guessin'."

Samuels leaned down and noticed that Roberto's rosary beads had fallen from his pocket. "Roberto didn't have enemies. Kept to himself. Whoever did this did it for killing's sake and killing's sake alone."

"A little birdie told me your cook was fed up to her ears with Roberto." Agnes had appeared out of nowhere.

"Thought you were calling the sheriff," Samuels said to his wife.

"Already did. Corn, go and fetch this cook."

"You will do no such thing!" Samuels shouted. "Leave Jo Brown out of this."

"I heard my name," a gnarled voice said, "and I don't like

hearing it unless I can see the face it's coming from."

"Where did you see Roberto last?" Agnes asked.

"Agnes!" Samuels said. "I'm in charge!"

"Under your watch," Agnes said, "two prisoners are no longer with us. So I ask this cook where she last saw—"

"I saw him taking out the trash," Jo said. "And, truth be known, I'm glad to see him gone home to his Lord. He already had one foot propping open the pearly gates and wasn't much enjoying his time on earth."

"So you helped him on his journey?" Agnes said.

"I've only killed one man in my life, ma'am, and that was my husband." She looked up at the sky.

"Yes," Agnes said, "I heard you poisoned him slowly like a—"

"Enough!" Samuels roared.

Agnes stepped back before shrugging. "Fine, Husband, but remember that if this murder goes unsolved, the governor might very well step in. That will be interesting, having one of the governor's lackeys hanging about the prison, investigating all the goings on."

Samuels considered what she'd said. It was hard to guess for which he felt more disdain, the idea of someone snooping about or his own wife.

"Sheriff Dobbs," Corn whispered, "is going to want to speak with Jo. Should I lock her up in her cell?"

"Lock me up?" Jo gasped. "You think I did this, Corn?"

"I didn't say that, Jo."

"Who'll fix supper?" Muldoon asked.

"Abbot could do it," Corn said. "Just for the night."

"No," Samuels said. "Abbot's leaving today for that rum-hole in Ocotillo."

"Tarnation!" Jo said. "How could any of you think I might do such a thing? To a man like Roberto?"

"I know you didn't do it," Muldoon drawled. Twisting his

freckled baby face, he turned to Samuels. "Jo couldn't have done this. Ain't possible."

"Maybe we should keep her locked up," Samuels mused. "Least until the sheriff talks to her."

Jo exploded. "I'm done! Done cooking for any of you. I'll spend my time rotting to death in the Hole before I so much as boil a pot of water for you sonsabitches. Accusing me of something so terrible? I may be a murderer, but I ain't ever been a liar. I didn't lay a hand on Roberto, here. And these hands ain't gonna lay a hand on another spoon! I don't have much power, but I'll take what I got. You all find someone else to cook, because it won't be me. Lock me up, Muldoon! Lock me up before I do kill somebody!"

"Please, Jo," Muldoon said. "Please don't—"

"Lock me up!"

Several Mexican inmates speaking a fast Spanish edged towards Roberto's body.

"Get back to work!" Samuels shouted.

"Lock me up, Muldoon! Lock me up now!"

"Back to work!" Samuels yelled again.

"They don't speak English, sir," Corn reminded Samuels.

Samuels rushed at the prisoners, his screams scattering them like pigeons: "Get your cussed whoremonger selves away from here!"

CHAPTER EIGHT

Like a child, Emma was sitting up as high as she could, her teeth shiny from smiling. "This buckboard's cooling me down like winter," she said. "Ain't it grand, Flossie?"

Flossie's tailbone ached as she remembered the pleasure of riding in broughams through the paved streets of Chicago. Even better were the quilted seats of her privately owned phaeton, once easing up and down the slopes of San Francisco, as she thrilled strangers with slight waves from her gloved hand.

No, traipsing across the rocky desert in an open buckboard wagon bearing the full force of the afternoon sun was not Flossie's definition of "grand."

Nonetheless, they bumped along toward Ocotillo. Breen Dwyer sat in the back with the two women. Oscar Primm held the reins.

Soon enough, they reached town, and Flossie's irritation blossomed to terror. So hard did she grip the edge of her wooden bench, several long slivers wedged themselves into her palms. Even for these, she was grateful, for the act of trying to tweeze them out with her short nails was a needed distraction from the stares of men who'd gathered in front of Jenkins's store. Flossie kept her head down and worried the splinters from her palm, but she could feel their eyes like needles on her skin. Surely they knew she was in the wagon since the buckboard had PROPERTY OF GILA TERRITORIAL PRISON painted in white letters on its side. Thinking on it, the wagon wasn't the only thing considered to be the prison's property. She should have those same words painted on her skirts.

"Look at all them horses and wagons front of the Golden Bead!" Emma shouted. "My gawd, Flossie, people must've come from all over the world to see you!"

"Will you keep your trap shut?" Primm growled to Emma. "We don't want them all spotting us. They'd be crawling all over the wagon quicker than gnats on raw meat."

As Primm eased the wagon behind the bright-red two-story building, Emma hushed. Instead, she hugged her knees and rocked back and forth excitedly.

Flossie touched the side of her face, the slightly raised skin a reminder that she was no longer the Flame, just a prisoner, a number. And this performance was simply additional punishment. The back of the Golden Bead lacked the luster of the front. The paint was chipped and the stench from the sewage sour. Primm yanked the reins, stopping the buckboard with a jerk. Flossie wondered what would happen if she leapt out and started running, running until her side burned and her lungs nearly exploded. She doubted Breen Dwyer would shoot her. But Primm probably would.

Clearing her throat, she hoped the owners of this establishment would offer her hot lemon water. Playhouses across the country were aware of her need for hot lemon water. It was the idea of the water, the craving for it, that finally gave her the strength to descend from the wagon and move toward the back stairs.

"You all head on up. I'll be back in a tick," Dwyer said.

Flossie took the rickety steps to the top of the even ricketier landing. Then she entered through a creaking door into a hallway lit by dirty kerosene lanterns. Primm nudged her past a door that bore a plaque carved with the words *Dressing Room*.

"Hey, Mr. Primm," Emma said. "Ain't we supposed to go in there?"

Primm shoved Emma back from the door. "Shut up. If it were up to me, you wouldn't be here nohow."

"I will need to change," Flossie said. "I can't appear on any stage looking like this."

"You get the closet," Primm barked. "No windows for you to be crawling out of."

At the next door, Primm lifted a lantern and entered, inspecting every inch. To Flossie, it seemed an inordinate amount of time to check a space not much bigger than the superintendent's desk.

"Awright," Primm said, "come in."

"I'm not going in there with you," Emma said.

"No," Primm said. "You're not. But she is. You're gonna wait out here while I help her change."

Primm reached for Flossie's arm, gripping it before she could pull back. She yelled out that he needed to let her go. "You are never to touch me!"

"What's going on here?" Breen Dwyer's voice called out.

Primm raised his upper lip, revealing a grin of mostly gums and only a few square front teeth. "Thought you had something to tend to?"

"I did," Dwyer said, "and it's done. Now get your hands off Miss Abbot."

"Just gonna make sure she doesn't try to escape while putting on her pretties," Primm said. "Someone's got to watch her."

"You'd best let her go and come away from there."

After Primm reluctantly released her, Flossie looked to the floor. Then she and Emma went into the closet and shut the door behind them.

"Sweet as candy," Emma whispered once they were alone.

"That guard's sweet on you."

"Rots your teeth, candy does," Flossie said.

"Sweet on you!" Emma sang.

"Shush," Flossie said, "or he'll hear you."

"Oh, lordy, will you look at that!" Vermillion taffeta skirts and a matching bodice trimmed in delicate black lace were draped over the top of a small wicker chair.

Flossie scratched at her hair, still not believing that this dress could be here in Ocotillo. "This was one of my favorites," she finally said, lifting the hem of imported London ribbon.

"That yours?" Emma asked.

"Wore it when I played Hermione," Flossie said, "in *The Winter's Tale.*"

"Sounds cold."

"Had dozens of frocks back then." Flossie remembered her trunks full of finery. "Dozens and dozens. Wish you could've seen them, Emma. You could have worn whatever you wanted. I believe we're about the same size."

Emma looked at her. "I reckon we are."

While pulling on the accompanying bloomers and cotton jersey, Flossie realized just how thin and sinewy she'd become since coming to Gila. Her arms were ropy, and her cleavage, once a soft white cushion, had hardened. She stepped into the skirts and slipped on the bodice. Only then did she look at herself in an old brass mirror, crudely balanced against several large crates.

"Why you crying?" Emma said. "This here's a happy day."

Flossie couldn't speak, lest the crying give way to sobbing. She felt ashamed as she cried over the sight of an old dress. Shakespeare's Hermione had endured far worse. A husband's false accusations. A son's death. And the unbearable separation from her infant daughter. And yet Hermione had swallowed the devastating injustice with grace. Flossie grew embarrassed thinking of all the inauthentic performances she must have given during the five-month Chicago run. How could her interpretation have rung true when Flossie, at the time, had not begun to know the sharp peaks of injustice?

Then, through the door, Primm's scratchy caw: "You ready yet?"

"We got hair to do," Emma called out. "Miss Flossie's gonna look like a queen when I get done working my magic."

"Best hurry," Primm grumbled. "Crowd's restless."

The two women sat down on the floor, one woman behind the other. Emma combed and twisted and knotted before opening the kit of face paint provided by Samuels.

"We're doing it—taking you back in time to when you was the Flame."

Flossie said, "Use plenty of pancake make-up. My freckles have overcome my complexion."

Emma, her tongue curled over her upper lip, was silent for the first time since Flossie had known her. Emma took her time despite Primm's pounding every few minutes.

"You best not cry now," Emma proclaimed after finishing. "Tears will ruin my work."

"No tears. I promise," Flossie said. "Am I ready?"

"Look."

"No," Flossie said, gathering her skirts and moving towards the door. "Let's just finish this nightmare."

"Nightmare?" Emma said. "You get the chance to do what you was made to do."

Flossie stared at her "dressing room," a closet full of lye boxes and crusty mops. "This isn't what I was made to do. Lord help me if this was what I was made to do. This is a far cry from my actual life."

Emma placed her hands on Flossie's shoulders and forced their eyes together. "You can't be comparing this to nothing but

now. You're locked up. High time you get used to it. No such
thing as an actual life and one that ain't. Good or bad, you only
got one life, you fool. And tonight, you got to leave our hellish
Sand Castle and come on out here and dress up in all this
finery. They even let us have our weekly bath three days early!"

When Emma released her and Flossie turned around, she got
a sidelong look at herself in the mirror. Like many mirrors, this
one had a thin crack parting one half from the other. She
wondered how it had happened, that crack. A careless move,
someone tapping on his or her own reflection, or maybe some
hard object launched from across the room. Perhaps someone
dropped it. Maybe it just appeared—a mystery. Maybe one
morning the crack was just there, and no one knew why. And
someone blamed the cold weather. Another blamed the heat.

She couldn't resist. She turned and glared at her two halves.
It was like seeing someone she used to know. She wanted to
greet the two halves as if they were old friends she hadn't seen
in years.

Instead, she turned and embraced Emma. In response, Emma
stiffened and backed away.

"Thank you, Emma."

"I'm good with the face paint," she said. "Wasn't lying about
that."

"No, you weren't."

"Think they'll let me watch?"

"I wouldn't know why you'd want to. Likely to be pure
spectacle. Keep in mind that tonight I'm an eccentricity."

"Don't know what that word means. Sounds entertaining."

Primm again banged his fist on the flimsy door.

"We're done," Emma shouted.

Flossie spotted her grit-caked prison garb. "Not quite," she
said.

Five minutes later, she was stepping down the hallway toward the stage.

"What the hell you got on?" Primm asked.

Flossie reached beneath her dirty dress—the one she'd worn on the ride in the buckboard—and tugged at her bodice, which continued to slip downwards.

"I asked you what the hell you're wearing."

"It's called a costume," Emma said.

"That grubby skirt's what you had on coming out here," Primm said. "Super went out of his way to ship in one of them fancy dresses you used to wear."

Flossie ignored him. She wondered if anyone would notice she was fifteen pounds shy of the cantatrice she once was.

"You look real pretty," Breen Dwyer mumbled. "I mean your hair and face and such."

"Thanks to Emma."

"You look like something the cat drug in." Primm wiped his nose. Then he poked Flossie with the barrel of his rifle. "Was supposed to put on the proper dress!"

Flossie stumbled forward, almost falling. As she caught herself, she heard a thud behind her. Turning, she saw the stocky Primm slumped on the floor, Dwyer lurking over him.

"You ought not to be pressing your rifle into people," the tall guard said.

Primm rubbed the side of his face, then snapped to his feet and started for Dwyer.

"Excuse me!" a voice called out.

A squat man wearing brown trousers, suspenders, and a cotton shirt stepped between Primm and Dwyer. Gold-rimmed eyeglasses, attached to a chain and hanging from his neck, were immediately raised to his face. "Is there trouble?" The man's voice seemed to raise and lower an octave or more with each word. "I told your superintendent I couldn't afford any trouble.

He assured me there wouldn't be any."

"This is Mr. Baxter, the Golden Bead's manager," Dwyer said.

Baxter glanced at Primm's rapidly swelling jaw. "Mr. Dwyer, I told you earlier I won't tolerate disturbances in the Golden Bead."

"Won't be any," Dwyer said.

"Where is she?" Baxter asked.

"Right here." Emma pointed to Flossie.

"But she's a prisoner," Baxter said. "I mean I knew she was indeed a prisoner, but this girl's wearing a prison rag. She's not ready for the stage." He leaned forward to examine the fabric, his top lip pressing down onto the bottom. "Why are you wearing that atrocity? We had one of your finest dresses shipped in special."

"Excuse me." Flossie ignored the man and brushed past him. "I don't want to keep my fans waiting a moment longer."

After a deep breath and a quick glance at Emma, who nodded encouragingly, Flossie glided out on stage, her nose raised and her neck stretched like a swan. The crowd booed and exchanged vulgarities, gawking at her stained outfit. The dust-ridden brown skirt and blouse released thousands of particles that defied gravity and sparkled in the light emitting from the gas lamps. The piano player, a leather-skinned man with a thin arch for a moustache, stared so hard at her, he stopped playing, fingers mid-air. As he squinted at the garb she wore, Flossie nodded for him to continue. Finally, he looked back down at the keys, and the tinkling of notes soon echoed off the saloon's lofty ceiling. The gas lamps had been fitted with colored shades, so a rainbow flickered across the stage, and Flossie swayed in and out of the red, green, and blue lights.

The audience had now stopped booing. The piano rang out "The Sidewalks of New York," reaching a crescendo. It was then that she began tugging on the brown cotton. The crowd gasped as she tore away the first piece of the prison frock. Every chord change brought the tearing of another panel, ripped away and flung to the floor. The crowd began to stand and press closer to the stage. By the time Flossie had shed the final remnant of her prison frock, revealing Hermione's dress beneath, every man in the saloon was whooping loudly.

Tossing back her head, the ringlets Emma had managed to create tickling the side of her neck, she now kicked the tattered and filthy fabric aside. The audience cheered as the piano pitched into a melody. Flossie began singing "There'll be a Hot Time in the Old Town Tonight." More than a hundred men and women stared transfixed, some stomping, others clapping. Then, as she sang out the last line, drawing out each word, imagining them as threads unspooling over the throng, a chorus of whistles pierced the air.

Instinctively, she bowed until the crowd quieted, and there was only the hiss of gas lights dimming.

Then the eruption of cheering: "Flame! Flame! Flame!"

"Here!" the piano player shouted over the chants. She turned just in time to see a cane—the prop that had made her famous—flying towards her. She caught it in her right hand and inspected it. It didn't appear to have the two-hundred yards of chiffon her old cane had, but it looked as though it had sufficient amounts.

At the first few notes from the ivories playing "After the Ball," the crowd hushed. Then, during the piano's glissando, Flossie began dancing around the stage, the red and orange chiffon trailing wildly behind her, as if flames sparked from the soles of her shoes. Flossie twirled, reached, and stretched, entwining herself in the yards of fluttering and gauzy material.

With the introduction complete, she and the piano player paused, their eyes locking. She winked, and he winked back. Then she stretched out her arms, and the chiffon fell into a billowy nest around her feet. The pianist slowed down the tempo and began playing "The Big Rock Candy Mountain," and Flossie sang, her heart nearly breaking.

When she'd finished, she noticed a guitar balanced against the piano. Rarely in her shows did she play the guitar, relying in the main on her pianist. Still, she knew how to play the instrument and wrote songs when alone. Before Judson Horner took everything from her, she'd thought about someday singing the songs she wrote. But that was just a fantasy. Women weren't supposed to write songs. And she'd never had the courage to admit she did. She'd had her reputation to protect. With her reputation now in ruins, she had nothing left to lose.

Flossie picked up the guitar. She'd play the song she wrote for Matty, who had never heard it. He never would. But she'd sing it to him now. The pianist dragged a bar stool to the center of the stage, and Flossie sat, the guitar's weight comforting in her lap. She'd written "The Rainy Sea" in minor chords—the maudlin chords, as she liked to call them. Matty Brewer had made the days better and lighter. Everything had been more fun with Matty. Now, as she sang, she was wishing he were still alive.

If it wasn't for her, he would be.

"I met you near the San Francisco Bay. I wasn't yours so could never stay. You aren't mine and would never be. I'm not yours, and we aren't we." Flossie shut her eyes as she flew into those last few months when she and Matty were free to do exactly what they pleased. "Secrets we tossed into the rainy sea," she sang. "In my lonely times, I remember your eyes blue. In my rooms alone, I remember you. You aren't mine and would never be. I'm not yours, and we aren't we. Secrets we tossed into the rainy sea."

Matty talked all the time of Ireland. He was from the west, County Clare. He said the best musicians in all of Ireland and probably the world came from County Clare. "You described Irish valleys and green fields," she sang. "Your brogue sweet new love revealed. You aren't mine and would never be. I'm not yours, and we aren't we. Secrets we tossed into the rainy sea."

By the time she finished, to keep from crying, she had to concentrate on the pain in her fingertips. It'd been so long since she'd played the guitar, the calluses she'd built up before had healed over. But she welcomed the sensation's distraction. Pain could be useful, she supposed. She wanted to linger inside her memories. It was as if she'd had a good dream and didn't want to wake from it. She didn't want to look up at the faces in the Golden Bead, either. Surely, if they knew her scandalous story, they'd know who the song was about. And they'd hate her even more for it. No matter. None of it mattered.

But she had to look up. Look the crowd in the eyes. And she saw how some seemed stunned into emotion. The boos and disapproval she'd faced when climbing the stage had stopped, and the room keeled with emotion. The few women in the audience were weeping, the men clearing their throats. Primm busied himself bullying those he deemed too close to the stage. Emma—vigorously clapping—stood next to Breen Dwyer, whose expression Flossie couldn't determine. Dwyer's left hand was behind his back. The right held the rifle. His wolf-like gaze held her in sight, unwavering.

After five more songs, she left the platform to deafening applause. Primm hooked his arm around the thirsty Flame and escorted her through the clots of people toward the closet.

"She won't need to change, now, Mr. Primm," Emma said. "Nothing to change into."

Primm, his breath smelling like whiskey, pressed his face into Flossie's. "You think you gonna be queen of the Sand Castle?" he asked. "Strutting around the yard in ruby-red skirts? You gonna be hot is what you gonna be. In that get up, likely to fall over dead from the heat."

He was right. The dress would attract warmth like syrup did ants. Flossie resolved to wear her cotton bloomers and jersey. The bloomers would be much cooler than her old dress anyway. At meal times, she could cover up with her apron. At all other hours, she would flounce around the facility in her undergarments. She wasn't concerned at all about exposing herself. Not anymore. For all she cared, the population at Gila could taunt her until their throats went dry.

"You're gonna have to wear that dress next time you sing, so you'd better keep the dirt off it," Primm said. "You ain't getting another."

"I wasn't aware your job included fretting over what the women wore," Flossie said.

"Look who's all high and mighty," Primm said. "You ain't no Flame no more. You're mud. The Mud of Gila."

Dwyer had disappeared to fetch the wagon. Flossie wished he'd hurry back.

Primm spat a hot wad of chewing tobacco onto the planked floor, the yellow juice spreading out over Emma's foot.

"Good thing I got shoes on," Emma said. "Before I came to Gila, didn't own a pair. Only good thing about our little hell hole, I'm guessing, is the government-issued shoes."

Two men had now meandered backstage and were fast approaching. The first was barrel shaped with a full red beard, the other just as portly but clean shaven and sporting a black bowler hat, a red kerchief snug round his neck. The pair pulled Primm out of earshot. Flossie saw the man in the black hat dig into his roomy pockets and stuff money into Primm's palm.

"You first, Emma," Primm said, returning. "Do what he asks, and he'll offer up some of what you've been craving."

Emma looked over to Flossie.

"Don't, Emma," she said. "Stay away from the opium."

Flossie could see that her cellmate was vivid with the hunger that rose too easily in her body, and she could do nothing to stop Emma from trailing the man with the red beard into the closet. Both helpless against Primm's rifle, she could only pray Dwyer would return quickly. Harnessing the horses and readying the buckboard, however, would likely take longer than fulfilling the two men's desires.

"Skinnier than I like," Black Hat said next to her, "but I ain't never poked no one famous."

She shivered as his leathery fingers brushed roughly against her cheek.

"That mouth ought to be good and warmed up from singing," he said. "Might not bother the other if you can use that mouth of yours. Wouldn't want to catch the prison mites they grow on the pussy over there."

Flossie recoiled, her stomach souring.

"What you doing, Primm?" a voice bellowed from down the hall.

Superintendent Samuels, Baxter a step behind, strode toward them.

"Where's Emma Partridge?" Samuels asked.

Primm's button-sized eyes widened.

"In the closet," Flossie announced. "Primm sold her—"

Before she could finish, Samuels swung open the door, practically breaking it against the wall. Inside the man had Emma, her skirt raised, backed up against a chair and was gruffly slopping at her face with a fat, pink tongue.

"I wasn't part of these shenanigans," Primm said.

"Yes, he was," Flossie said crisply. "The bastard took payment from these two animals."

His fists clenched, Primm stepped forward. "Don't listen to this dirty whore."

"What's the truth, Miss Partridge?" Samuels said.

101

Emma lowered her skirts and wiped at her face.

"Miss Partridge!" Samuels pressed.

"Primm set it up," she said. "Said I'd get me some of the dragon."

"Goddamn liar!" Primm shouted.

"Shut up, Primm," Samuels growled.

"Sir," Flossie said, "Miss Partridge is speaking the truth. She was to service this one with the beard, and I was to pleasure this simian gentleman, something I had no intention of doing. I am afraid you would have had yet another murder, or perhaps an unfortunate maiming, on your hands had I been forced into that closet."

Samuels glowered at the red-faced and sweating Primm.

"Despite what you might have heard, I am not in the business of conducting myself in such a manner," she said to the man in the black hat. "You would have ended up a eunuch after our little encounter."

"What the hell's a unuck?" the man asked.

"That," Flossie said, "is something I hope you discover for yourself one day."

"You two get the hell out of here," Samuels said to them, "before I haul you back to Gila for a permanent visit."

"You'd like it there," Flossie said. "The men do most of the servicing. Especially the new prisoners. With no money exchanged, either. Just get to live on to the next day is all."

The men darted out the back, nearly running over Dwyer, who was stepping inside. "What's all this about?" he asked.

"Came to collect the proceeds," Samuels said. "Did you know this was occurring, Baxter?"

"Most certainly not!" Baxter said. "This is the last thing I want in my establishment. I take good care of all—"

"I was told Miss Abbot would be provided for," Samuels

snarled. "One look at her, I can tell she hasn't even had a drink of water."

"She is a prisoner," Baxter said.

"And I am the superintendent of Gila Territorial Prison. I gave instructions. The owner assured me all would be taken care of. He will be notified of this, Mr. Baxter. As for you, Primm, you can just go ahead and hand over your rifle. A lying hothead like yourself has no business guarding other lying hotheads."

Primm stalled. But when Dwyer leaned toward him, the man relented and handed over his rifle.

"I'll have your badge and uniform once we get back to Gila." Samuels turned to Dwyer. "You take the two women back on your own. I'll escort Primm myself."

CHAPTER NINE

When Samuels returned to the cottage after midnight, he found Agnes stark naked inside. Every lamp had been lit, and she was scrubbing the parlor's floor, her bare rump facing the door.

"Paid a visit to Adair, eh, Agnes?"

She turned toward him, making no effort to cover her heavy breasts, which were distending from her tiny frame like the unmilked udders of a dairy cow. Samuels couldn't remember the last time he'd seen his wife naked. It'd been a good while, and he drank in the current sight.

"I didn't want to soil my dress," she said. "This floor was a foul pond. Could you order your guards to scrape their offensive boots before stepping into my parlor?"

"I could," he said, "but you wouldn't notice if you didn't have so much of Adair's medicine."

She rose and lugged the sloshing bucket to another corner of the room. "You're home late." Now she dropped to her hands and knees and started scrubbing, the muscles taut on her arms from the sheer energy behind it.

"I went to town, saw the Flame."

"The proceeds? You collect the money?"

"Every cent owed." He felt a measure of relief as he patted the thick stash of bills in his breast pocket. It would be enough money to stave off the bill collectors who had been for several months threatening and bullying him with telegrams and letters. He settled into his rocker, and his wife dipped her brush into the bucket, splattering soapy water onto the toe of his boot.

"She did that thing with the cane, spinning 'round like a dervish," Samuels reflected. "It was something else."

Agnes looked disgusted by the idea.

Samuels heard a thumping on the porch and the scratch of hound claws. He knew by the sound it was Christ H., the prison dogs following him as was typical.

"Get some clothes on, woman."

"After I've finished my floor," she said, her scrubbing maniacal. "Go speak with the cripple outside if you're so worried about me in all my glory."

"Might need access to my office." He considered telling Agnes about the guard he'd just discharged but thought twice. She needed no more fodder to complain on.

"If Christ H. sees me in my natural state, then so be it."

Christ H. continued knocking. An odd symphony followed. *Scrub, knock, scrub, knock.* Samuels's head hurt as he yanked open the door, shoving Christ H. back and out of the way, hoping the guard didn't get a peek at his wife's bottom.

"What?" Samuels demanded, slamming the door behind him.

"Too late to be disturbing you, sir?"

"No," Samuels said.

"Saw you just rode in," Christ H. said, the dogs panting. "That's why I came running."

For the ordinarily lethargic Christ H. to be running, the news had to be bad.

Christ H. glanced toward the shut door. "She awake?"

Samuels nodded.

"Might be best," Christ H. said, "if we talk this over elsewhere."

Trailed by the three hounds, the pair moseyed over to the yard, Christ H. still trying to catch his breath.

"Out with it," Samuels said.

"We gonna be having trouble come morning." The guard's voice was low and cautious.

"Why's that?"

"I'm just about in a panic, sir," Christ H. huffed. "Don't quite know how to tell you . . . well, sir, your wife's gone and insisted we toss old Jo in the Snake Den."

"Goddamn that woman!" Samuels said. "Go and fetch Jo out of there."

"Can't, sir."

"You sonofabitch, Agnes doesn't run this prison."

"It's not that sir," Christ H. said, stroking the bony skull of the largest dog. "It's Governor Zulick."

"Zulick?"

"Your wife called him up, sir, on that crank phone. Minute you left. Told him that you was gone and that Jo had confessed to the killing."

Samuels's headache flanked both temples, his eyes burning from the grit of the road. "*Did* Jo confess?"

"Not that I know of, sir. Minute you was gone, Mrs. Samuels got on that contraption and spoke directly to the governor. Sent a guard out on his horse to catch the sheriff before he made it back to Ocotillo. Dobbs drew up the charges himself, so they could be handed over to the judge. Threw Jo in the Snake Den. We gave her a few blankets and something to eat on. But Mrs. Samuels was spying on us and hollered at us to fish those blankets out." Christ H. paused, removing a cigarette from his pocket. "You mind?"

"Go ahead, long as you rolled an extra for me."

Christ H. handed him a crudely shaped cigarette. Samuels lit his own, then Christ H.'s with the wooden matches he kept in his breast pocket.

"There's more, sir."

"Figured." Samuels took a long pull of the cheap tobacco.

"What else?"

"She . . . Mrs. Samuels . . . well, she . . . she . . ."

"What?"

"She made us take Jo's clothes. Jo's buck naked down in that hole, sir. We been waiting for you to get back, so we could give her a dress. Don't seem right, an old woman down there like that. Guard you hired last week already quit. Walked away after Mrs. Samuels told him to guard the Snake Den. Muldoon, well, he's all choked up."

"Goddamn that woman!"

"Your wife's pushing for Jo's execution, sir. She's got it in the works."

"Never been a woman executed in the Arizona Territory."

"We know that," Christ H. said. "And that's what made your wife smile. She said your name would go down in history."

"Get Jo out," the superintendent ordered. "Now!"

"What about the governor?"

"Unless he'd like to come on down tomorrow morning and cook up two hundred bacon biscuits, the governor can go to hell."

Christ H. limped away with the dogs at his side. Samuels tossed his cigarette to the ground before climbing the hill to his cottage. His head was splitting, as if it were a wormy log struck by lightning. Walking in, he saw that Agnes now wore a skirt. Still, nothing covered her chest, which was heaving from all the cleaning and maybe too many doses of Adair's medicine.

Samuels wanted to wrap his hands around her thin neck.

She smiled at him, however, and he took himself away from the cursed moment, forced himself to a time when she'd offered him those nipples as if he were a nursing babe. Back then, she'd cradled his head before wrapping those magnificent legs around him. Early on, she'd been so sweet on him, she'd done nearly anything to stay in his good favor.

The first year of their marriage was full of promise. The second year, Agnes became pregnant, and she lit up from the inside. Losing their baby boy only two days after the birth broke Samuels's heart. It did something far worse to his wife.

She'd started weeping whenever she was awake, which wasn't often, because she rarely rose from bed. Then he'd gotten her the medicine, a medicine that somehow infused her with the energy to at least live. But it wasn't a real life. And then Agnes disintegrated into the thing she was now.

Samuels felt a tug of loyalty toward Agnes. He blamed himself. He'd been the one who first approached a doctor and secured the medicines that had surely rotted his wife's soul.

No matter. His wife must now leave the prison. He could no longer tolerate the kind of trouble Agnes agitated. He'd put her on the next train to Missouri. He'd tell her in the morning after some of Adair's poison had worn off.

"Sweet dreams, Agnes," he said, stepping into their bedroom and softly shutting the door.

CHAPTER TEN

Though tired enough to long for her cell and its flea-infested mattress, Flossie refused to complain. Still, her arm burned as she attempted to prepare an edible breakfast for the entire cast of cranky inmates and guards, all famished from going without so much as a nibble the night before.

"We getting fine cuisine?" Corn asked. "That what ladies cook while wearing their underwear?"

Flossie didn't mind the head guard's teasing, especially after he'd fetched Armando Madrigal to help. The doctor had built the best fire she'd seen in weeks. Moreover, he'd smeared a cool liniment on her arm and said it would soon ease the pain.

After Corn stepped outside, she turned to him. "I don't know how long we can make it without Jo." She rolled out yet another clot of dough and went on to tell him how they'd sent her to Jo's cell this morning. Flossie's goal, according to Samuels's orders, was to "coax her out." Flossie had failed. And Jo had been plain in her refusal, swearing she'd never until the end of time cook so much as one bean for any of them.

"I don't blame her." Flossie pressed down on the rolling pin. "Accusing Jo of such a crime is preposterous."

As he organized the utensils in the drawers, Dr. Madrigal said he agreed. "Señora Samuels has no tolerance for women."

"Señora Samuels should hike up her silk skirts and take a few cooking lessons." Flossie was aware of how petulant she sounded. "There's not a person here, guard or prisoner, who thinks Jo killed that man." Flossie now abandoned the dough and set to beating together four dozen eggs and three pounds of beans, intending to fry the whole mess up at once in the big cast-iron skillet. She'd seen Jo prepare something similar.

"How was Golden Bead?"

"Full house."

"Bien?"

"Mostly," she said.

Flossie relayed the incident involving Primm, leaving out the part where she was to be prostituted, too. She'd fallen far from grace into a land of utter disgrace. Still, she couldn't stomach the fact that she'd almost endured being prostituted. She doubted she'd ever tell anyone. It would be easier to pretend it never happened.

"Opio." He shook his head. *"Es malo."*

"Emma," Flossie admitted, "didn't resist."

"Ah, *sí*. Drug *es amor.*"

Corn re-entered and sniffed at Flossie's sickly brown creation, a mess that didn't look at all like the dish she'd seen Jo prepare.

"What in Sam Hill is that?"

"That," she announced, "is breakfast."

"Lord help us."

"I am not a culinary genius," Flossie said. "I am an entertainer. A singer. An actress."

"Then *act* like you're cooking."

Muldoon, his shoulders slumped, eyes swollen red, entered the kitchen though the back door.

"She's been officially charged." He poured himself a mug of bitter coffee. "They could hang her."

"You should get on home, Muldoon," Corn said. "You've been workin' twenty-four hours straight."

"I'm stayin' on 'til Jo's back in the kitchen, where she done belong."

"No you ain't," Corn ordered. "You get on back to town."

"Jo would like it if I stayed around."

"Jo don't make the decisions 'round here about which shifts the guards work. I do. You look beat."

Muldoon's tone now took on a hopeful note. "I heard that the superintendent's sendin' his missus away. That true, sir?"

"I'm not much for prying into the superintendent's business," Corn said. "But even if the super wants to ship her off, Agnes Samuels will fight tooth and nail. She's waited a long while for a hanging, especially that of a woman. With one on the horizon, she's not likely to miss out."

"Can't hang Jo for somethin' she didn't do," Muldoon said.

"They do what they please," Corn said.

Flossie trembled as she poured her concoction into the hot cast-iron pan. The gunk sizzled and splashed over the sides.

"Jo wouldn't like you messin' up her stove like that," Muldoon said. "She keeps a clean kitchen."

After Muldoon vanished the way he'd come, Flossie leaned in toward Dr. Madrigal. "Would they do it?" she whispered. "Hang Jo?"

"Might."

Flossie poked at the eggs.

Dr. Madrigal moved toward the washbasin, which was as far away from Corn as he could get in the mess hall. Out of sight, he motioned for Flossie to follow. To cover their words, he poured water from a pitcher into the basin. "Is my time to leave," he whispered. "Jo, too."

Flossie tensed.

"Must be done, *sí*?"

She listened intently as he—in a quick flurry of English and Spanish—detailed precisely a plan that might work. But she would need to help.

"Your *cuisine*," Corn said, startling them both, "smells like I

111

left my boot in a campfire."

Flossie quickly returned to the stove and scraped the cooked edges from the sides of the pan.

"I believe I'll have a cup of that coffee," Corn said.

"*Sí, señor.*" Dr. Madrigal reached for a mug.

Corn sniffed again at the pan and then screwed up his face. "I better get some extra guards in this mess hall. This here fare's likely to send the entire population into fits the likes of which we ain't never seen."

"Josephina Brown's been a model prisoner," Samuels said to Sheriff Dobbs. "She works hard to keep this prison afloat. Her philosophy is akin to mine. She believes this is a small town. And Jo's one of its best citizens."

As if Samuels were a small child, Sheriff Dobbs shook his head. "Only thing this hellish plot of land has in common with a small town is a murder waiting to be avenged. The very idea of giving a convicted killer access to kitchen knives and such arms is absurd."

Samuels poured two stiff drinks. He'd preferred to rough the sheriff up, but he'd try finesse and liquor first.

"I am a teetotaler, sir," Dobbs said, waving away the whiskey. "And you yourself would be best served by avoiding the tippling during these trying times."

Samuels put one drink back onto the table. Then, with one swallow, he downed the contents of the other.

Dobbs offered a wry smile. "The citizens of Ocotillo will not tolerate a prison run amok. It could be disastrous for the entire territory. Under weak leadership, the prisoners might take the penitentiary over."

"Aren't you getting a little ahead of yourself, Sheriff? Prisoners here are nowhere near an uprising, especially being half starved as they are. Even if they were plotting along those lines, hanging the woman who feeds them isn't going to assist in their placating."

Agnes entered with a tray. She served the sheriff tea, pouring with her pinky finger erect. The sheriff thanked her, and she joined the men, sitting neatly on a tiny wooden chair, fanning herself as if she were an innocent child. "Well, I certainly feel much more secure now that Mrs. Brown no longer has at her disposal all those wicked knives and such." Agnes's voice was shrill and biting. "Wonder if I had been her victim?"

Samuels considered. The thought was growing more appealing.

"Did you know, Sheriff," Agnes said with a pout, "that my husband is sending me home on a train?"

The sheriff's face turned red. "Why so?"

"My dear husband thinks I should live with family until he regains control of his prison."

"Is this true?" The sheriff's feminine eyebrows twisted toward the small space between his eyes.

"It's a precaution." Samuels lifted the whiskey he'd offered Dobbs and took a sip.

"So you do think the prisoners are out of control?" Dobbs asked.

"My wife," Samuels stammered, "hasn't been well."

"I've been fit as a fiddle."

"She looks healthy to me," Dobbs said. "A woman shouldn't be too plump. At least that's my firm opinion."

Samuels slammed his glass down on the buffet, the liquor sloshing over the sides. "Stay out of my personal matters, Sheriff. Stay out and get out! Get out of my goddamn home."

The sheriff backed toward the door.

"Now listen here," Dobbs said, "you don't need—"

"You goddamn sonofabitch, good for nothing cow-fucking piece of horseshit!"

Samuels kept at it until Dobbs stumbled backwards out the front door of the cottage and was climbing onto a sorrel that Samuels thought looked as well groomed as the sheriff.

"You watch out, Samuels. I will speak with Zulick. He shall be informed of your short fuse and obstinate refusal to execute a murderess. Before long, despite what you think of me and my notions, your hands will be tied regarding this matter. Of that, I am certain."

The sheriff made a click with his tongue and shook the reins. The horse cantered off, leaving Samuels on the porch. His head hurt again, even more so with that unforgiving sun hitting him square in the eyes. When he turned, it took a moment for his eyes to adjust. But when they did, he saw Agnes smiling broadly.

CHAPTER ELEVEN

"Don't you be talking about what the good Lord wants," Emma said. "The good Lord wouldn't want you dangling blue from a rope. Not if he's good like you say."

That morning, Flossie had finally been able to cajole Jo out of her cell. She sat with Emma and Flossie in the prison library. It was the one day of the week the women were allowed, and the men were not. Having been built underground, it remained reasonably cool on the hottest of Gila's days. Flossie knew the room would typically be teeming with inmates, not because they enjoyed reading, for many were illiterate, but because the room offered relief from the relentless heat of the sun-soaked yard.

"You must do what the doctor says. His plan is sound." Flossie glanced toward the gate. Assigned to guard Jo, Christ H. had stepped away for a cigarette. He could be gone for a minute. Could be a half hour. Knowing his penchant for dawdling, Flossie figured she had enough time to persuade the stubborn woman. Still, she kept watch.

"I've no use for the outside world," Jo said. "And it ain't got no use for me. I was fine thinking I'd be doing the rest of my living and dying here. You won't understand this, none of you, but Gila was a fine home to me."

"You've more use in the outside world than you can ever imagine."

Jo stiffened when Flossie wrapped her arm around the small

115

woman's shoulder, shrugging off Flossie's affection. "We wouldn't make it two feet. Even if we did, there's the river, and I can't swim. Never did learn. I like the parts of the earth that are hard and dry."

"Listen," Flossie said, "you have my word that you won't have to swim that river. Dr. Madrigal has connections. And I can convince Breen Dwyer to help us. I'm sure of it."

Jo was unmoved. "You still think you're a fancy princess in a carriage, don't you?"

"I most certainly do not. I was dethroned long ago. But I still have my wits."

"Then why are you wearing those undergarments?"

"Feel this cotton," Flossie said. "These were custom made."

"Someone as famous as you should've been able to afford more fabric."

"Egyptian cotton, Jo, the finest, the softest possible." Flossie touched it and closed her eyes, remembering a time when she slept on sheets made of the same textile. How cool those sheets had felt against her skin.

"Wouldn't be caught dead wearing my underwear in public. Don't much care where they grew the cotton."

"Then you can wear whatever you want," Flossie said.

"How? Won't have two pennies to spit on. Be eating lizard soup if we survive the Apaches. Be lucky if the lizards don't eat us first."

"The doctor has some money. Enough to see you through to California."

"I ain't never owed anyone anything, and I don't plan on owing anyone now."

Emma had been looking at the pictures in a children's book when she glanced up. "You better take what he's offering. He might burn all that cash in a campfire if you don't. And everyone here knows how you hate waste."

Jo rose, called out to Christ H., and then left without another word, for she didn't like to waste those either.

The Stone Circle

Josset called out to Cutter. He said nothing without saying a word for the flame, like to warm those yellow

CHAPTER TWELVE

That night, after all had their fill, both the men and women, Flossie's only company was the stacks of crusted dishes and Breen Dwyer. As she lugged to the basin one tower of plates after another, he silently lurked near the dark-yellow door that had been propped open to let in the night breeze. Just looking at the stacks of plates made Flossie swoon. She aimed to speak to the superintendent about the matter the very next day, reasoning that if she was making money for the prison by singing at the Bead, they needed to find another inmate to clean up after supper.

For now, she balanced as many tin plates as she could and deposited them into the soapy water. Several slipped off before they reached their destination and clattered to the floor.

"Let me help," Dwyer offered. He came over, kneeled, and began gathering the plates. "I could ask one of the other ladies to give you hand, but I'd be going behind the superintendent's back. He's the one got to arrange such things."

"Why can't one of the men do these dishes?" she snapped. "Why one of the *ladies*?"

He didn't answer her irritability and kept helping. She should watch her tongue. At least tonight. She had to convince him to help her, and she wouldn't be able to do that with harsh words.

She shouldn't be complaining about the amount of dishes, either. The more dishes to wash, the more time she'd have to talk him into it. So, really, this was a dream come true, these pots and pans lining up on the counter like a cityscape. The flour and egg encrusting the stove. The more than a hundred tin plates waiting to be cleaned, many of which were still piled high with Flossie's meal of undercooked corn bread and beans hard as teeth. Though inmates were required to scrape whatever remained on their plates into the trash, they were steaming mad over the poor-tasting food, leaving the uneaten globs for her to clean their only method of protest.

"We'll take one counter at a time," Dwyer suggested.

He did the heavy lifting, and she dipped the plates in the cool water, washing them with a rag.

"Hot in here," he said.

She agreed.

He reached over her head, pulling an additional rag from a shelf above the basin. "Pardon me."

As he lowered his arm, she purposely turned and wound herself in an awkwardly positioned embrace. "May I ask you something?"

He stepped back, nearly stumbling.

"Why'd you hire on at Gila?" she said. "Christ H. said you were once quite the cowboy."

"Not much to cowboy after the big winter killed off most the cattle, Miss—"

"Call me Flossie, and I'll call you, Breen, yes?"

"No need to talk about such things that are in the long ago category. Plenty of plates to scrub in the here and now."

"I can listen and wash simultaneously," she said. "Certainly, you know of my many talents."

He lifted a heavy iron pot off the stove and set at it with a steel-wool pad. "You and Jo sure must be strong lifting such things."

"Mr. Breen?"

"Yes, ma'am." He didn't look up at her.

"You miss being out there? Riding free? Being a guard at the Sand Castle must be a shock."

He blushed and backed even farther away, bumping his shinbone on the left of a butcher-block table. Flossie splashed her face with the dishwater.

"That water's awful dirty," he said. "Could make you sick."

"Dirty water's the least of my troubles. And I don't know why you should fret on my health."

Flossie scrubbed hard on a particularly filthy dish, her fingers red and raw.

"I'm just watching out for you. The way I watch over all the prisoners. A sick inmate's a burden on us all."

Flossie held up a plate and inspected it. "Haven't noticed you watching out for anyone but me."

He lowered another stack into the water, then wiped his hands on his blue uniform shirt. Flossie ran her soapy fingers through her hair and looked straight at him.

"I watch over 'em all," he grumbled.

"Emma says you're sweet on me. I hope that's true," she lied. "A little sweetness could go a long way in such a bitter place."

He turned away, strode toward the stove, and began to chip away at the dried food with a knife. She hesitated once his back was turned but was determined to go forth with Dr. Madrigal's plan. She stopped washing, neared the guard, and touched his arm. He whipped around as if someone had held a lit match to his skin. Prisoners were never allowed to touch the guards. Flossie stood on her toes and pecked him on the cheek. It was clumsy, but she knew it could achieve more than words. He, clearly nervous, peered from side to side.

"No one saw," she whispered.

He brought his hand to his face.

"I mustn't do that again," she said. "I know."

"You shouldn't." He returned to scrubbing the stove's black

120

surface, the muscles in his arms hardening to ropes from the effort.

"Why are you watching out for me? A man died due to my 'unbecoming behavior.' Didn't they inform you of that when you signed on?"

He lifted an iron pan off the stove and hefted it toward the counter.

"Are you going to answer? I can be quite pesky with my curiosity."

He returned to the basin and began briskly scouring the plates. Flossie approached and stood next to him. Side by side, she sank her hands into the soapy water, found his right hand and held it. He didn't snatch it away. Instead, he turned it palm up. She squeezed before moving her hand up and out of the water to caress his arm.

"How's your injury?" He stared straight ahead, as if she weren't touching him at all.

"I'm feeling quite well," she said.

"Glad to hear."

"You?" she asked.

"Like it never happened, except my finger's shorter than it used to be. Still works."

She leaned into him.

He shut his eyes for a moment before wrenching both hands out of the basin and putting some distance between them.

"Where are you going?" Given that this was her only chance to save Jo, she was afraid she'd somehow muddled it.

"I'm getting another guard."

"I don't want another guard. I prefer you."

His whiskered jaw sharpened into a steep ledge. "Don't matter what you want. You're the prisoner at Gila, not me."

"Emma said you were sweet on me. I suppose she was right."

"Sweet on you?" He wiped his wet hands on his trousers. "I

want nothing to do with you."

"If that were true, you'd have gotten the other guard the moment I kissed your cheek."

"You're an aggravating woman," he said. "You're aggravating in this prison, and I'm damn sure you were aggravating outside it."

"You should speak softly. Corn's in the next building."

"Don't got nothing to hide."

Flossie tossed her steel scrubber down and strode toward him. Reaching up, she pulled his head down with surprisingly little resistance and kissed him on the lips with the passion she'd once had on the stage. And that passion, what she thought had been a still pool of muddy, mosquito-infested water, still frothed, heated, and roiled.

When she pulled away, his expression hadn't changed. But he'd wrapped his long arms around her with seemingly no intention of pulling away.

This time, it was he who kissed her.

Flossie shut her eyes and traveled to wherever his mouth took her. A treed land where branches blocked the sky and ferns protected them from the sight of other guards. She'd played her role as coquette perfectly. She'd given one of her finest performances.

He pulled away and looked down at her with those glacier eyes.

"You've something to hide now," she said.

"We all got secrets."

"We do. We surely do."

He kissed her again, this time on top of her head, before turning back to his scrubbing. Flossie, behind him, considered and weighed her next words. "Would you be willing to add yet one more secret to your cache?"

She reached for him again, unsure for a moment if drawing him closer was for Jo or for herself . . . not sure at all.

He only let her go after hearing footsteps outside the mess hall. Or perhaps he'd imagined the steps. Maybe he'd imagined everything. His head felt tangled after he'd listened to her proposition. This wasn't part of his task, the one he was being paid for. This was unplanned and dangerous and could undo all he'd arranged so far. Still, in order to follow through with the orders his benefactor had given him, he'd probably have to go along with the plan she, Jo, and Madrigal had devised. But it was risky and could very well be the dumbest thing he'd done at the prison, if not in his life.

Still, here she was squinting up at him, waiting for his answer, trying to kiss him again.

"You don't have to do that," he said.

"Don't you want to?"

Her voice was too sugary, too much like some of the soiled doves he'd come to know when he was living in Montana, the women who'd drained his pockets and hardened their sweetness after the poke was done. "You can stop talking that way," he said.

"Can't help being taken by you. You're tall and handsome, and you saved my life. A girl doesn't forget a man who saved her life."

He watched as she walked her small fingers up and down his chest before finally finding the gumption to push her hand away and turn from her. "Just stop all this. I'm not one of your fans, Flossie Abbot. I'm here to guard you."

She stayed put. And he was glad for that, though he wanted her mouth again, wanted to lift her up and carry her back to his room above Jenkins's store. Wanted her legs wrapped around his waist. All that want was making him antsy.

"If you won't do this, Mr. Dwyer, then I beg you not breathe a word of what I just said."

"Didn't say I wouldn't do it." He kept his back to her and observed a fly landing on a cast-iron pan. "But I'm not taking the risk because of your kisses and false words. I'm taking it because it's the right thing. That's all."

Now he turned and saw that she stood in the same place. In her cotton bloomers and camisole, now stained the same color as sand, her nose freckled, her ginger hair matted and tossed on top of her head like a nest of mud swallows, she merely nodded and began scraping the plates into the bin. He didn't like the idea of magic, no, but he felt as though he'd been bewitched by this bedraggled and desperate woman, who, in all her filth and captivity, still seemed like the most beautiful creature who'd ever walked the earth.

"But we're doing it my way," he added.

When Corn walked in, neither flinched at the presence of the burly lead guard. "I'm headed to the men's bull pen," he grunted.

After he left, Dwyer strode toward Flossie, yanked the plate from her raw hands, and kissed her hard on the mouth.

As he held her in his arms, her head on his chest, he could have sworn she trembled. But, when he thought on it later, he considered it might have been him who was doing all the shaking.

Chapter Thirteen

Kane had eventually slaughtered the Palomino Giannahtah had left him. Until the meat had rotted, he'd eaten well. The few times he'd risked ducking into Ocotillo at night, he'd found scraps of grub—potato peels, half-eaten corncobs, meat bones—in the trash bins outside the Golden Bead. The risk had been worth it. Firstly, the fare had helped some in staving off starvation. Mostly, though, he'd found information he needed. Broadsides claimed the Gila whore was singing at the Bead. And he had the date and time. Now he could get this job done, collect the rest of his money, and move on with his life.

The past week, he'd spent his days hunting snakes. Listening for them in the mesquite or sage and then, once discovered, crushing their throats with his boot. Didn't matter what kind, but the rattler was tastiest. The meat from a snake could get him through a day. Two snakes, the pangs would hold back their aching gnaw for longer. The best meals, though, were from the river. If sure no one was around, which was rare, he'd try to catch a bass or trout. Typically, he only had time to fill his canteens. But having water was a must. Roaming the desert for as long as he had, he knew the perils of heat sickness. Fast it would come. Death would follow shortly. He'd seen it, always considering that any fool traveling the desert without water deserved a dirt nap. He saw their deaths as an amusement and felt the same even with those lost companions he'd known well. An unspoken code in their gang was to never share water. Didn't belong in the desert if you couldn't ration it right and provide for yourself. And if it were him dying of the thirst and heat, he wouldn't expect any to hold out their canteens to his dry lips. True he might try to just take the water, killing the man in the process. But their unspoken code didn't forbid killing.

Glad for two full canteens, Kane considered today hotter than most. For the past few hours, he'd been crouching behind a juniper watching the road for a Gila wagon. If the broadsides were right, today was the day. They were waiting on her at the Bead. But his plan was to make good and sure she never showed.

He stood and tried to look into the sun. Before she'd died, his mother once told him he'd go blind looking at it, but he'd never believed her. He figured it couldn't be true, or nearly everyone would have been stumbling around, their worlds black and noisy. So he stared at the sun and then blinked away the white spots it left behind. When he opened his eyes fully again, he noticed a wagon ambling towards him. A man, older and bearded, clutched the reins. Next to him, a plump woman, plain to look at, but with rolls and folds on her stomach, arms and hips. The back of the wagon held three children, the girl having inherited the ripe fleshiness of the mother. He so enjoyed carving through flesh, the more of it the better. The feel of his knife, one Giannahtah had saved for his inevitable escape, carving through the textured layers of skin gave him a satisfaction little else could. The girl couldn't be yet ten, he decided, craning his neck. Two boys, tall and broad-shouldered, would cut open quickly.

Standing now, Kane waved at the passing family. The bearded man glanced over, refusing to slow for the wild-looking fellow on the edge of the road. Kane's clothes, a poorly fitted suit that Giannahtah had provided, were stiff with sweat and dirt, his long, black mane matted and crimped. The man flogged the horses harder. Then when he saw the rifle rising up to Kane's

126

shoulder, he whipped the horses mercilessly. But Kane shot the lead steed. As it fell, the wagon tilted with the horse's weight.

The oldest boy leapt out before the wagon tipped completely, but the rest of the family spilled to the ground like birdseed. The mother wailed, blood rushing from her nose. She grappled about for her children. The man, who seemed to have no gun, stood and positioned himself in front of the fallen wagon. Kane again aimed the rifle he'd taken from the guard, Dwyer. With a bead on the man, he stepped forward and cut the father down.

The others started to plead, scream, and pray. Kane had missed this music. The woman and two children backed up against the overturned wagon. The mother attempted to push her offspring away, imploring them to run, as the other had done. But they only huddled closer.

As she tried to slip between the vertical seats, her leg twisted like the string of an apron. "Run!" the mother screamed.

Finally, the girl broke, a lone quail. Pausing, the boy then took flight, too, blood dripping down his temple, trickling in rivers down his neck.

"Run, Sara!" the mother yelled. "Run!"

Sara. He was glad to know at least one of the children's names. He'd be taking his time with her.

Then he remembered the other boy, the one who'd leapt out before the wagon teetered over.

Kane left the woman to her shouting and whimpering, rounded the wagon, and headed toward the fleeing figure, whose head he could make out just above the red-rust dirt and cloudy sage.

He cocked the rifle and fired only once. The bullet wheeled through the boy's back.

The other two were a good ways down the road by now. Kane trotted after them. They were moving fast for ones so young. Kane sped up. Now within range, he shot. The boy ran a few steps before falling face first into the road. Kane practically tripped over the prostrate figure as he closed in on the girl. In another minute, he saw her short legs began to tire. Nearly upon her, he leapt, taking her down in a heap.

"Hello Sara," he growled.

Kane pinned her arms with his knees. He bent down and ran his fingers through her hair. Tears dropped from her eyes, but clumps of gritted sand caught them. Kane was out of breath, partly from the chase, partly out of exhilaration. His chest heaved, his eyes moving from the child's unformed breasts to her face and back again. But then he felt an odd sensation spreading out over his left temple. He wiped what he thought was rain or mud from his eyes, not remembering that the desert offered neither.

The mother lifted the board from the broken wagon seat again. She cracked it against his skull—this time the wood hit a softer spot of bone. The blow sucked the air out of Kane's throat, and he dropped in a heap to the left of the girl. He couldn't urge his eyes open or stop a buzzing sound that overcame him. So loud was the sound, it seemed as if a thousand wasps had swooped into his ears.

With the chaos inside the prison, the two prisoners, Quanto and Pike, agreed the time had come.

They'd wait until the Flame and the guard Dwyer headed for Ocotillo in the afternoon. Then they'd take out Muldoon, steal the water wagon, and catch up to Dwyer. The two of them would butcher the guard, swipe his money and his rifle, and commandeer the less cumbersome buckboard and ditch the water wagon. Then they'd head to Mexico, the Flame a plaything with which to pass time to the border.

Their weapon, a spiky stone honed to a razor-sharp edge, had passed its first test on Roberto. Pike was sure as shit it would do the job on Muldoon.

During the morning, Pike had Quanto stash the shank inside his black and whites before heading to the quarries. As the day wore on, Quanto kept bitching that the edge of it had sliced several gashes in his hip. Every time Quanto lifted his pick, he moaned and screwed up his ugly face, which Pike had always thought was as flat as a barn owl's.

"Feel like pouring my canteen down my britches," he grumbled. "Hip's on fire."

"I don't give a rat's shit about the pain," Pike said. "It bleeds anymore, Muldoon's gonna see the blood soaking through."

"Blood's dripping down my leg, puddling in my shoe."

"Just keep your fat ass turned. Hit the rock like you always do. Muldoon won't notice, if you don't turn around and show him."

"It almost time?" Quanto's lip trembled.

"Should see 'em coming out the sally port soon. When you spot Dwyer's hat, set on Muldoon right quick."

"Why's it gotta be me who kills Muldoon?" Quanto whispered.

"You got the rock." Pike scratched at his chin. "You want me digging around in your pants, so I can do the killing?"

"Why do I have the rock?"

Pike didn't answer. The two men kept hammering, driblets of sweat winding down their faces.

Another hour passed before Pike eyed Dwyer's buckboard moving out. "Looky there," he whispered. "They got another gal with them. In the back."

"That's a girl a piece," Quanto said, grinning.

Pike smiled back. "I get first pick."

Jacob Hoddle, the softest and most talkative convict Pike ever served time with, had eased up behind the men. "You two could work this pile faster. We don't go in until you break up all this rock. And the rest of us are almost done. I sure wish you'd take to it faster."

Pike considered killing Jacob on the spot, just to shut him up. But killing him would ruin the whole enterprise.

"Who you think they got cooking tonight?" Hoddle asked. "Huh? Flame's gone to town. Jo won't do it. You think we might starve? Go hungry till morning? I like the Flame's cooking alright, but it ain't Jo's. Jo's grub was tastier than angel fare, I tell you what. There's the durn truth. Better than they serve up in heaven."

"Shut your damn mouth, Hoddle," Quanto said, spitting as he did.

"Mosey on back to your work, now, would you?" Pike pressed, attempting—despite a murderous urge—to be polite. "We got to finish this like you said."

"Oh, sure, guess you can't talk and work at the same time, which would make things more pleasant around these parts. I've a mind to ask about switching cells, what with you two not being up for much conversing. Where I come from, people like to have a good chat now and then—"

"We got to finish," Pike interrupted.

"Right." Jacob shuffled off with a whistle.

Pike glanced out and saw Dwyer's buckboard head down the road.

"Now or never," Pike said.

Quanto nodded and trudged off toward Muldoon, who was pacing back and forth, stopping every few steps for a chug of water from his canteen.

"What you need, Quanto?" the guard barked.

"Just a little thirsty, is all."

"Water break in fifteen. You can fill up your canteen then. Not before."

"I'm feeling poorly."

"You'll be feeling extra poorly you don't get back to them rocks. You and Pike slow as snails today."

Pike watched Quanto finger the shank in his pants.

"Get back to work, Quanto."

Quanto dug it out too slowly.

"What the hell are you doing?" Muldoon said, then swung his barrel up to fire.

Quanto moved forward, closing the distance, probably making a shot impossible. But as Muldoon swung up his rifle, the barrel happened to clank against Quanto's head.

To Pike, it sounded like a thick book had dropped to a hard dirt floor.

"Corn!" Muldoon shouted.

Pike was glad Quanto was able to shake off the blow. He watched his partner thrust his weapon towards Muldoon's chest. As he did, Corn leapt for Quanto, tackling him into the dirt. Muldoon pressed the barrel of the gun against Quanto's head.

Pike saw a wide-eyed Quanto staring up at the barrel of the rifle and thought his partner was about to meet his maker. But Muldoon shifted it away from Quanto's face. Quanto leapt up at once and began to struggle again. All the inmates, including himself, considered Muldoon one of the easiest guards to fool, so it surprised Pike when Muldoon reared up and punched the prisoner three times in the face until Quanto fell like a tree at his feet.

"Looks like you broke the dimwit's jaw." Corn sounded surprised.

Pike was curious, too, because Muldoon didn't come off as all that rough compared to some of the other guards.

"Have a couple of the boys haul him to the infirmary," Corn ordered. "I'll bring in the rest of the gang."

Pike looked away and shook his head as two inmates dragged

off his partner, the lower half of Quanto's face swinging, as if on a hinge.

Dwyer headed slowly out the sally port. When he saw what looked like trouble back at the quarries, he stopped. Corn soon waved him on with a gesture that said order had been restored.

Just like the thick and windless air around him, the reins remained idle in his hands, the worry about what lay ahead giving him pause.

"Get going," Flossie said. "Please."

Dwyer nodded and shook the reins, the horses responding with a quick trot. A mile down the road, he decided they'd put enough distance between the buckboard and prison. "Go ahead and pull them off," Dwyer said to Dr. Madrigal and Jo, who'd been lying flat underneath several layers of scratchy government blankets. "No one's around."

With Emma's help, Dr. Madrigal and Jo shook off the blankets and sat up. Each breathed deeply, with Jo looking pale and shaky in the harsh mid-afternoon heat.

"Second they see we're missing," Jo said, "they'll come after us with Christ H.'s hounds. We'll be filling for one of my pies before long."

Dwyer could only hope Jo was wrong. "That ruckus in the quarries will be keeping them busy long enough."

"Don't you be so certain. That wife of Samuels has it in for me. Wants the hanging just for hanging's sake, and she's got her goose-necked lover Sheriff Dobbs to see the deed is done. She's been taking daily strolls past my cell. Came by just this morning. Taunting me with a rope. Dangling the durn thing in my face. She finds out I'm missing, she'll be caterwauling from here to Montana."

He couldn't argue with the woman, so he urged the horses into a faster canter.

In the distance ahead, Dwyer spotted three buzzards circling. As the wagon drew closer, the horses whinnied. Dwyer yanked the reins, and the wheels dug in with a crunch.

"What is it?" Flossie asked him.

"Don't know." Standing at his full height, he thought he saw a wagon wheel. To see for sure, he leapt to the ground and walked a ways forward, scanning ahead. Soon enough, he homed in on the accident. His first instinct had been to rush toward it, knowing those aboard probably needed help. But with his obligation to Jo, Flossie, and Dr. Madrigal, he held off and headed back to the buckboard to share what he'd seen.

"We hide, yes?" Dr. Madrigal said when hearing of the upturned wagon. "Anyone see us, Josephina will hang." The doctor climbed into the back, and Jo lay next to him, both still as coffins. Once Flossie and Emma had pulled the blankets over the pair, the horses moved forward. The wheels digging up small pillars of dust, Dwyer closed in quickly on the overturned wagon.

Dr. Adair gingerly examined the unconscious Quanto, determining that the patient had undeniably broken his lower mandible in two locations. Though an excruciating injury, he nevertheless decided against dosing the convict with morphine or giving him ether. To him, dulling a convict's pain was illogical. A criminal should be punished, and Adair was of the mind that Gila Territorial treated its prisoners too well. Some in Ocotillo referred to it as a country club. And that floozy, Flossie Abbot, was even allowed to sing again, traveling to and fro as if she were free as prairie grass.

The break was as bad as any Adair had ever seen, barring one instance in Idaho, when a log had sprung loose from its rope, flipping up and smacking a fellow. It sent the man airborne, and he'd landed some thirty feet deep into the woods.

He hadn't lived through the night, choking on his own vomit after Adair had attempted to wire the jaw shut. If Quanto met the same fate, Adair wouldn't be altogether surprised. A jaw broken this badly had little chance of healing.

Setting the mandible through sheer manipulation was tricky, but Adair accepted the challenge. Leaning over Quanto, he cradled the criminal's head in his left arm and took hold of the misplaced bone in his right. Slowly, he pushed the mandible back in place, setting it by wrapping twine around the man's head, pushing it tightly over the lips, nose, and right eye. Adair chuckled. Quanto looked like a chicken ready to be roasted. Seconds later, however, the twine loosened, and the jaw swung loose again.

Sighing with frustration, Adair tossed the twine to the floor and stomped on it. He was so looking forward to an evening of sherry, laudanum, and the newest Sherlock Holmes he'd received in yesterday's post. And his cat, Solomon, would be waiting for him as well. He could think of nothing more pleasant than an evening in his favorite high-backed chair, Solomon on his lap, the tall glass of sherry, the lovely laudanum, and the new Holmes. But it looked like those luxuries would have to wait.

Quanto would need surgery. Adair would have to pry open the convict's head and set the jaw with wire. For surgery, Adair would not risk the dangerous man waking. He set out for ether. He was certain he had some stored inside the infirmary, though he'd had little use for it since his appointment at the prison. He'd almost always insisted on carrying out the most painful procedures with patients fully cognizant of their ordeals. Rummaging through a cupboard above the washbasin, he removed several large bandages and searched behind a jar of menthol. He found nothing. Not even chloroform. He was almost certain he'd ordered chloroform.

He peered into an adjoining cupboard, this one filled with Mrs. Samuels's medicines. He was certain he hadn't put the ether or chloroform in there. A quick check proved him right.

Finally, he figured he had forgotten to order either anesthesia. Surgery would have to proceed without. Or, he thought, perhaps he should just let the man give up the ghost. Unfortunately, the superintendent had specifically ordered Adair to not let the man die.

It angered Adair that Samuels, wanting Quanto alive for questioning, had first decided Madrigal should perform the necessary repairs. But then Mrs. Samuels insisted upon a real physician. Of course. Only a real physician could handle a complicated procedure such as this. Before Samuels relented, he'd made Adair swear to do what he could to save the animal. So Adair had promised to do whatever was within his means to patch up the man. How he hated Samuels.

Looking upon Quanto now, Adair surmised that the patient would certainly expire if his jaw remained in its current crooked state. If he didn't die, surely he would never speak audibly again. Truthfully, Adair wasn't certain he'd be able to speak *with* surgery, for a break this bad sometimes damaged the vocal cords. Vacillating between performing and not performing the surgery without chloroform or ether, Adair fleetingly wondered if he should get Madrigal to assist him. This would achieve two goals: he'd have some help with the tricky procedure. Also, if anything went awry, Adair could blame the Mexican.

But Adair didn't want to give Samuels this particular satisfaction. Plus, he didn't dare admit to any of the guards that he feared a man broken up this badly. Finally, after several minutes of contemplation, he convinced himself Quanto would remain in a stupor long enough for the procedure. Besides, Corn was right outside the door.

Adair leaned over the patient and pried open his eyes for one last check. He waved the lantern in front of the fixed eyes, testing them against the light. Neither shrinking nor growing, the pupils remained as tiny as Russian caviar. Confident, Adair raised his long knife and pressed the blade into the tissue surrounding the mandible. He began to hum Handel's "Messiah" as the first layer and then the next gave way. God was speaking through his blessed surgeon's hands. Wedging his long fingers under the flap of tissue and gum, he reached toward the jagged fragment of bone.

Quanto opened his eyes. It took only an instant for the blade to transfer hands.

And only another few seconds before Quanto jammed the sharp instrument into Adair's temple, hammering it into—from what Adair could recall from medical school—his frontal lobe.

Once Dr. Madrigal had flung off the blankets, he had the nerve to ask Dwyer for his gun. *"Por favor."*

"Hush, you," Emma said to the doctor. "Just stay hidden. We'll give these folks a hand, then be on our way."

"What if a ride is needed? Or if injured are among them? I am first a doctor. Second a man. I am a prisoner last."

Helping inmates escape was one thing, Dwyer thought. Handing over his rifle was another.

"You should let him have it," Flossie urged. "If we're caught, they'll believe we're hostages."

"Lo siento. For you, this way it must be done."

Flossie urged Dwyer with a nod. But he didn't feel comfortable handing the convict his rifle. This seemed as careless a thing to do as anything he'd ever done. Jo was creeping out from under the layers of blankets, kicking them away from her spindly legs.

"Ain't no choice, Mr. Dwyer." She wiped the sweat from her face. "If any of us is to have a chance at life."

Still, he hesitated.

"They catch you carting prisoners around on your own accord, you might be strung up right alongside me."

"Jo!" Flossie said. "Don't imagine such a thing."

Jo snorted. "All I'm saying is you'll have a storm of trouble they see you're helping us. Besides, if Madrigal, here, wanted you dead, he'd have done it a ways back. Wouldn't take much to snap a chicken neck like the one you got holding on that head of yours."

Dwyer released his fingers from the gun and passed the rifle to the doctor, who then had the gumption to climb up onto the driver's plank next to Flossie.

"I'm just praising the good Lord to be out from under these sandpapery blankets," Jo said. "Sweating so much, I'm about to shrink to nothing."

They closed in on the broken wagon, upended on the side of the road, half of it tipping into a shallow gulch. The heat swiped at them, as they scanned the heap for movement.

When Dwyer noticed the body, he halted the horses. Evidently, this wasn't an ordinary accident, for the man had been shot. What remained of him lay halfway in the gulch on a tuft of scrub.

Dr. Madrigal leapt down from the buckboard and walked around the accident. "One dead steed." He leaned over the Appaloosa. "Wagon tongue rigged for two."

Whoever did this killing took the other horse. "Was the mount shot?" he asked the doctor. "Or did it die from injury?"

"Shot. Rifle," Dr. Madrigal said.

Looking around, Dwyer soon caught the horrible sight of the boy prone in the road. The doctor headed over, and Dwyer joined him. Looking down on the child, his stomach soured, and a taste of bitter leaves clenched his throat. Dwyer rubbed his eyes, as if trying to scrub the vision and its memory from his head. He had the urge to reverse time. To turn the wagon around and start the whole day and maybe his whole life over.

"Many things not to understand." Dr. Madrigal turned and slowly headed back to the women.

Reeling, Dwyer leaned against the belly of the upturned wagon. He stared up at the sky. The same sky he'd seen every day for all his life. It was a frank blue today, as smooth as the back of a spoon. Another day, it would be cloud stuffed, the sun a white pumpkin in its corner. And yet another day, it would swell into a purple hive, near bursting. How could something so pure languish over such a world?

Madrigal returned to swaddle the boy in one of the blankets before carrying the child back to the buckboard.

Dwyer helped him do the same with the father. The work was grueling, bloody, and sadness drizzled down on the five people until all were soaked to the bone.

Corn was surprised when Quanto stumbled outside, Adair's bloody scalpel clamped in his fist. The head guard watched the prisoner shiver, what was left of his mouth chattering. It was over a hundred degrees in the yard, but Quanto looked to be freezing to death. Corn considered shooting the inmate and had even raised his gun, shouting at the man to stop. But Quanto, in a zigzag motion, stumbled toward the sally port anyway. He didn't seem to notice the other prisoners clearing the way and staring at him as if he were a carnival freak.

But Corn never had to shoot, for Quanto fell onto the unbending earth before making it another step.

When Corn rushed back into the infirmary, he was confronted by two terrified Chinamen, both confined due to tuberculosis. The men hacked and coughed over Adair's body and explained to Corn with a lightning-quick Mandarin what had happened to Adair, whose eyes were wide open, as if he were looking at the Grand Canyon for the very first time.

Words were failing, so the pair turned to pantomime: one of them lay on a gurney, as the other leaned over pretending to operate. Then the Chinese patient sprang up and pretended to stab his friend in the temple.

By the stiff gestures toward the door that followed, Corn knew they wanted out of the infirmary. They stood near the exit, wheezing and attempting to take long breaths despite the strenuous coughs. But Corn couldn't let the contagious men out. Luckily, Muldoon showed in time.

Corn ordered him to stay with the sick men. "I'll give Samuels the news."

It had been Flossie who'd rounded the overturned wagon to fetch Dwyer. "I'm afraid we've no time for weeping now," she said as she kneeled down toward him and reached out to gently touch the side of his face.

He wasn't weeping. But the boy's death bore down on him.

"I wanted to let you know I won't be escaping with my friends," she said. "I'll be staying with you. In truth, I have no intention of escaping. Not today or any other day."

He tried to shake off his grim thoughts and listen. She'd never said anything about escaping, and he would have never gone along with this if that had been her intention. His job at the prison depended on keeping her close and then bringing her to Tucson when the time was right. Flossie escaping with a political prisoner and cook wasn't part of the detailed instructions he received every month.

She was looking into his eyes. "Aren't you glad I'm staying?"

He was about to tell her he wouldn't have let her go if she'd tried but stopped himself. Her personality lent itself to a rambunctious rebellion. He was convinced she would have gone off with Madrigal out of spite had he said such a thing. "I'm very glad."

"Good." She nodded quickly, as if she were in charge.

They joined the others, and Dwyer was surprised it had been Emma who'd devised a plan to right the family's wagon and use it for an escape. "We can unhitch one of our buckboard's horses," she said. "One horse and a wagon will be faster than walking. Even if we have to ditch it somewhere down the road. It'll at least help us get to a cooler climate with some shade trees."

Emma escaping hadn't been part of the plan, either, and Dwyer didn't want to risk it. He was glad the doctor now took his side.

"You stay with Señor Dwyer."

Emma shook her head. "I'm going with you, Doc."

"Six months is all you have left of your sentence," the doctor said. "Go back. Survive the months."

"Six months could turn into six years," she replied. "I'll take my chances, stay on with you. I can help."

"I forbid it," Dwyer said. "You're piling onto my burden by joining up with them."

"Looky here. I got one man in the world who treats me like I'm something besides dirt. And that man is Armando Madrigal."

Dr. Madrigal looked down at his hands.

"Can't talk me out of it," she said. "You'll have to hog tie me if you don't want me going with the doc. This desert's hateful. I'm a daisy, not a cactus, and don't belong in a place without grass."

Did he even have the authority to keep her with them? Dwyer wasn't a *real* guard. Emma and the others had caught on to that fact faster than Corn or Superintendent Samuels. Still, maybe he should hog-tie her. It'd be easy for him to do.

"They got some grain in here!" Jo shouted. She'd been inspecting the wagon. "Must've just picked it up from the docks. Lord have mercy! They got a whole barrel of cured meat. Someone's taken a chunk, but enough here to feed us for a month."

Dwyer stared at the road-stained, barefoot soles of the boy. He knew the meat was meant for more than just the father and son.

Dr. Madrigal handed the rifle back to Dwyer. The weight of the weapon felt good in Dwyer's hands, but he briefly wondered if the doctor should keep it. Their trip to the California coast, which is where they were headed, would be long and dangerous.

"I've never seen the ocean," Emma said. "I always wanted to see them big waves. They say it's made of salt. Did you know that, Flossie? That the water's salty? That you can't see the other side?"

Flossie pulled Emma toward her. "The law's going to implicate you in the killing of these people," she said. "Traveling around in a murdered man's wagon and eating his goods lacks prudence."

Dwyer figured Flossie was right on this. "Might want to pack as much grain and meat as you can carry and try to walk it."

Jo shook her head. "We got this thing. Our chances of dying are smaller with it. Let's right this wagon. You can tell old Samuels the horse went missing while you was in the Golden Bead. Story will fit right in with his missing prisoners."

Dwyer decided to go along, as he didn't have the energy to argue. The image of the boy wouldn't leave him.

After they'd righted the wagon, he inspected it. The axles seemed in working order. One of the benches in the back was broken, but it was otherwise road worthy. He and the doctor harnessed one of the mares. Dwyer stroked the side of its long face and wished it luck. After the wagon was readied, Jo said nothing as she climbed up into it and stared straight ahead.

Flossie reached up and tried to hug her. Jo reluctantly returned the affection.

"Emma," Flossie said. Now she embraced her cellmate.

Emma kissed Flossie's cheek and climbed up to the wagon's bench. Dr. Madrigal, with the reins already in his hands, clicked his mouth. The horse started down the road, pulling them sluggishly along.

Dwyer watched it ramble away, looking on as the three grew smaller and smaller, the way people do when they get too far to see or think on anymore.

Agnes screamed in her high-pitched, bloodcurdling way before rushing into the bedroom and throwing herself onto the bed, kicking at the quilts and pummeling the pillows with tiny fists.

"Right through the temple," Corn proclaimed. "Looked like his brain'd been stirred."

Samuels remained seated behind his desk. He thumbed through a stack of papers about new prisoners who were headed to Gila in a couple of months. A few petty thefts. One Indian caught with liquor.

His ledger was open on his lap. There, the news was bad. Agnes had been spending with a ferocious energy, ordering delicacies and fabric that she'd never eat nor use. His wife was bankrupting the prison, and if it weren't for the Flame singing in Ocotillo, the whole lot of them would starve.

Hell, what did it matter? With Jo up for execution, they may well all starve anyhow. Now Adair and Quanto were dead. Kane was long gone, it seemed. And now this. Samuels slammed the ledger shut.

"Sir?" Corn pressed.

Samuels did not answer. Contemplating the call he'd have to

put into Dobbs, he blew air from his mouth.

"We gotta do something right quick," Corn kept on. "Muldoon's waiting in the infirmary with the sick fellas who got the T.B. so bad it's thicker than a swarm of bees. You know how Muldoon's afraid of sickness."

"His mother died of tuberculosis." Samuels's eyes couldn't focus on the papers anymore. The words seemed as vague as a forgotten language.

"Sir?"

"Nothing." The superintendent shoved the ledger into his top drawer, locking it with a small gold key before rising with conviction, his stomach growling from the lack of good cooking. Light headed, he made his way over to the crank phone.

Before he could make the call, however, Christ H. appeared.

"There's something else," the lame guard said between heavy breaths, "that you need to know on."

Though it was slow going with one horse, Dwyer and Flossie, wearing their silence like heavy pelts, eased toward town. Traveling with the bodies of the man and boy weighed into them as well as their remaining mare. He could tell the horse was piqued by her heavy steps and constant head shaking. All he needed was for her to make it to town.

As Dwyer squinted toward their destination, gauging the distance between their location and Ocotillo, he spotted two figures on the side of the road. Drawing closer, he made out a woman and a young girl whose thick braid wagged against her stained pinafore. The woman, dragging her left leg in the dust, gripped the girl's shoulder as they walked along the road.

He soon reached the pair. The woman stopped and turned, her round face tear streaked and veined. The girl's clothing and face were stained with dirt and blood. Dwyer drew up the reins.

The woman heaved and coughed. The girl shivered.

143

"My boys!" she cried. "Got to go back to them. My boys!"

She collapsed on the road, and Flossie scrambled down to help her. Through her weeping, the woman told the story of the longhaired man. How she finally struck him in the head and killed him. "I took Sara and ran as best I could. Jack was in the road. Staring up at the sky. Oh, Lord. Lord."

Flossie held the canteen to the woman's shaking lips.

"And Owen," she wailed. "Both my boys shot down."

She moaned and shook, rocking back and forth in Flossie's arms.

"Ma'am," Dwyer gently said.

The woman, her eyes bulging with grief and pain, peered up at him.

"Your boy," he said, "he's here. We got him and your husband. Your boy passed on. You should know. We didn't see your other son."

The woman shrieked and tried to stand on her one good leg, clambering toward the back of the wagon, where she flung herself on the legs of her husband and son and wept.

Dwyer let the woman exercise her grief. Folks handled death in different ways. Some wept. Some angered and struck out at objects or people. Some tucked it inside as if someday they might find use for it. Others turned foot and lived out the rest of their lives as a ghost. He could always notice these people— their steps lighter, their voices clipped and quiet. He hoped the woman could carry on for the sake of her only child.

Square on his shoulders was the knowledge that he'd been the instrument of their demise. The woman had described Kane. He was sure of it. And it was Dwyer's stolen rifle that had done all the damage. But Kane couldn't be dead, as she believed. They would have found his body.

CHAPTER FOURTEEN

He'd had longer days on the range. Still, this day, filled with sorrow and nerves, had been one of the longest Breen Dwyer had ever lived through.

For most of the rest of the way to town, the woman and her daughter sobbed. Then, eerily, the weeping stopped. The daughter, as if her roots were becoming entangled with the creosote's own complicated system, looked out to the desert. The creosote, short and misshapen, did most of its growing underground. Dwyer suspected the same would be true for the girl, Sara. The girl's mother went into shock before they reached Ocotillo. Dwyer had whipped and cajoled his one horse, hoping to save the woman before she also died, leaving her daughter an orphan.

When they finally arrived, Dwyer pushed the horse toward Dr. Fowler's office, which was at the far end of town. The doctor accepted the two, speaking gently to the woman and calling her June. She stirred at the doctor's familiar face, and little Sara clung to the gray-haired man.

"I'm headed over to the sheriff's," Dwyer said. "I suspect he'll be out here sooner or later asking on what happened."

"Tell Dobbs to give the woman time," the doctor said.

Dwyer dreaded his own confrontation with Dobbs. But the sheriff would need to know about the murders of the family and the likelihood of Kane's involvement. Too, the sheriff would surely ask on the escaped prisoners, as Gila Territorial had

145

likely noticed Jo and Dr. Madrigal missing. Dwyer would swear he knew nothing. And if they investigated further, he'd deny his involvement even more.

It unnerved him, though. He'd never been much for lying. His mother could tell by his eyes, saying they changed from gray to blue with each false word. But for his sake, for Flossie's sake, for Dr. Madrigal's sake, Jo, and Emma's, too, he'd tell tales taller than the Rockies.

After situating the buckboard, he brought Flossie along into Dobbs's dark but clean office. "What brings you and the songbird?" Dobbs looked as though he was dressed for a fancy ball.

"Emergency you need to be dealing with," Dwyer said.

"Out with it." Dobbs stood from his desk, where he'd been polishing a pistol.

Dwyer gave him as many details he could about the murdered family.

Dobbs squinted at the guard. "So that's what they've been up to."

"Who?"

"The prisoners who seem to be leaking from every hole at Gila."

"Only had the one escape."

"You'd be wrong on your count." Dobbs went on to explain the call he'd just received from Samuels.

Feigning surprise, Dwyer looked accusingly toward Flossie. "You know anything about this?"

"I'm not shocked, but no, I was not aware that my dear friends were about to flee that wretched, ghastly, inhumane hellhole." She hadn't said much since they'd picked up the woman and girl. But she seemed to be carrying around the sadness and fear for the lot.

Dobbs seemed to find her outburst amusing, because he was

146

grinning and looking her up and down in a way that made Dwyer want to beat him until his hide was black and blue.

"They didn't talk to you?" Dwyer said, instead. No choice but to act surly toward her. He only hoped she'd understand.

"They talk to me all the time. Of course they do," she said without a hitch. "But they didn't tell me about this."

Dobbs had lifted his gun belt off a hook on the wall. "Escaping is one thing. Murdering young boys is another matter entirely."

"Dr. Madrigal didn't do this. He may be out, but he ain't no killer. Besides, it was Kane the woman described. And it was the rifle he took off me that was used on that boy. You can go talk with the mother herself when she's feeling up to it. June's her name. Or you can just take my word."

Dobbs pointed at him. "I'm not apt to take your word, Mr. Dwyer, not yours nor anyone else's."

"Hard way to get along in the world, if you don't mind me saying. Wouldn't last long on the trail."

"And you won't last long at Gila Territorial," Dobbs said.

"We'll be going," Dwyer said, "unless you're needing something else."

Dobbs had turned his back on the pair. He was making himself a cup of tea.

Dwyer canceled Flossie's show at the Golden Bead, watered and fed the mare, and then began the slow journey back to the prison.

"Thank you," Flossie said, exhaustion weeping into her voice.

He glanced at her profile in the twilight. Twilight in the desert was his favorite, the way it made everything glow, the way her face was doing now.

"If you ever doubt the virtue of what you did today, know that you did the right thing," she was saying. "They've no business going after Jo. Nor Dr. Madrigal or Emma."

He nodded.

"Lord have mercy, I'm tired. I wish I could just go home and sleep for a hundred years. And I'm not talking about the prison. The Sand Castle is not my home."

"Didn't think you were," he said.

"You've gotten yourself in the middle of trouble, trouble with the steepest of consequences. The best thing you can do from this day forward is stay clean of me."

"Think so?"

"Don't talk to me unless necessary," Flossie said. "It will behoove you to avoid me altogether."

"*Behoove* me? You think I kiss all the prisoners?"

"Whatever it is you want," she told him, "you cannot have it."

"Why's that?"

"You're not a fool," she said. "Kissing you was purely meant to bend you to my will. I had to save Jo, no matter the cost."

Dwyer ran a free hand through his hair and laughed. He scratched his long neck and slowed the horse, pulling the buckboard to the side of the dusty road. "What's your will now?" he asked her.

"I've not an inkling what you mean."

"I'm guessing you'd like to kiss me again. Right now. I know I'd like to kiss you." He leaned toward her, and she did as he'd hoped and expected, moving her mouth to his. They lingered there, his hand on the back of her head.

He straightened, releasing her from his embrace and picking back up the reins. "Just so you know, I've freed your friends, and you're next. Not anything you can do or say to stop me."

"I told you back there I have no plans on escaping. As loathsome as Gila is, it's safer for me inside than out here at the mercy of Judson Horner."

"You're not at the mercy of anyone or anything," he vowed.

She scooted to the far end of the bench. "If you do not tell this horse to get moving," she said, wiping her mouth on her bare arm, "I'll get out and pull the wagon myself."

Muldoon was minding the sally port when they reached the prison. "Samuels wants a few words before you head back to town." The guard was so distraught, likely about Jo, he didn't notice the missing horse. If he had noticed, Dwyer was going to say the mare's shoe had come loose, and he'd left her stabled in town. Muldoon looked nervous as a tick on a shaved dog. The person who cared for the horses, Mabel, would surely wonder right away, but he was counting on her not asking on it. In any case, he had the story about the shoe if she did.

Before Muldoon took Flossie into custody, she gave Dwyer one last glance, one he couldn't understand. And he felt wrong having to leave her, knowing another guard would come along to guide her back to her cell. He should be taking her himself.

Despite his misgivings, Dwyer did what he had to do and left her in Muldoon's charge. While waiting to be escorted to the women's cellblock, she sat on a bench near the sally port. Her hands were folded in her lap. How odd she looked sitting there in the moonlight, as though she were waiting for a train. After storing the buckboard in the wagon shed and leading the remaining mare to the stables, Dwyer trudged over to Samuels's cottage. His legs felt as heavy as tree stumps as he climbed the cottage's front steps. Pleased that Agnes was nowhere in sight, he was still unnerved at the idea of talking with the superintendent. After all, it was his rifle Kane was doing the killing with. And the escapes were his doing. It wasn't possible, he surmised, that a man as experienced as Thaddeus Samuels hadn't considered that Dwyer might be involved in the disappearances of Jo Brown and Dr. Madrigal.

149

Hunched over his desk, a tall glass of buttermilk at his right elbow, Samuels sat in his back office and scribbled on paper with a fountain pen. The ink blackened the heel of his hand and drizzled down his forearm. Seeing Dwyer, the superintendent scowled.

"Too early for the show to end," he said.

"The sheriff call?"

Samuels nodded.

"Then you know."

He nodded again. "But you had a job. It was to get Flossie to the Golden Bead. Bring home the proceeds. I need those proceeds." He pounded his fist on the desk.

"The Flame couldn't sing tonight if I held a gun to her head. We found that family, the child shot. You can't expect Flossie to sing after that."

"I expect her to sing under any conditions. I never once saw Jo complain about cooking, no matter what the day served up."

"I canceled the show. Flossie had no say in it. Figured you'd need her for questioning, anyhow."

"I need her for money. That's what I need her for." Samuels's face reddened.

"What's done is done."

"For you, perhaps."

"Can I head on home?"

"You can head home after you tell me where Jo and Madrigal are."

The silence was the same as if someone had just cocked a gun and was about to fire it into a crowded room. Dwyer didn't wait for the bullet, however, and answered the superintendent with the words he'd already prepared. "Emma Partridge is gone, too. I was about to let you know. She disappeared somewhere between finding the victims and my visit to Dobbs."

Samuels gulped his buttermilk, the yellowish liquid dotting

and webbing his moustache. "Emma Partridge wasn't much use at this prison. But I need Madrigal for his doctoring, especially now that Adair's . . . not that he was much good . . . never took to that son of a bitch . . . and the inmates are hungry," he rambled. "And I am, too. Goddamnit. Hungrier than I've been in a good while." He slugged the rest of his milk and slammed down the glass.

"I don't know where any of them are, sir. Don't know much about it. Except that Emma Partridge is likely somewhere in Ocotillo."

Samuels examined Dwyer's face. "You've been a good guard, far as I can tell. Always been glad I hired you on. Always have. Think you're a fine lad. I do."

"Thank you, sir."

"Sure wish you would've brought the proceeds back with you. Sure wish you would've gone ahead with the show."

"The proceeds?"

"Would've helped your cause, here. Would've gone a long way toward helping your cause. Yes," Samuels said. "It certainly would have."

"What cause you speaking on?"

"Well, the way I'm seeing it, after thinking on it, I'm guessing the only way they could get out of here was in the back of your buckboard."

They both turned upon hearing the door of the cottage open. "Where's Dobbs? Where is he?" Agnes screeched.

"That's the only way unless you got a different version of the events," Samuels reiterated.

Agnes appeared in the office, her face splotched, her eyelids swollen. "Isn't he here? He should be here," she muttered before spotting Dwyer. "Why's he back so early?"

"He canceled the show," Samuels said.

Agnes bared her teeth like an angry dog before racing out of the cottage into the night.

"Don't pay her no mind," Samuels said. "Adair's been murdered, and she's lost in her grief. They were quite close."

"Adair?"

"Expired while trying to repair Quanto's jaw. Muldoon's stronger and meaner than we all thought. He's a good guard. Like you. A nice young boy. If I had sons—"

"Where's Quanto?"

"Oh, he's dead, too. Dead. We got Pike in the Hole. He can rot down there for all I care."

"Sorry to hear about the doc."

"Never had much use for him, myself. But I can't have folks dying here like they have been. No, can't have that. Though I suppose it doesn't much matter anymore."

"I'd like to be dismissed, sir. It's been a long, hard day."

Samuels looked up, sweat beading his forehead.

"May I head on back to town, sir?"

"There's something . . . what were we discussing? Can't remember . . . doesn't matter."

"I'll be back tomorrow, daybreak."

Samuels stood and again pounded his fist against the desk, ink splattering his face with dark tick marks.

"Yes, that's an order. Report at daybreak."

"Yes, sir."

"Git, then! And next time bring my money!"

"I will, sir."

"When I give you an order, I mean it. I'm in charge of this prison."

"Yes, sir."

CHAPTER FIFTEEN

Although the trip was quicker on Gabby than on the buckboard, it still wasn't fast enough. Dwyer was weary, his shoulders, head, and back all throbbing. The town was emptier than usual. Seems that word had spread about the murders. Dwyer spotted Worley, who by all accounts made his living from arm wrestling any stranger who came to town. Dwyer himself had accepted Worley's challenge upon first arriving. Accepted and lost, as if his own arm was made from string. He'd taken the loss with a grin and a tip of his hat, much the same as he did now to greet the burly man.

"What you hearing?" Worley asked.

"Bad as they say."

"That man named Kane?"

"Could be," Dwyer said.

"I'll keep an eye out."

Dwyer rode on through town, noticing a brown three-legged dog staring at him from in front of the Golden Bead. Determined to ignore the dog, he lumbered on toward the dry goods store. He climbed the smooth, worn planks of the staircase to his room. Jenkins had warned him about how slippery the steps became in rain, but it hadn't rained since his stint at the prison began.

Once at his door, he saw that Jenkins had left him another parcel. His fifth. Just as discussed before hiring on.

Inside the unventilated space, he sat on the edge of the straw mattress and removed his shirt. The room was sweltering, so much so it was hard to breathe. A few nights before, the heat had been so bad, he'd taken Gabby and set up camp on the outskirts of town for some fresh air.

Tonight, he shoved open both his windows, and a bullet-sized horsefly buzzed in, as if the filthy insect had been waiting for him to come home. Though the open windows offered little in the way of relief, he wouldn't be sleeping outside tonight, not with Kane on the loose.

Making Kane suffer in intolerable ways filled his mind. What the animal had done to Flossie was enough to kindle violent fantasies of vengeance. Now that he'd murdered a child, Dwyer, if given the chance, could imagine tying the man to the back of a wagon and dragging him naked across the hot sand until Kane's skin scrubbed off.

Only after he'd peeled down to his undergarments did Dwyer open the parcel. Money was there, as it always was. So, too, a letter.

He dreaded these letters. Each one brought new misgivings and something like regret. He'd accepted the job though, and he'd follow through. His father had taught him as much. Regardless of how bad a job got, a real man finished the work he'd taken on. Why the stranger had contacted him and not another down-and-out cowboy, of which there were plenty, Dwyer couldn't be sure. The only knowledge he had was that the man had known his father. This wasn't mentioned right off, but the first handwritten question asked if he had the same mettle as his father.

Dwyer wasn't sure he did. Especially tonight. Doubt about his mettle now mingled with the stuffy heat and nearly suffocated him.

He went ahead and counted the cash before placing it with the rest of the money he'd stored in a square silver box that had belonged to his mother. He'd saved every cent, knowing he'd need the money for what lay ahead. Besides, a man couldn't spend that much cash on himself unless he was prone to whoring, drinking, and gambling. Thinking on that, a year ago, he might've been able to go through the wad as if it were water poured into a sieve.

He wasn't that man, now. Those days of giving up all his earnings after a long drive were long gone. What's more, it didn't matter who sent him to Gila or why he'd decided to take on the task. Not anymore. He'd be breaking her out one way or the other.

Laying his head down on the stiff pillow, he thought about Flossie. The horsefly alighted on his cheek. After swatting it away, the tickle remained. Lying awake on the lumpy bed, he longed for her, as he had never done before for any other woman. The loneliness, something he never much minded, now unbearable. Even though he'd never lain with her, he had something akin to the memory of her body, a memory born from so many nights of dreaming her up, considering what it would feel like to have her near him. Worse than the loneliness was the worry and guilt at having to leave her at the prison. That she was locked up in a cell tormented him. But he couldn't show his cards yet.

He cursed at himself for these thoughts, wishing he could return his mind to why he'd taken the job in the first place: the money. The money, alone. More money than he'd ever known. How simple it was then.

He'd tired of the droves and the roundups and the travel, sure enough. But what he couldn't stand anymore was the rough treatment of the animals, especially the horses. A cow seemed to have little in the way of feeling. After being branded, dehorned, and castrated, the calves would simply wander back into the pasture to nurse off their mamas. Still, it bothered him some when the other boys adopted the harsh methods of making a stubborn cow move by tossing sand in its eyes or twisting its tail until it broke. But it was the way many treated their horses that irked him most. Some cowboys didn't think much of their horses and would ride whatever was placed underneath them. If the horse bucked, it would get a fist in the face. If the behavior was worse, the horse would sometimes be shot and eaten. Dwyer was teased day and night about his devotion to the horses, but few would cross beyond teasing.

Taller than almost all the men he rode with, a distinct disadvantage, Dwyer had earned respect by being an expert with a rope, the lariat almost an extension of his body.

Still, he would lie awake on those long drives and listen to the cowboys' songs and the bellowing from the cattle and wonder if this was all he'd make of his life. As a cowboy, he was always moving toward something, always in the grips of the next destination, the next stop, the next start, always in a state of being when often enough he just wanted to be.

And it was while he was in this state of mind that he received his first letter. It had been waiting for him in Abilene. And whoever had left it had known about Dwyer's acquaintance with a prostitute called Honeyjar Jane. Dwyer would never deny that he'd been relieved of much tension in Honeyjar's arms, but the friendship between the two persisted beyond the pleasures she'd brought him on her small feather mattress. As time wore on, Dwyer stopped meeting her on that mattress and began sharing meals with her instead. Throughout the years, they'd confessed feelings and ideas they wouldn't have told another soul, for both spent most days pretending to be unruffled by the dealings around them. His benefactor must have understood that Honeyjar was the best person to be trusted with such a letter. He'd always wondered how the man had figured that out, given that few knew about Honeyjar and Dwyer's relationship or would have guessed it was anything but a man wringing out his desires on the softest thing he could afford.

He'd never had feelings this strong for Honeyjar Jane. If he had, he would have married her, whore or no whore. No, what he was feeling right now wasn't familiar. A very slight breeze cooled the room by a few degrees, but Dwyer still swooned from the heat—whether the desert's or not.

CHAPTER SIXTEEN

"To have one of your escaped convicts go on such a rampage in my county, thereby terrorizing its citizens, is entirely unacceptable," Sheriff Dobbs said. "In addition, Mr. Samuels, you are now missing three more inmates. Do you plan on letting them all run free?"

"Even your no-good deputies should be able to locate an old woman and a Mexican traveling together," Samuels replied. He hadn't even led the sheriff back to his office. He kept him in the front room, Agnes's so-called parlor, closer to the door in case Samuels had the urge to throw the man out.

Dobbs sniffed in disgust. "I've a choice. Order my men to hunt down your newest escapees or look for a man who delights in murdering children. I don't have enough manpower for both. So, I'm going after the murderer."

Samuels nodded. Earlier, Dobbs's deputies had found the other boy who'd been shot in the back. The deaths of those boys leaned hard on him.

"You send your own men to look for the most recent Gila fugitives," Dobbs said. "I, for one, don't have a soul to spare."

"Why is it you have no concern for Jo Brown, whom you just yesterday wanted to hang?"

"Jo Brown murdered a prisoner, a no account—"

"She did no such thing." Samuels's eyes burned, and he rubbed them with his right fist. "And the no-account prisoner who died was probably more innocent than you and your lot."

158

"How dare you!"

"I didn't dare anything. I came out and spoke truth. Ah, hell, I'm sour on this particular conversation. I'm soured with just about every goddurn thing in this godforsaken place."

Samuels escorted Dobbs to the door.

"Where's your wife?" Dobbs asked, once on the porch.

Samuels yawned. Agnes was in the infirmary, cleaning out Adair's cabinets. She'd be up all night. Maybe she'd leave him alone for a while. Just a few hours. So he could get some rest.

"I asked where Agnes was," Dobbs pressed.

Samuels's thoughts returned to Breen Dwyer. No, a fine lad like Dwyer wouldn't have gone along with such a scheme. A forthright young man. If he had a son, he'd like a boy like Dwyer. Yet, Dwyer should've checked the back of the wagon as was standard. Yes, it was standard to make such a check. Must've forgotten. It happened. It certainly did.

"Did you hear me?" Dobbs said. "Where's your wife?"

"Mrs. Samuels?"

"That is the wife I'm speaking of, unless you've another stored away in a drawer."

Samuels shook off his muddy thoughts. "You've no business with her."

"She sees things you no longer see," Dobbs said. "Her insight is ever so valuable."

"Mrs. Samuels is detained. You've no business talking to her."

"I do," Dobbs said. "I've a great deal of business with her."

The darkness had brought a stretch of stars, the day's wind blowing aside most of the cloud cover. Samuels rolled his neck side to side, wishing his thoughts would become clear as this night sky. When his thoughts became sickly, he always tried to look up at the sky or out at the horizon. The place did seem touched by God when he did that. But it was his job to look after the folks around him, and so he was surrounded with all the ugly that God seemed to ignore.

"Dobbs, I'm feeling poorly. Just get on back to Ocotillo where you belong."

"I believe I'll have a good long chat with Agnes first, as is my custom."

The Colorado, particularly loud tonight, raged in Samuels's ear, rushing through his blood like the strongest current he'd known. Drowning, he couldn't stop himself from lunging towards Dobbs, pushing the sheriff off the porch with a bull's force. Dobbs fell onto his back. Samuels shoved a forearm up and under Dobbs's chin and then whipped out his Colt, pressing it firmly against the man's temple.

"Tell me," Samuels said, "what type of chats do you have with my wife?"

Dobbs attempted to wrench free, but Samuels was stone.

"If you don't remove your firearm," Dobbs said, "you'll be imprisoned with the very men in your charge."

Samuels slammed the man's head into the dirt.

"This is . . . hardly . . . necessary," Dobbs sputtered.

"Tell me," the superintendent raged, cramming the tip of the barrel deep into Dobb's fleshy temple.

"Allow me to stand, and I shall tell you."

Samuels moved his weight off but kept the Colt trained on the sheriff.

Dobbs rose and brushed off his clothes. "I shall be leaving now. And I know you wouldn't dare shoot me. You're all talk. Agnes has said so on more than one occasion."

Dobbs started for his horse, but Samuels lunged for his collar and pulled him back as he sputtered and choked.

"You better damn well tell me what business you had with my wife," Samuels said, seething. "I will shoot you. I will most certainly shoot you. I've a right craving to shoot you dead."

"Let go!"

"Tell me, you fool!"

"After your wife . . . after she—" Dobbs paused to cough and clear his throat, Samuels having released him.

"After she what?"

"After your wife had that incident with the Gatling, killing that guard," Dobbs said, "folks . . . they wanted a trial."

"What folks?"

"Particularly," Dobbs said, "the family of the guard Agnes killed."

"What?"

"I persuaded them," Dobbs said, "to drop their efforts against Agnes."

"And in return?" Samuels lunged toward the sheriff again, but Dobbs backed away.

"I convinced Agnes to show me her . . . her . . . *appreciation.*"

"You sonofabitch!" Samuels grabbed the sheriff by the back of his head and smashed his face into a post. "Tell me what you mean by that!"

Dobbs, blood flooding up between his eyes, said in a muffled voice, "I don't see how the details would improve your situation."

"I'm not worried about my situation. It's your own that should concern you. Tell me, or I'll shoot you dead. I swear to the good heavens I'll kill you on the spot."

"Afternoons." Dobbs wiped the blood from his eyes. "Many afternoons . . . she had this . . . this—"

"This what?"

"This book from New York with all sorts of lurid positions. She's limber, your wife, so limber."

Samuels took aim between Dobbs's eyes. He cocked the trigger.

"But . . . you demanded . . . you demanded I tell you."

Growling, Samuels lowered the barrel, pointing it instead at the sheriff's privates. He fired to the left, the bullet burrowing into the blood-splotched post. Then the superintendent spun around and stalked off towards the infirmary.

Samuels stumbled on a rock and dropped to his knees on the hard sand. For just a moment, he recalled how he used to pray. That was before he'd become contaminated by all the filth in this cursed place. Praying wasn't possible anymore, not with all he'd seen. The God he'd prayed to as a child couldn't have possibly created Gila Territorial Prison. Couldn't have possibly have created Agnes in her current state.

He rose, brushed the dust from his trousers, and stalked toward the white building, his Colt swinging at his side.

Only dim light emitted from the crack under the infirmary's door. Samuels approached and slammed it open. "Agnes," he said to the near-empty room, as the two tuberculosis patients had been relocated to another cell.

He received no answer.

"Agnes!"

And there she was. Near Adair's medicine cabinets. A dozen small bottles had been opened. Emptied. Agnes still clutched one near her vomit-stained pinafore. Held it tightly as if it could seal the holes in her heart.

Samuels kneeled down, the odor of the chemicals dizzying. "Agnes." He touched her once plump cheek. He remembered that sweet plumpness. Now her face was hard, cold, as if chiseled from wood. His wife was dead on that floor. But he knew that she had died long before now. She'd died with their babe.

Samuels stood and backed away. From what he could see, the infirmary was spotless. Agnes had scrubbed all of Adair's and Quanto's blood from the floors and walls. He hated to sully the room, her last bit of work.

The only soiled spot was next to his wife. The spilled

medicines. The vomit produced by a body struggling to purge itself of those final poisons.

He veered back toward her and sat next to her on the clay floor. Wrapping his left arm around her, he raised the right— still clutching the Colt—to his head.

He held her tightly, as if both were riding on a runaway wagon. He would stop her from falling or being thrown. He would take her home.

CHAPTER SEVENTEEN

Dobbs wanted to go home to his fat wife. He never thought he'd want such a thing, but, after fourteen hours at Gila Territorial, he longed for the comfort of his red-cheeked wife's pillowy embrace.

Lois Dobbs had only been thirteen on their wedding day. He remembered fondly the first few years with his young bride, skinny as a stick with a sprinkling of freckles on her nose. After birthing three children, however, she'd swollen to the size of a Conestoga. Dobbs kept her around for her cooking, mothering, and superb management of the household but remained drawn toward thinner women, the straight-hipped variety with ribs poking through and faces sharp as ploughs.

And it was those particular cravings that got him embroiled in this thorny predicament. A predicament he aimed to pass on to some other fool as soon as possible.

He'd had the superintendent and his wife carted over to the icehouse with the rest of the dead. Bringing in the coroner was impossible, because Adair had served that post in addition to being the prison physician. Dobbs acknowledged that the idiot had been skilled at neither, and his death was no great loss, except that he, as sheriff, was now required to perform the sickening task of inspecting and writing a report on Agnes, a woman he'd bedded on countless occasions. The two had abused every orifice, every moist corner on the human body, to pleasure themselves.

His teeth chattering, Dobbs tried not to look upon his former partner in the art of making love. She was coated in vomit, bile, and Samuels's brains, and Dobbs was highly annoyed that someone so divinely delicious in life could become so hideous in death. For causing him so much trouble and for the recent fustigation, he wanted to slap the dead superintendent's face. Since only a portion of the man's face was left to slap, that deed was impossible. Astonishing, Dobbs pondered, how one bullet to the temple could wreak so much damage. Scrubbing Samuels's head off the white granite had taken four inmates most of the night.

Ah, the heat was a glory to God once he left the icehouse and returned to the cottage. Yet the odor inside—so permeated with the sickly-sweet gardenia smell of Agnes—sent his stomach quivering.

Leaving the front door open, he hoped that some of the smell would waft out.

Once in the office, he sat down at Samuels's desk. Governor Zulick's secretary had called earlier and vowed a hasty replacement. Dobbs wasn't certain how long it would take to find a new superintendent, but unquestionably the governor would process the paperwork quickly. Surely, he wouldn't expect the sheriff to remain at the prison away from his family any longer than he'd already been. Perhaps, Dobbs thought, he should use his authority to appoint one of the guards as a temporary replacement. That way, he could go home. Reflecting on this, Dobbs realized that would be impossible. He knew all the guards, and none was up to the task.

"Oh my." He wiped the sweat from his brow, the chill he'd experienced earlier having completely dissipated. Now he was burning up. After finding one of Agnes's ornate paper fans, he began to vigorously fan himself.

"Sheriff," a voice called from outside.

Dobbs saw Breen Dwyer's lanky silhouette in the doorjamb.

"Why hello, Mr. Dwyer. Last we met, you had been scraping the dead from the road. What might I do for you? I am quite busy you see."

"Boys sent me to ask who the new super might be. They're threatening to walk off. A few of the younger ones already left. Not used to all this killing and dying. That's what I'm guessing."

"Exactly what Zulick needs—prison guards striking."

"They're not up to striking," Dwyer said. "They're just wanting to leave. Whole prison's gone to hell in a handbasket, and I don't think you'd be disagreeing with me on that matter."

"I certainly wouldn't disagree with you. But I would hold you accountable for a great deal of the hell inside this particular handbasket."

"You got an answer for the boys or not?"

"Tell them Samuels's replacement is on his way. Anything to shut them up and keep them doing their jobs."

"I ain't gonna lie to them."

"Tell them whatever you please. Meanwhile, you should do everything possible to make this transition an easy one. Samuels may have been tricked into believing you had nothing to do with the most recent escapes, but I'm not quite as addled. And, if I am here for any longer, you will certainly be parting ways with Gila Territorial, and not on your own volition."

Dwyer stomped off the porch without another word and headed back to the yard. Dobbs watched him approach the guards who were pacing the catwalk. Their rifles cocked, Dobbs could tell they were edgy. He'd ordered the prisoners to stay inside their cells and be fed slices of cured meat for breakfast. How long he could keep them inside he didn't know. Even he understood that six men to a cell would certainly start killing each other, given enough time.

Wringing his hands, he was about to shut the door when he saw a carriage in the distance. The cottage, positioned on a hill, looked down upon the prison and the road leading to it, so he was able to watch the carriage easing up to the sally port.

The gate swung open. The carriage rode in.

Dobbs stepped down from the porch, straightened his ascot, and thanked God that someone had finally come to relieve him.

The man came out into the sunlight and squinted toward the gleeful Dobbs. Clad in brown wool despite the heat, the man's bronzed skin was capped with silver-white hair. He strode through the doorway and ducked to avoid hitting his forehead on the beam. He didn't bother to shake the sheriff's hand, which Dobbs held out in greeting.

Instead, the man crammed his papers into the sheriff's palm and requested he step aside.

Dobbs did so, for the man didn't seem the type to toy with. "I'm at your service, sir, despite my lack of rest."

"Where'd Samuels keep his files?"

Dobbs pointed toward the small office to the side of Agnes's parlor. Glancing over the man's shoulder toward the carriage, he decided that this one didn't come with a fetching wife. Or at least she wasn't with him. That was unfortunate, but at least he'd be able to leave this hellhole.

"Aren't you going to inspect my papers?" The man sounded incredulous.

"Oh yes," Dobbs said. "Of course. Of course. I should look over these documents at once."

"I should think so, Sheriff."

"Harper Jones," Dobbs read aloud.

Jones didn't respond. Instead, he marched into Samuels's office and immediately began rifling through prisoner files. Finally, he yanked one out from the middle of the stack and flattened it on his desk. Disregarding the superintendent's pricey swivel chair, he stood stooped over, tracing his finger down the various pages.

"Perhaps I can assist you in locating something?" Dobbs asked.

Jones straightened. "Are my papers in order?"

"Quite."

"Then you are no longer needed. Before you go, send in the head guard."

"That would be Cornelius Hammond, sir."

Jones ignored him and started rooting through Samuels's drawers.

"I'll send in Corn before I depart, then."

"What?" Jones asked, glancing up.

"I shall send in the head guard, Mr. Hammond, sir."

As Jones nodded and slammed shut one drawer, Dobbs backed out the door. He was so happy to be leaving, he nearly cried.

CHAPTER EIGHTEEN

Dwyer didn't have to sneak. He just walked past Christ H., who was snoring near the gate. Mable whistled as he strode by her cell, and Rosa, Mable's neighbor, said something in Spanish. Mable's cellmates, Berthalea and little George, were sleeping on their shared cot. Dwyer opened the iron gate a few inches in order to drop inside a sack full of fruit, meats, and a toy top he'd bought in Ocotillo to keep the child occupied.

Reaching Flossie's cell, he stood in front of the iron straps and blocked the sun. Though the sun burned down on the back of his head, the cell's interior was entirely in the shadows. He craned his neck and squinted but didn't see her anywhere.

As if by magic, Flossie materialized, her long fingers with their oval nails curling around the lattice. He warned her to speak in low tones, and she nodded, tears and weariness in her coppery eyes.

Holding his keys steady, so as not to jangle them, he let himself in, quietly closing the barred door behind him.

Side by side, they sat on her bunk.

"Sorry about the lockdown," he said.

"I'm sorry for us all."

"I brought you something." He removed an orange from his pocket, one he had purchased in town before riding in that morning.

Flossie took the fruit and immediately began peeling it. When the sweet citrus wafted into her nose, she breathed deeply.

"Smells delicious. Heavenly." She broke the fruit into wedges and held them in her lap, all except one, which she raised to her face.

"Aren't you gonna eat it?"

"I miss the sweet smells more than almost anything. Perfumes. Fruits. Roses. The cypress that grows on the Pacific coast."

"You can have them all back," he said.

"That is an impossibility." She finally popped the wedge into her mouth and shut her eyes as she tasted and swallowed.

He moved closer to her, but she gently pushed him away. "Not in here."

"I can wait," he said.

"You'll be waiting forever."

"I want you to listen to me," he whispered harshly. "We're about to get ourselves a new superintendent. Might already be here. The man could be good, could be bad. Chances are high they'll send in someone tougher than Samuels."

"He's really dead then? I heard the rumors."

"He and his wife. Samuels shot himself, it seems." Dwyer was uncomfortable with the idea of suicide and had fond thoughts about the superintendent. Some guilt played into what he felt given that those last escapes, the ones that had likely sent Samuels over the edge, had been his doing.

"What did she die of?"

"Got into Adair's medicines. Swallowed as much of the poison as a body could take. And then she took some more."

"She deserved to die."

He shrugged. "Some deserve their lot. Some don't."

"Some must accept their lot."

"Don't plan on letting you rot in here."

"You don't have a choice," she said.

"I do. You do," Dwyer insisted. "I'm one for making choices. That's the way it's gotta be."

He yearned to pick her up and carry her out, shooting anyone who stood in their way.

He studied her eyelashes as she blinked. "You do realize," she said, "I want out of here, desperately want out of here. But . . . can't."

"You can."

"I *am* an adulteress, you fool. And a man died. Matty died. My friend. However it happened, it was my fault."

"I'd like to know how it happened." He pulled her toward him and wrapped his long arms around her slender frame. She leaned into him for a moment before retracting. "And I'm set on freeing you from this cell, no matter the circumstances." His eyes having fully adjusted to the shadows, he could see how drawn and thin Flossie was.

"How?" she asked.

He was about to explain when he heard Christ H.'s voice and the hounds barking. Dwyer swiftly crouched up against the back wall. If caught, Dwyer wondered if the seasoned guard would even make a remark. Given the current bedlam, Christ H. might choose to ignore him. Yet, he had no urge to burden the guard further. Despite his ulterior motives for being employed at Gila, Dwyer had acquired a great deal of respect and fondness for many who worked here, Christ H. among him. Also, he pitied everyone at the prison, guard and inmate alike, what with the place in such an uproar, an uproar he should really be helping to ease.

"You can go," Flossie said.

"I hate leaving you."

"I am quite capable of being alone. In fact, I prefer it that way."

"You can talk like that all you want, but I know you like having me around."

"Just leave, please, before they see you." She popped another slice of orange into her mouth.

Dwyer paused before the lattice, the light in the cell as murky as weak tea. "The man you were married to, what's he like?"

"What does Judson Horner resemble? Or what's in his heart? Shall I compare him to a Shakespearean character? Because I would say he is as pompous, self-righteous, and as loquacious as Gonzalo or Polonius. And he's certainly as cruel as Iago. But he wasn't as smart as any of them. As far as intelligence, I would cast him as Dogberry."

Dwyer didn't know what she was talking about. "I don't know much about Shakespeare."

"Well, if you ever decide to learn, you will be most identified with the Earl of Kent, or perhaps I don't know who you are. As you certainly do not know me. I'm no Hero. Nor am I Cordelia."

The smell of oranges swelled before he spoke again. "I intend on getting you out of here, and I want you to get ready for that day on account of it coming quick. Gila Territorial's a dangerous place, and folks will start killing each other fast if this new superintendent doesn't shape it up."

"Death is only one of the fates I fear," she said. "However, I am certain that particular fate waits for me outside these walls, not inside."

Exasperated, Dwyer shook his head. "I'll head on back this afternoon. They'll likely let me work an extra shift with all these rookies quitting."

"No need."

Before he left, he bent down and quickly pecked her gaunt and dusty cheek before she could stop him from doing it. "All that affection must've been a dream," he said when she didn't respond to his kiss.

"Then I see Queen Mab hath been with you. She is the fairies' midwife."

"We need to feed these inmates some real food." Harper Jones had just heard of Dobbs's imposed lockdown and the trouble it was causing. "Where's the prison's cook?"

"We're self-sufficient, here," the head guard said. "All the work, including cooking, is done by the prisoners."

"Then please do fetch the prisoner who cooks out of his cell and send him to the mess hall immediately."

"*Woman* who fixed all the grub escaped. Can't blame old Jo for that."

"Ah," Jones said. "The woman up for execution. Just read her file. Samuels had made a notation at the bottom. He'd written the word 'innocent.' "

"We're darn sure it was Quanto who killed her helper. We got the weapon to prove it, too. Pike won't say much, but a few more days in the den should loosen his lips."

Jones looked down at the files. "But this Josephina Brown did kill her own husband? Yes?"

"By all accounts, yes."

"Then she *is* a murderer."

"Had some rough beatings by her old man," he said. "Hear tell—"

"So you believe there are reasons to kill?" Jones asked. "Good reasons? An eye for an eye, that sort of thing."

"Don't think my beliefs got much to do with the law, sir."

"That will be all," Jones said, without looking up.

The guard started to leave.

"One more thing," Jones said. "I wanted to ask on this fellow, Abe Kane. I've studied his file, but I'm not certain all pertinent information was included."

"If the file says the man was a crazy, no-good cur who should be shot down or strung up, then everything's there."

"Did Kane have any belongings on him when brought to Gila?"

"We got all his things in storage. We take their personals. Some of them get back books and letters and such with good behavior. Kane never got nothing."

"Bring his personals to me," Jones ordered. "At once."

Kane scraped the blood and pus from his right eyelid before attempting to pry it open. It was the same routine every morning.

Wandering the sandhills with only one functioning eye was aggravating. And the pain was so intense in the other socket, he spent much of his time searching and rooting for herbs to soothe the throbbing. Resigned to the infection and slight fever it brought, he intended to complete the task he was being paid to do, so he stayed near the river, in walking distance of Ocotillo. He needed the other half of the payment he'd been promised and would wait as long as it took, living off creatures and vegetation that few men would consider edible. Suffering now seemed worth it, as five thousand dollars was enough money to live like a king until his death and into the great yonder.

He'd avoided detection for a month now. In that time, he could have traveled deep into Mexico and back, but, with the money he'd receive, he planned on going to places he'd never been and never returning. He'd eat and bed native girls, a different one every night, and pay one to knead oil onto his back and shoulders and temples. Maybe sing him to sleep and fan him. If he had a hankering for food, any he wanted, servants would bring it out on platters. The place in his mind was green and wet and never got too hot—not like the brown, dry, and blistering landscape he wandered now.

So, despite the pain, he'd stay nearby until he'd accomplished what he'd come to do. Because he could climb the sandhills as easily as the scorpions, it had been easy to evade lawmen. But even the scorpion became hungry, and Kane was no different. His stomach empty and his throat crackling with dryness, he veered back to the Colorado. Standing on the banks, he leaned toward the water and waited. Patience is what had kept him alive this long. It's what had kept him alive his entire thirty-eight years of being. After an hour or so, he watched with savage glee as a school of fish neared. One flick of his hairless wrist brought him a fish, which he ate raw, scales and all.

The contents of Kane's personals had been spilled on Samuels's desk. "See this," Jones said, lifting a flask.

"Fancy item for a rough convict like Kane," Corn said.

Jones agreed, and Corn remembered packing it up with the rest of Kane's belongings when they brought the demon in for holding up a wheelwright. Shoot, Corn thought, durn rascal turned out to be more than just a clumsy thief.

"Mr. Hammond—"

"You can go ahead and call me Corn, sir."

"Nicknames are for cowboys, hooligans, and whores." Jones examined the flask under a lit gas lamp. "Did you wonder when he was brought in why he would own such a thing?"

"No, sir. Figured he liked to imbibe."

"Pure silver, this is. Kane look like a man who could afford a solid silver flask?"

Corn examined the small markings on the back—a woman's profile, a large *M*, a lion, and a sideways anchor. "Figured he took it. The man was brought in for trying to take things that didn't belong to him."

"John Lawrence and Company. Fully hallmarked," Jones said.

Corn thought it was a nice bit of silver, but, if put upon, he wouldn't have been able to pick out silver from gun metal.

"This is a very dangerous man," Jones said. "Should have

been hanged."

"If ever anyone deserved a lynching, it'd be Kane," Corn agreed.

Jones lifted and examined a spur-sized cross that hung from a rough chain. "Perhaps Mr. Kane thought Jesus would save him."

"You a religious man?" Corn asked nervously. He hadn't served under a religious superintendent since old Taggot was in charge. Taggot had a religious streak two roads long. He was prone to forcing even the Chinese inmates into sitting through hellfire sermons, though they understood little of what was being said and had their own peculiar religions. Taggot even had the prisoners bowing their heads for grace before each meal. After a while, he went beyond simple grace and required all inmates—Chinamen, heathens, you name it—to go down on their knees and pray for their souls every night during head count. But Taggot's most irritating edict was aimed at the guards. He proclaimed that no guard would be allowed to smoke or drink, and he recruited the town's then-sheriff to keep track of offenders. Naturally, the guards refused. And Taggot discharged a few before being replaced by another less devout superintendent, who simply hired the offenders back. The way Corn saw it, a man couldn't do a job like the one at Gila without getting liquored up on his free time.

Jones seemed to disregard his question, continuing to root through Kane's belongings.

Feeling the ache of exhaustion in his head and legs, Corn asked the new superintendent if he could head on home.

"Certainly, Mr. Hammond. I'll introduce myself to the remaining guards."

"You're sure you don't want me around for that?" Corn was attempting pleasantries, something he'd never been very good at.

Jones stared hard at him. "You look ready to drop where you

stand, Mr. Hammond. Best go."

"Yes, sir." Corn got to the door and was hoping to slip out into the night without further conversation. But, before he could wrap his hand around the knob, Jones's voice reached him.

"Did Kane ever threaten or hurt any other woman besides Flossie Abbot?"

Corn thought on this and talked aloud about how Kane had threatened and cursed everyone he came into contact with. "Didn't have much contact with the other women, truth be told. Abbot was exposed by helping old Jo."

"Had he threatened her before?"

"Can't say that he did. But Abbot's in her cell; you want me to bring her to you?"

"Not at this time," Jones said.

"You could discourse with Breen Dwyer on that there incident as well." Corn was trying to choose his best words, as Jones seemed more refined than other superintendents he'd worked for. "He came face to face with the devil. Nearly was kilt."

Jones didn't answer or look up from the files he was staring at, so Corn finally left. As he stepped off the porch, he considered doing a walk-through to check on the inmates and then thought twice. He'd had enough of Gila Territorial for now and needed one night away from the cursing and moaning of the inmates. When he had thoughts like this, it always struck him sideways. The prison could get hot as a furnace, and the days in the quarries were long and hard. But the worst part, to his way of thinking, about being sentenced to the Sand Castle or any other prison was simple. It was the single fact of not being able to leave. Even for one night. To him, confinement in itself seemed punishment enough for any crime.

Dwyer was whispering to her in the dark. "They sent in a

replacement. Likely let the prisoners into the yard tomorrow, according to Christ H."

Dwyer stood on one side of the lattice, Flossie on the other. He'd hooked his fingers around her hands. "Wish I could come inside, but the guards are getting jumpy, especially at night."

"I wish I could come outside."

Dwyer stroked her thumb. "Soon."

The dim lantern light scraped against the left side of his face, as if he were a portrait, and the artist had deliberately left half in the shadows.

"You think they're safe?" she asked him.

"We'd have heard by now if they weren't. They're wanted, all three, but if they lay low, they should be able to live out their lives without much trouble."

Flossie let go of his hands and leaned the right half of her body against the lattice. "I hate the idea of living out my life, as if it were something I must endure."

"Better than no life at all, which is what they had in here."

"I prefer neither."

"We can think up another sort. But it's got to be one out of this place."

She retreated into the darkness of the cell, where he wouldn't be able to see her.

"If you're thinking getting out of here is dangerous, it is," he whispered. "You got fellas like Kane roaming around, and you'll have the law hunting you, too. But it's got to be done. You ain't got no sort of life inside Gila. And you never will."

Flossie returned and wedged her hands through the bars. "Can you feel my pulse?"

He lightly touched her wrist.

"It is a life, isn't it? I'm alive. I'm breathing and eating. I've all five senses. I can see you and hear my fellow prisoners' dream sounds." She lifted his hand to her mouth and kissed it. "There,

I can taste the salt on your skin. I can smell the metal from your gun and the leather bridle you earlier held. And I can feel . . ."

Through the bars, he trailed his hand down her neck.

"Yes, I most certainly can feel," she said.

"You're living, true," he said. "But you're not living right."

"I'm not concerned about living right."

"I meant a life like you used to have, doing what you please, singing where you want. Acting if you get the urge."

"I act all the time inside Gila. Have you not noticed? You, perhaps, have witnessed my finest performances on Gila's dusty stage."

His head snapped in the direction of keys clanging. They both stopped talking and listened. Soon the sound faded.

"I think they're gone," he whispered. "Whoever it was."

"Good," she said. "I don't want you to leave."

"Don't want to leave." He stooped down, so his eyes were aligned with hers. "I got plenty of money. It would see us through for a good while on the road."

She released his hands. "This has nothing whatsoever to do with money. I'd rather be free and eating dirt than locked inside Gila. But here I am. And here I'll stay. I've no choice."

"I need to know what happened, Flossie. Every detail. I need to know why you're so afraid. And then we'll have a little talk about choices."

She turned and walked to her cot.

"Come on back here, Flossie," he hissed. "Can't talk above a whisper, and you know it. Everyone'll hear."

She stayed quiet.

"Damn you," he said. "You're as stubborn as they come."

"I am damned." Flossie paused. Why was she punishing him? She couldn't end the night like this. She wouldn't be able to sleep. And she didn't think he'd be able to either. She rose and went to him. When she reached her hands through the iron lattice, he clutched them and tugged her toward him. "I'll tell you my story but not in here. Do you think we could risk going to the library?"

He looked around before quickly inserting his key. Without opening the gate any wider than a foot, he pulled Flossie out onto the worn path.

The flame on his lantern barely flickered, but their shadows still twitched on the library's textured walls. "I was seventeen when my parents died." She noticed a shadow of sympathy on his face so quickly continued. "We weren't close, so you don't need to look at me like that. I barely knew them. They'd sent me away to school for most of my life. Before that, I was raised by a nanny. I remember thinking my mother was very beautiful, but that's about all I knew about her. My father had a grand moustache. And that's what I remember about him. Imagine dying and all your only child can recall about you is your moustache?"

"Can't."

"No matter. They died. That's the important part. And I inherited a fortune. Not your imaginary fortune, a real one. Almost immediately, Judson Horner, a friend of my parents, began sending me flowers and showing up unannounced to my parents' home. Well, it was my home now. He was an Englishman and living in San Francisco, and the accent was charming. Well, somewhat. It wasn't all that different from some of the accents back east. Still, he had different ideas than most men in the city who'd wanted to court me. He wasn't nearly as handsome, of course, but he seemed more polished. He was much older. Twenty years older. His ideas just seemed cleaner. I was only seventeen, after all. What I found most appealing about Judson Horner was that he supported my choice to go on stage.

He not only supported it; he helped arrange for those early shows and assisted me with details. You see, unlike Judson, most of my younger suitors had insisted I quit performing."

Someone had left a map of Europe open on the tabletop, and Flossie leaned over it, Paris near her right elbow. Maps were a favorite among the inmates, who would stare at the land formations and seas while dreaming about being free. Some who'd been at Gila longer than five years probably had a difficult time believing such places still existed. She'd overheard one inmate telling some others that the whole world was covered in gritty Arizona sand, and that the devil had eaten all the trees. She wondered if this would ever be the way she saw it. And she supposed there was a chance.

"As my star grew, Judson stayed close, fetching me anything I needed, behaving more like a servant than a suitor. If I cleared my throat, he would show almost immediately with a glass of hot lemon water. If I shivered, he'd be there with a coat. I didn't find him handsome, smart, or charming, but, back then, he was indeed helpful. And over time I became accustomed to his dull stories and insipid observations. And my life was exciting enough on stage. I had no need for excitement off stage. I believe this may be one reason I accepted his proposal of marriage eight years ago on my twentieth birthday.

"Despite my wealth and fame, we had a small wedding. Sadly, it didn't seem important. I couldn't take his name, as I had already become well known as Flossie the Flame Abbot. In any case, Judson had been a constant in my life, and it seemed natural he would continue to be. I believed this entirely until my wedding night." Flossie stared at the bindings of the books in the library. She spotted *Ivanhoe,* a novel she'd read when she was fourteen.

"What happened on your wedding night?"

"Why, Mr. Breen Dwyer, can't you guess?"

"No ma'am. I don't want to guess or imagine you with another man, as you may have figured."

"There was the usual wedding night consummation, in the most clinical sense of the word, but Mr. Horner added much more excitement. Evidently, though I was entirely ignorant of these strange proclivities of his prior to the wedding day, during relations he enjoyed striking women and choking them to the brink of unconsciousness."

Flossie had lived through the violence so many times, describing it didn't undo her. She endured it as another would have to endure an itch behind the knee or cracked lips in the winter.

With his expression caught between anger and compassion, Breen reached for her and pulled her to his chest. Her hope was that this type of violence seemed unusual and strange to him, but her suspicion of men was bright as fire.

"This is simply how it was," she said, dismissively. "I was fortunate to have wealth and the escape of the stage. I continued to perform and travel and live my life as the famous Flame of San Francisco, as you know. All of me was left on that stage every night. This was purposeful. I wanted him to have nothing of me, nothing from the real me. You should know that. He didn't know me, even though he watched my every move and insisted on knowing my whereabouts every minute of every day. When I woke in the morning, he would be standing over my bed and staring down at me. Occasionally, I would be bruised very badly, and he would bring me cold poultices to hold on my cheek or jaw. On the nights I was to perform, he was careful not to leave marks where others could see.

"It was several years before I realized he was the only person I ever conversed with in any real way. I didn't have any family. Any friendships I had prior to our marriage were forbidden. He eavesdropped on all my interactions and intercepted my correspondence. He hired several people to follow me around and report back to him. This I didn't know until later."

"Doesn't sound much better than the Sand Castle."

He was right. Her life with Judson Horner had been a prison of sorts. Still, she had been able to perform. She'd been able to eat what she pleased and bathe every day. Her clothes were soft and comfortable. Her feet were clean, and her ankles weren't rimmed with dust. Her nails weren't filthy and splitting. Her hair was silky smooth. She could read whenever she pleased and cool herself down with a fan. She could sing in her garden and cut roses to bring into the house.

Living with Judson Horner had been dreadful, yes, but it was certainly preferable to the here and now.

When they heard shouting from the cellblock near the yard, Breen stood quickly. "Might need me," he said.

"I'm sure they do."

"Going to get you back to your cell for now. We can talk later."

"We can talk tomorrow," she said. "I'm tired. Feeling as tired as I used to feel in those days. Just tired of it all."

He embraced her quickly and kissed her gently on the mouth and then on the top of her head. "I'm getting you out of this prison and making sure you'll never go back to the kind of life you had with that son of a bitch Horner. I don't have fancy words like you, Flossie Abbot, but I do keep my word. Always have."

CHAPTER NINETEEN

The following afternoon, the ordinarily dry heat became unbearably humid. Dwyer was overseeing the burial of Mr. and Mrs. Samuels, as well as that of Adair and Quanto.

The prison bone yard was dotted with wood markers and body-length piles of stones, which had been set upon the graves to keep the coyotes from digging up and consuming the dead. Neither the markers nor the stones would stand the test of time, the lives under the sand doomed to be forgotten by most. He knew not much more would be done to represent the lives of its newest residents, despite some of the newly departed having a somewhat higher station in life. Samuels's kin in Missouri were repulsed by Agnes's overdose and the superintendent's subsequent suicide. So repulsed, they refused to collect their belongings or tainted bodies.

On the edge of Prison Hill, Dwyer surveyed three prisoners shoveling out the unwieldy desert soil. Usually, a grave-digging assignment was met with dread. Yet, after spending an entire day and night locked in their cells, the three inmates assigned to the duty, one shaggy-haired outlaw who'd tried to steal a crate of liquor and two Chinese who'd operated an opium den, seemed downright chipper to be out in the sunshine, despite the morbid task.

Striding over the opposite hill, the new superintendent, Harper Jones, called out to him. "Mr. Dwyer, may I have a word?"

Now the long-faced, silver-haired Jones, his gait as stiff as wood, was moving toward him. Dwyer thought the man looked like a preacher.

"What can I do for you, sir?"

"I understand you were in close proximity to Kane before his exodus."

"Exodus?"

"A Biblical term," Jones replied.

"Well, in cowboy terms, the sumbitch got away." Dwyer didn't think he'd ever forgive himself. "Should've shot him when I had the chance but didn't. Now folks are dead. Children."

"Please," Jones said. "I am not here to ask on your guilt. It's Kane who concerns me. If we are to stop him, I need information. I need to know where he went and how he left Gila."

Dwyer told him as much as he could remember, how Kane had attacked Flossie Abbot, how he'd lost the tip of his finger. "Should've shot him."

"Yes, you already shared that."

"I was lucky to live through it, according to Doc Madrigal."

"Madrigal the prisoner who escaped?"

"Yep." Dwyer liked picturing the doctor, Emma, and Jo happy, well rested, and fed, though he doubted that was the case.

"And you wouldn't have had a hand in this escape?" Jones said.

"No, sir."

Jones cleared his throat of the dust that was being swept up into clouds by the gravediggers. "Tell me, what do you know of Flossie Abbot's crime?"

He flinched. This man had better not touch Flossie. If that happened, he'd have to kill him. "You can read the details in her file. Don't need to be asking me."

"I do need to ask you because I believe you have a special relationship with Miss Abbot."

"You'd be wrong. It's just my job to take her to Ocotillo to do her singing, and that's the extent of it."

"I believe there's more to it than that," Jones said. "Has she told you anything else about her crime? The events surrounding it?"

"Flossie Abbot's innocent."

"I believe that to be true," Jones said. "Nevertheless, in order to help her, I'll need to know the facts behind the death of her pianist and about her marriage."

Dwyer turned away from Jones to look down at the gravediggers. It occurred to him that Jones might have been nearby when he and Flossie were in the library last night. He tried to recall if he'd said anything that could get them in trouble.

"I do want to help her, Mr. Dwyer. I give you my word."

"Your word?"

"It's good."

He was realizing suddenly how ignorant this sounded and wondered if he had sounded as full up on himself to Flossie last night.

"I have nothing without it," Jones said.

"That might be true. Might not." Dwyer noticed that the convicts hadn't dug deep enough for Quanto's oversized pine box. He yelled down to dig deeper. The last thing the prison needed was Quanto's half-chewed corpse dug up by coyotes and dragged around the grounds.

After he was assured they'd resumed their digging, he turned back to Jones. "Where do you hail from?"

"I've lived many places."

"You plan on sticking it out here at Gila Territorial?"

Jones fixed his eyes on the Colorado. A steamboat meandered down its center. "I am merely a temporary replacement."

Dwyer nodded at this and continued watching over the scene below. The stench of death drifted up the hill and assaulted the air. He wished the prisoners would hurry up and finish.

"I must," Jones said, "insist you tell me everything you know."

"Still not deep enough!" he shouted to the men below.

"My motives are benevolent. That you must believe."

Dwyer looked hard at the man, whose face was built from stiff edges and angles. "The heat's something today. Don't have a lot of humidity, normally. Least I haven't experienced it."

"If you know nothing else about her crime, then say so. I'll leave you be."

"If I did know more, doesn't mean you'd need to, superintendent or not."

Jones dug into his pocket and pulled out a piece of hard candy. "You like horehounds?"

The irritation at having to discover who his benefactor was in this underhanded manner must have shown on Dwyer's face.

"I had to be sure," Jones said.

"Sure of what?"

"That you'd be loyal to her and protect her." He was still holding out the horehounds. "You don't like them? They're good candy."

Without thinking, Dwyer stuck out his hand and took the candy, though he had no intention of actually eating the treat.

"Please do tell me." Jones's voice was as solid as the stones in the quarry. "Tell me everything she has shared with you."

"I have a few things I want answered," Dwyer said. "A few things I've been wanting to ask on."

"For now, for her sake, we'll postpone that conversation," Jones said. "I'll need all you know to help her and to arrange things."

"You tell me who you really are and what this is all about." Dwyer stubbornly kicked at the dirt.

"I am an owl of the desert." Jones looked out with eyes the same color as the sky. "I have eaten ashes like bread and mingled

187

my drink with weeping."

Dwyer began to step away from the man's queer words and even queerer nature.

"I am here to help her. Not just help her escape. Help her clear her name. She was married to a murderer. Judson Horner didn't just kill her pianist."

Dwyer didn't know who else Horner had killed, but he wasn't taken aback by such an accusation. Flossie's story detailed a man who was a skilled confidence man. That Horner was also a murderer didn't surprise him. "She's spoken some about it."

"Good," Jones said.

Dwyer didn't stall any longer. He wiped the sweat from his brow and shared all she'd told him last night, not knowing which details were important and which ones weren't. The beatings. The way he had her watched. The fact Horner was an Englishman. The change in Horner's character after the marriage. Everything. By the time he'd finished, he looked below and saw the graves were ready for their occupants. From where he stood, snakes or rabbits or even ants could've made the holes. The creatures of the desert were always burrowing underneath the sand, and he wondered about this other underground world, how maybe beneath his feet was an entire new set of problems.

"Get those folks inside the graves before they rot in this sun!" Dwyer shouted down. The heat was an enemy. It spoiled the food and blistered the skin. Even the dead died more under its fiery stamp.

Harper Jones, however, had hardly broken a sweat. The only thing heated seemed to be his eyes, which flickered and burned and seared as Dwyer had relayed Flossie's story. His attention focused on Jones, Dwyer didn't see Quanto's bulk sliding out of the poorly-built coffin as the convicts attempted to heave it into the grave. But one of the gravediggers screamed like a young child, which caused him to look down again.

"Pick the damn thing up!" Dwyer yelled.

"I can see this job entails more than watching out for Miss Abbot," Jones said.

"That it does."

"But you're being well compensated?"

"Money doesn't much matter now. I'll be following through with or without your packages or letters."

Jones nodded.

"Say," Dwyer asked, "how'd you get to be the new superintendent?"

"You might say I'm an opportunist, Mr. Dwyer. When the position became open, I happened to be nearby, as you already knew. So I simply arrived at the prison and took it. It was quite simple." Jones turned and began striding back over the hill.

Dwyer called out before Jones disappeared behind a creosote bush. "Will Flossie still be traveling to Ocotillo this week?"

"She will indeed," Jones said. "You'll guard her well, yes?"

Dwyer said he would and pulled his kerchief up over his nose to block the smell emitting from the bodies below.

"You'll make sure she travels safely," Jones said. "Even if the journey is longer than usual?"

"I'll guard her with my life."

189

Chapter Twenty

Breen Dwyer had been assigned to guard her. And though they'd opened all the doors, the heat gripped the mess hall, and sweat pooled on her neck and the small of her back as she lifted the pans and bowls to the counter.

When he asked, she didn't play coy with the rest of the details of why she ended up in prison. Sure the story would make him think less of her. But last night, while she lay alone in her cell, she'd decided that was all the more reason to tell him. Once he heard about who she really was and what she'd really done, he'd want nothing to do with her and leave her alone.

"Things changed when Judson's father back in England grew ill, and he had to travel there to attend to him. At first, he'd ordered me to travel with him. When he saw how much money we would lose from canceling shows, he ordered me to stay. As you may have guessed, he had several people watching over me and reporting my whereabouts and activities to him via letters."

"Who?"

"Servants. My driver, for one. He'd even asked Matty. But what Judson never understood is that everyone disliked him. He regarded servants poorly—was rude and demanding and never paid them on time. My carriage driver, who treated his own wife in much the same way Horner treated me, was the only person who carried out his wishes. In any case, the driver was easy to avoid, as I love to walk. And I simply hired a different carriage when I needed one."

Flossie laughed at this, at the small revenges she'd taken on the man who'd stolen her life. How, back then, she'd gather her skirts and haughtily stride down the street, her chin in the air, stopping to speak with fans if they recognized her. Judson hated her speaking with anybody and would chastise her if she even looked in the direction of another man. Even if it were accidental. Out of spite, too, she'd eat platefuls of cheese and fruit and bread, even if she wasn't hungry. Judson Horner was keen on keeping her from getting fat and boasted about how much he hated large women.

But with Judson Horner out of the country, it was as if she'd just untied her corset and could breathe after a long night of singing and recitations. She grew bold and brave and went out on the town after her performances, chatting with other actors and young men and women who were enjoying San Francisco's nightlife. She'd once or twice stayed out until dawn, drinking champagne and dancing with strangers. A few of these strangers she'd bedded freely and with a fierce, reckless energy.

Judson would send her letters, but she wouldn't read them. Rather, she'd wad them up and toss them in the fireplace. She enjoyed watching the edges blacken and then explode into a quick fire before transforming into ash. As the weeks wore on, she grew accustomed to the freedom. And she decided she could never go back to the life she'd been leading with Judson Horner. She had money, after all—her parents' fortune as well as the one she'd earned as the Flame. She would give Judson enough of it to go away forever. Once he had money, her hope was that she would never see or hear from him again. She stupidly believed it would be that simple. She thought he'd go back to live in England. Or perhaps he'd sail to Paris or some Polynesian island. He could do whatever he wished, as far as she was concerned. As long as his future didn't include her.

She'd been performing five nights a week at the Nightingale.

Every night she'd pack the house. Matthew "Matty" Brewer could play more instruments than most were aware. He played the accordion, fiddle, and tin whistle. Flossie had heard him play all these instruments, though audiences knew him for his abilities as a pianist. He only had to hear a song once to learn it. Then, after a half hour of practice, he'd add flourish and flare. Sometimes, on stage, Flossie would stop singing, motion toward him, and listen to what came from the baby grand he'd be hunched over, his arms and fingers flying up and down the keys. His speaking voice, with its Irish modulations and musicality, charmed all the women. And he told the best stories, stories that would captivate the crowds. Many a night, he'd held an entire roomful of people's attention at the Palace. Because of this, Flossie was often relieved of any attention she might otherwise receive from fans, which she welcomed. In bed, Matty cooed and cuddled. He tenderly relished the pleasure they gave each other. Matty was her friend and her lover, but she didn't think she was in love with him, nor was he with her. It was the affection and fondness for each other that she treasured. The lightness and joy.

They'd never considered becoming lovers until Judson left for England. But after it happened, Flossie didn't regret one moment together. Making love, laughing, drinking champagne, and making music were good pursuits. If a heaven existed, she hoped it would include all those things. And the two met frequently in her husband's absence.

Flossie wasn't sure when Judson would return, nor did she know what would happen after her divorce. Marriage with Matty wasn't out of the question. If Matty had asked, she would have likely agreed to the union. And she might have been happy with the result. She didn't know. Would never know.

She'd essentially stopped living at her house on Castro. Rather, she and Matty resided at the Palace Hotel. The Palace was luxurious, with its fireplaces and private bathrooms in each room, and redwood paneled rising rooms so one didn't have to walk the stairs. Staff at the Palace met their every need, and the food and drink were delicious and abundant. With all that, they stayed there for a different reason. The privacy. Though almost completely assured her own servants, except for her driver, would keep their secret, the peace of mind staying at the Palace offered was irreplaceable.

She and Matty had slept in until noon one day and were still in bed. The hotel's staff had brought them up a tray of omelets, hot bread, sausages, fried potatoes, and coffee. When she rose nude to throw back the curtains on the bay window to see the street below, she remembered how Matty looked, his black hair askew and blue eyes sparking. She leapt back in bed with him, and he draped a long leg over her hips. They fed each other some of the food and talked about writing a song together.

When Judson walked in, opening and shutting the door with a click, as if he came into this room every day and the room was his own, she recalled the feeling distinctly. It wasn't shame or fear. Instead of leaping up and distancing herself from Matty, she moved closer to him, wrapping them both in the cream-colored quilts of the hotel.

"I was told I'd find you here," Judson said crisply. He removed his hat, revealing that he'd lost even more of his hair while in England. His head was unusually square. Hair sprouted from his ears and nostrils, and his nose was shaped like a small gourd. Then he frowned with lidded eyes before removing a pistol from his coat pocket. "Good sir, you should likely find your own pistol if you would like to live on."

Flossie knew Matty had a temper. She'd seen him curse at a windy day and lash out suddenly when a lout from one of her audiences shouted a crude comment at her. She felt him under the quilt tighten and straighten. Then he was out of bed, freely striding toward his belongings. Until that moment, she hadn't known he owned a gun.

When Matty removed his Colt from a suitcase, Flossie screamed at them both to stop. But no one could hear her scream over the gunshot, for Judson Horner had shot her lover in the back of the neck before Matty had a chance to turn around. She tried to help, lunging toward Matty, cradled his head, using clothing from the luggage to stop the bleeding. Matty wouldn't move. Then Judson grabbed her by the hair and dragged her toward the door while she kicked and screamed.

Judson kneeled down and grinned at her. "I'm afraid you've inadvertently killed your pianist, my dear. For that, and for the adultery, I must ask for a divorce. Of course, as your husband, you will be destitute. All belongs to me, as you are surely aware."

Flossie wanted to lie down with Matty, wanted to cover him with the quilt. Wanted him to look up at her.

"When he began to hit me, I hadn't even realized how much I'd been screaming. He told the police he was slapping me to calm me down, and they'd accepted this as the natural response, even though he'd split my lip open and blackened my eye."

Breen was whispering how sorry he was while wrapping her up in his arms. For a moment, she fooled herself into feeling protected before breaking away. As she stashed the bowls and cups in the cupboards, she described what happened next.

"He told the police that, after he arrived home from England, the servants told him I was staying at the Palace. As my husband, the staff at the hotel gave him the key and room number without question. His story to the police was that Matty was reaching for his gun, and that he had no choice but to fire upon him. Detailing my adultery was easy, given that I had been staying with Matty at the Palace for weeks. Everyone had seen us together, as we hadn't hid our affection. I was a fool. I'm probably still a fool. You should know that.

"They jailed me instantly, and Judson Horner tortured me by sitting outside my cell. He relished in tormenting me with how much money he had now that I would be going to prison. He delighted in relaying repeatedly the death of Matty in all its grisly details. He blamed me for the death, as did the judge. I blamed myself, too."

"It wasn't your fault."

"If Matty hadn't been in that room with me, he'd still be alive. I had no right."

"Man makes his own choices. Some women are worth dying for, anyhow."

She shook her head and had to bite the inside of her mouth to keep from weeping. A man as talented and as full of good cheer as Matty should have lived a long and full life. She would have gladly sat in prison for the rest of her own life if it could bring him back.

"Some women are worth dying for," Breen repeated, looking at her. "I'm sure of it."

"Every time he came to my cell, he'd bring me tea, cookies, slices of pie, and he'd be smiling in this sinister way. He kept saying I had two choices. Either come back and live the rest of my life as his devoted wife or rot in prison. He let me know that if I didn't return to him and offer him every night all the pleasures a wife should give to her husband, he would never stop until I was ruined and dead. He would do whatever it took to destroy me completely."

The gaslights started to go out one by one in the cellblocks and yard. "I hate that I have to take you back," Breen said. "Hate that more than anything."

"Nothing that bastard did shocked me. I'd deluded myself thinking I could divorce him and be free. I should have been careful with Matty. I should have known. You know what did surprise me? The public's reaction. I was utterly deluded that they would be on my side and the trial would go my way. I had too many fans to be convicted. I was the Flame of San Francisco, after all. But it was as if they'd just been waiting for me to fall from grace. My fall seemed to lift them higher. They were anxious to hear every salacious detail and to condemn me. Those who'd attended the trial delighted in my 'debauchery,' as the prosecutor had called it. The women who attended sat on the benches of the courthouse fanning themselves and glaring at me with their stony, self-righteous eyes."

Dizzied from the heat and memory, she gripped the edge of the butcher block.

He rested his hand on her shoulder and sighed. "Folks are full of hate and loathing, Flossie. Mainly for themselves and their own bad deeds or thoughts, or even their inabilities and disappointments. Given the opportunity to hate or loath another, they'll jump on that wagon. Way of the world, way it is everywhere I've been. Now, let's get you back to your cell before we raise any nerves with the other guards by dawdling."

After dousing the lights in the mess hall, he led them up the granite stairs into the yard. In the moonlight, Flossie saw a wood rat scuttle under an outhouse. She then spotted Christ H. limping up prison hill with all three hounds following him, headed toward the superintendent's cottage. Breen soon let her into the cell, and she disappeared into its dark recesses. She missed Emma tonight and wished they could talk together like schoolgirls. Emma would have liked that.

"Come out where I can see you," Breen said.

"Do you understand, now?"

"Understand what?"

"Tell me you understand," she said.

"Always did. Come closer. I want to see you before I head out. Won't sleep if I can't."

She did as he asked, their faces inches apart. "I'm not asking you to understand why I'm in here. I want you to understand that you can't possibly help me escape. What happened to Matty cannot happen to you."

"You can't decide for me."

"If you help me and they catch us, I'll merely end up back here, same as before . . . more time, yes, but same as before. Your fate will be entirely different. Something terrible will happen to you."

"I won't be caught," he gruffly insisted.

"You should know, too, that if I were ever to experience again the wondrous world beyond these walls, it does not naturally result in my taking up with a young, skinny guard such as yourself."

"That's prideful talk," he said. "And it's wearing on my temper. When I get you out of here, I expect you'll stick by me, at least for a while, just to keep from being shot, if for no other reason."

"Is that what you want? A woman who stays with you for protection alone. Or do you want more?"

"Don't matter what I want."

"What do I have to say to you? I've turned you away. I've insulted you. I've warned you against the almost certain dastardly results of helping me, yet you persist. Now leave me be."

"Keep it down," he warned, dropping his voice. "We are leaving. And you will never return to this place."

Flossie stumbled back, nearly kicking over the bucket serving as a latrine.

"It's got to be done," he said.

"I'm tired." She lay down on her bunk. "Leave me alone."

His keys knocked dully against the iron lattice. She knew he was trying to see her in the dark. "Goodnight then," he said. It seemed it was all he could think to say.

She didn't respond. She didn't want him leaving, but he'd been gone too long. The other guards and the new superintendent had probably noticed how long he was taking. Inside her cell, the night was thick, even with the moonlight. And the silence was making it even darker. Shutting her eyes, she welcomed the dark. It was total and abundant, same as her belief that she could never allow him to help her. Someday he'd be glad about this. He'd understand. He'd be alive and well. Maybe married with children. And she'd be nothing but imagination.

CHAPTER TWENTY-ONE

A kingdom of stone-colored clouds plugged the sky, and the air reeked metallic, the heat swampy and bloated. The two piebald mares pulling the wagon would every so often twitch and buck, uneasy about the rumbling clouds in the distance. Still, the horses kept a good pace, tugging the buckboard toward Ocotillo, seemingly as anxious to beat the storm as Flossie and Dwyer were.

Flossie's arm ached more than usual this afternoon, and the rather ungracious grooves in the road offered no comfort to her tailbone. She wondered if her arm would forever be her own personal, albeit painful, weather vane, as its steady throb drew her away from Breen, who sat next to her on the bench.

When thunder bellowed and gulped behind them, the horses lurched and shook their manes, the wagon veering to the left. He took the quirt to the pair, urging them to outrun the storm that galloped behind them.

Flossie let go of the bench to massage her arm. "Think we'll beat this?"

He looked over his shoulder at the bruised clouds behind them. "Sure moving fast. Storms here save themselves up. That one back there looks like ten rolled into one." He made a clicking sound with his mouth and shook the reins at yet another crack of thunder. "Good thing you're used to traveling," he said.

The wheels rolled roughly across the road, and the horses,

their fear mounting, tugged awkwardly.

"I am certainly not accustomed to this type of travel."

"Suppose you had fancy carriages and such."

"Elegant. Plush. Inside, there would be ladyfinger sandwiches, lemon tea, and someone to wash my feet. Would you stoop so low as to wash my feet?"

He ignored her, shouting "haw" at the horses, which were good and spooked, their hooves switching between canter and sudden stops.

A sudden crack in the sky caused one mare to rear up on her hind legs. The wagon shimmied. One wheel lifted off the road, and Flossie slid toward the tense Breen, who struggled with the reins in an effort to control the frightened horse.

"We should go back," she said.

"Nothing back there but downpours, floods, and a life inside."

"We *will* return after the show," she insisted.

He shouted "Gee!" at the horses. They increased their pace.

"We *will* return," she repeated.

With the rein still wrapped in his fist, he reached over and squeezed her hand. The only noise now was the sound of the wheels on the road, but the sky was a swollen gray.

"Will you answer me?" she asked.

"I think you need to float through this day, Flossie, and let me do the planning."

"I don't float," she said. "Not anymore."

"Read once about you. Was waiting for a shave. The magazine said you didn't walk on stage, you floated. Floated and hovered like a damselfly. That was the word they used. I remember being glad they didn't compare you to an angel."

"Why?"

" 'Cause that's what they'd said on all those broadsides of you I'd seen. 'Voice like an angel,' they claimed. Truth is, I don't have much use for angels. Want someone I can hang onto, someone I can touch. Sure wouldn't want to fall hard for someone with a giant pair of wings jutting out her back. Hard to get my arms around a woman with wings like that."

She couldn't help but smile when he laughed.

"Gee!" he called to the horses, which had started to pull in opposite directions.

"I'm no angel." She glanced down at her bloomers. "Doubt I would qualify for that particular occupation."

"That magazine said you died good, too. I remember that. Said you died perfect."

"Yes, in my day, I died better than most."

He squinted at the road ahead. "Almost there."

"I hope I don't know how to die too well," she said, as the first fat raindrops started to fall.

By the time they arrived at the Golden Bead, hordes of theatergoers, despite the rain, lined up outside. To avoid being noticed, Flossie lowered her head before the wagon drew too close. Then Breen quickly swung it around the back of the establishment. He allowed a young Mexican boy to take the nervous horses to the livery stable, and he and Flossie hopped down onto the soil, which was veined with dozens of muddy rivulets. Breen assisted her up the slippery stairs, and both were damp to the skin by the time they got inside.

Easing down the hall, which reeked of mold, they approached the same closet Flossie had used before. As Breen began to turn the knob, a pulpy man in a blue, pinstriped suit approached from the other end of the hall. The man introduced himself as the owner of the Golden Bead, Mr. Duane Cummins.

"Where's Baxter, manager you had before?" Breen asked.

"Baxter has found other employment."

"I see," Breen said.

"I'm so pleased you could come tonight. Especially with this weather. Regretfully, I missed your last performance, Miss Abbot. I had business in Santa Fe that particular week. But folks from near and far are raving."

"We apologize for canceling the last show," Breen said. "Had some troubles on the way in."

"It was I who was the most disappointed. I was so looking forward to the Flame's performance. But many held their tickets over rather than request a refund," he said. "As you probably noticed, we've a full house tonight."

Flossie turned to the closet, ready to get this over with.

"No, no, no, you'll not be allowed in that closet, Miss Abbot." Cummins wagged his finger, as if scolding her.

"Listen here," Breen said. "She'll need privacy to change. After our last visit, she's not feeling altogether comfortable."

Cummins smiled, his lips oily from some sort of meaty supper. "This way. This way." He led them back down the hall toward the actual dressing room. "I believe this is more appropriate. If I had the means, you'd have much more. Much, much, more. The very idea that Baxter forced you to use the closet sickens me! I would have never allowed you to change in there—no, no. Heavens no. Prisoner or not."

He held the green door open for her, and she hesitated for a moment before Breen guided her inside. Red velvet upholstered the walls, and from a pink ceiling a crystal chandelier hung. A dressing table, equipped with lipsticks, rouges, silver combs, one wide hairbrush, and a tall glass of hot lemon water, jutted out the right wall before a giant brass-framed mirror. A cloud-shaped seat, also upholstered with dark-red velvet, was tucked under the table. Too, a new dress awaited her, laid out near the window next to the one she'd worn before. An iridescent gold lace wove through the garment's fabric, and the skirt was topped with a violet corset. With relief, she looked upon the new, crisp undergarments that had been provided, for her own had turned gray with the past few weeks of wear.

"Will this do?" Cummins grinned, the shadow from his long nose lifting from his upper lip.

"Most definitely." She allowed him to kiss her hand.

Cummins, leaving the door ajar, scuttled back down the hall.

"Shut it, please," she said to Breen. "We can't have anyone see me dressing."

"Okay, I'll leave you be, then."

As he started to leave, she said, "I'd rather you stay."

"I'll be right outside. I won't go anywhere. You've got my word."

She shook her head. "I'd rather you stay in here. With me. I don't want to be alone. Besides, I'll need your help fastening this corset. With my arm aching like it is, the hooks appear smaller than mites."

His face reddened, and he stepped back inside, shutting the door behind him.

She examined the dressing table. "Look at this brush. Do you know how many times I've dreamed of having a brush?" She ran her fingers across the bristles. "Queer, isn't it? The things you miss?"

He nodded, setting his rifle down near the table.

Without another word, she began undressing, stepping from her bloomers and jersey rather quickly, letting the cloth drop to the floor.

Breen's eyes sprang open and then shut tightly—almost at the same moment.

"Whatever's the matter? You've surely seen a naked woman before. A man your age has jostled with a few whores along the way."

Breen spun around and stared at his drippy reflection in the rain-flecked window.

"Don't ignore me," she said.

"Put something on. Anything."

"I will, darling. I most certainly will. Could you be so kind as to hand me my new undergarments?"

He gathered them up and shifted toward her without looking up.

She'd lifted his rifle so slowly, he hadn't even noticed.

"This is a sight," he said calmly.

"I knew you were a gentleman," she said. "I was counting on that fact."

"Why are you doing this?" He hadn't backed away, hadn't shown the smallest bit of surprise or emotion. It was an instinct he hadn't been aware of having before this moment.

"I am ordering you to stay inside this room," she blurted. "I am about to experience freedom, glorious freedom, just as you desired. But you will not accompany me. If you try, I will shoot you. Might just shoot you in the foot or leg. But I'm not a good shot."

In his mind, she was welcome to shoot him. Being without her or being dead were the same evil. But he was sure as the sun that she'd never pull the trigger.

"Do not doubt me."

"First, you'll give me the rifle back. I'll need it out there. Then you'll put on some clothes."

"I am leaving," she said.

"You won't make it a quarter mile."

"That's right. That's exactly right. I won't make it. They'll catch me within an hour. Take me back to the prison. Toss me in the dreadful Hole. And if I live through that, I'll be guarded closely for months, perhaps years. You will be incapable of freeing me. You'll be safe."

"What happened to Matty won't happen to me." He was speaking softly and removing his coat.

"Don't move."

He wrapped the coat around Flossie's shivering body. "I don't want you sick. We've got a long journey ahead."

"I have a long journey."

"Set the gun on down."

"I won't allow you to do this for me," she said.

He wanted to tell her she was the only person in the world he cared about. He wanted to confess he needed her. He gently removed the rifle from her loosening grip and placed it on the dressing table. "Trust me, please," he said, finding her mouth, his fingers tenderly resting on her lower back. As the rain pattered on the roof of the saloon, he felt her leaning into him.

"What if I lose you?" she asked.

"Won't let that happen." He sat on the chair and drew her down with him. Her mouth was wet as the rain and trailing down his neck. His coat slipped off her shoulders, exposing her breasts and neck. He took one of her breasts in his mouth, his hands on her hips.

When Cummins tapped on the door, she shifted off him and tugged the coat up.

"I've brought you a refreshing beverage," he said through the door. "I'll just leave it out here."

Dwyer thanked him and turned back to her. But she had already started getting dressed.

The rain reminded Abe Kane of the only happy day he could recall from his childhood. He'd heard other inmates and some folks he'd robbed talk about whole childhoods of happiness, but Kane could only recall the one day.

He and his older brother, Jeremiah, were all that was left of the Kanes. The rest were killed off by Apaches. He wished they hadn't killed his mother, but his pa had been as mean as the Mojave green, so he didn't grieve long for him. Not like he did for his sister. It stung for a long time that they'd taken his sister, only eight years old, and hung her alive from a meat hook jammed under the base of her skull.

He and Jeremiah left Silver City with no one and nothing, but he remembered one day when they, starved with throats dry as summer grit, stumbled upon a family who'd drowned in a flood caused by a sudden desert downpour. The family had been traveling and were washed away almost before knowing it. He and Jeremiah knew to get to high ground and watched it happen. The rain was hard and the creosote sweet smelling, and the family's wagon washed up practically at their feet. Inside was enough food to see them through for weeks. Money, too. And canteens and bladders of water. The Apaches would eventually kill Jeremiah, and Kane would be alone, but he was glad to have shared that day with his brother.

The rain tonight was refreshing. Weeks of filth and sweat drizzled off his skin into the mud behind the Bead. He considered going inside, as hiding in a crowd was often easier than hiding in an empty field, but his disfigured eye might make folks stare.

He'd wait for now. He might head into the back of the building if that guard Dwyer had left her alone, but he'd have to wait and watch. He would certainly kill her before the pair traveled back to the prison. And he'd probably have to kill the guard to get to her. He was glad he had a rifle. Shooting was easier than cutting people up. Even if the latter gave him more pleasure.

Standing in the rain, he watched the shadows and lights on the second floor of the Bead. He wondered which room she was in. He wondered if she were still afraid of him. It would help if she were. Most of all, he wondered why she would have ever married someone like Judson Horner, a man who would have been easy to kill, as even his handshake was buttery and slack. And, though Kane would have to kill the Flame, he wondered if

206

it would be possible to keep her around for a while. He craved a little conversation after so many days alone. But, knowing himself, it was more than likely he'd just poke her, then kill her quick. He was patient about most other things but had trouble controlling his urges in that regard.

207

CHAPTER TWENTY-TWO

"You made me cry, ma'am." The sniffling Cummins trailed Flossie and Dwyer down the hall toward the dressing room after her performance. "Made me think on my sweet Annie, God bless her soul, and I won't forget that. You need anything, you let old Cummins know. She was a good one, my Annie. The Lord's enjoying her company, I expect."

Dwyer handed Cummins his handkerchief. It was all he could think to do with the emotional man. Cummins raised it to his nose and blew, all the while raving and insisting that if there were anything he could do, ever do, he would. "Anything! All I ask is that you promise to come back and sing again."

"What's your meaning, sir?" Dwyer asked.

"I just want to repay this lovely woman, this chanteuse! This canary!"

"What is it you'd like to do for her?"

"Oh, my," Cummins said. "I merely meant that I'd be thrilled, simply thrilled to bring a drink and something delectable to the Flame. I would bet my last silver dollar she hasn't had good beef in a long while, a long, long while. Am I correct in my presumption, Miss Abbot?"

She nodded.

"Would you like steak? Maybe some fresh green peas? Delicious, just picked from my garden. And you, of course, Mr. Dwyer, I would be delighted to feed you as well."

"How thoughtful," Flossie said. "You've been so kind. Kinder to me than almost anyone else in a long time."

"Anything for you, anything at all," he reiterated before heading back down the hall toward the kitchen.

This gave Dwyer a thought. "Think he'd want an extra wagon?"

Flossie didn't answer as she began pulling pins from her hair.

"I was planning on ditching it up the road a bit, but it'd be safer if Cummins kept it. Don't you think?"

"I thought you had this planned out," she said. "And now you're asking me? I know nothing about escaping from a prison. Nothing at all. Besides, I never agreed to it and still haven't. How many times do I have to tell you this?"

"Mark my words, Flossie Abbot, if I have to roll you up in this carpet and toss you over the rump of my mare, we're leaving tonight."

"My fate is to live out my sentence at Gila. And then I'll likely die alone, destitute."

"That's not dying well," he said.

"If it gives you a measure of comfort, the gates will open someday, and I'll shuffle out and stand and rage at the storm just like old Lear did."

"Don't know what you're rambling on about, but your fancy talk won't turn my mind about this," he said. "We're leaving tonight. We won't be caught, if that's what you're worried about. And I'd rather be dead than living, knowing you're in that cell, even if you're the most stubborn woman I've ever known. And I got my reasons for feeling that way, just like you got reasons for staying put."

He took the few steps toward her and kissed her gently.

"How long have you been planning this?" she said.

Before he could answer, Cummins rapped on the door, though it was still open. He stood there holding two glass mugs.

"Your dinner's cooking, but I brought you sarsaparilla to wet your wait."

He handed each a mug.

"I would've brought some spirits but didn't think you'd be allowed, Miss Abbot. And I recall the superintendent saying that guards weren't allowed to imbibe. Ah, yes, the superintendent's not having much of a say now, is he? In any case, I'm certain your new overseer is just as fussy."

"Miss Abbot has a favor for you to think over," Dwyer said.

"What is it?" Cummins asked. "I'd be pleased to help you."

"She was wanting to ask if you'd keep our wagon."

"Is there something wrong with it? I can have someone look it over."

"Mr. Cummins," Flossie said. "There is nothing the matter with our wagon. It is perfectly maintained."

Cummins began to show the slightest trace of a smile.

Dwyer added that they'd like to keep it somewhere, away from people's prying. "Folks are likely to make a spectacle of something Flossie Abbot's ridden in," he said.

"That they would," Cummins agreed.

Dwyer let Cummins think on it while he drank his sarsaparilla in silence. When the man didn't respond after a few minutes, he asked again. "Think you could do this for us?"

"I've an outbuilding where I could store it, for a while at least. Long enough to be sure."

"We only need long enough," Dwyer said.

Cummins wedged his thumbs behind white suspenders, a wide grin of satisfaction spreading across his red cheeks. "You like the sarsaparilla? I make it myself."

"Oh," Flossie said. "It's rather delicious."

"I'll go see about those steaks. A full belly might see you a ways."

Cummins left, and Flossie gripped the back of the upholstered chair at the dressing table.

From behind, Dwyer wrapped his arms around her. "You trust me?"

"Yes," she said. "I do."

Dwyer was glad for that. He'd need her trust to have confidence in what they were about to do. That morning, before they left for Octotillo, he'd shared Flossie's story with Jones. Upon hearing everything, Jones told him the journey might be even more dangerous than Dwyer could predict.

He wouldn't be telling Flossie this. He couldn't. She'd never agree to escaping if he did. Maybe he'd tell her later. Maybe he wouldn't. It almost seemed too late to tell her about Jones or the real reason he'd first hired on at the Sand Castle. But he'd have to tell her. He just didn't know how or when.

When Cummins entered around ten minutes later, Flossie had already changed into the practical riding clothes Dwyer had brought along for her—tan trousers, a man's cotton shirt, and a wool shawl.

Cummins carried two enormous plates, each piled high with steak, buttered bread, and, as promised, fresh garden peas. The pleasant smell wafted around the small dressing room.

"This should tide you over." Cummins's eyes twinkled.

"Thank you for your kindness," Flossie said.

Cummins started to leave. Before he did, he spoke with his back to them. "Regarding your wagon, I have made the arrangements."

Knowing it could be weeks before they had another hot meal, Dwyer dug into the food, and they both ate without speaking.

The gold pocket watch his father gave him showed it was time. The river steamboat would be arriving at 12:30. Jones had spent the evening studying files, creating lists, and then revising the lists, scratching off a name here and there, adding another.

Finally, he was satisfied that the list was complete.

He set off toward the main cellblocks with a little less than an hour to complete his task. Knowing it would take several hours for the guards to protest, he'd purposefully waited. By the time they fully understood his actions, the deed would be done, and he'd be long gone.

Soon he was at the cells, list in hand. He unlocked the main gate, startling a sleeping guard, Christ H. if he remembered correctly. One of the hounds at the man's feet woke and barked, and the guard offered a half-dazed greeting in a gravelly voice as Jones brushed past him.

He headed to cell three and unlocked the barred lattice.

"Chadwick Nelson," he ordered.

The man stirred, frightened, on his top bunk.

"Please come with me."

The nervous prisoner, in for vagrancy, slid down and followed Jones out of his cell. Jones proceeded toward cells five, eight, eleven, fourteen, sixteen, nineteen, twenty-two, and twenty-three. He opened each and called for the men on his list. One jailed for stealing seeds. Another for taking three oranges from the grocer to feed his pregnant wife. Yet another, a black prisoner who had been accused of being a suspicious person after accidentally wandering onto a white family's ranch. In all, Jones rounded up thirty-six prisoners from the main cellblock.

Jones ordered the men, who'd politely followed him to the bull pen, to wait. He left them standing in the rain and headed toward the infirmary. Once there, he released two men dying of tuberculosis. When he ordered the small-boned Apache called Niyaha to come with him, the gaunt Indian didn't move. Jones wondered if the man had already died. After nearing him, however, he saw that Niyaha was breathing and quite awake.

"Come with me," Jones said.

Niyaha just stared.

"I will be forced to carry you if you do not rise off that cot and follow."

Niyaha finally shifted, stumbling forth into the rainy night, his blanket wrapped tightly around his bony shoulders.

After reading about him, Jones had decided that Niyaha's was perhaps the saddest of all the stories in those files. In 1871 at Camp Grant, Arizona, he'd seen and survived the murders of his father and grandfather as well as the rapes, murders, and scalping of his mother and older sister. Then he'd witnessed his older brother being taken away to be sold into slavery and his baby sister being bashed to death against a rock. He had tried to fight back, but the men, a group of citizens from Tucson, had laughed at him before shooting him in the foot. After he'd miraculously survived, he'd sneaked into Tucson. Niyaha searched for the man who'd shot him. Unable to find the shooter, he settled on the corpulent, red-faced man who had flung his sister against the rock. Rushing the sleeping man, he attempted to stab him in the heart. His small knife, more a toy than a real warrior's blade, merely cut through the man's jacket. The man awoke, and Niyaha was promptly arrested and accused of attempted murder. He was to spend the rest of his life at Gila.

That wouldn't do, Jones thought.

The men from the infirmary joined the others in the yard, and Harper Jones wound his way toward the women. Except for Wilhelmina Yeoman and Jesus-Marie Rodriquez, he released them all. Jesus-Marie *did* seem dangerous. As for Wilhelmina, he wasn't sure. Still, she'd murdered a man. He ordered the convict Berthalea to bundle up her toddler, George, "as if he was going on a journey." She complied, and George, used to the strife, didn't cry out. The rest of the women, rubbing the sleep from their eyes, stumbled forth.

The assembled prisoners huddled in the men's bull pen, their eyes shiny with fear. He handed each a parcel. Inside the parcels were clean clothes, jerky, hard tack, dried fruit, peanuts, horehound candy, a full canteen, and enough money to last each a month.

A few guards, Cornelius Hammond among them, had stepped up to him.

"Sir, this is highly irregular," the head guard said.

"Oh, indeed," Jones agreed. He looked upon the befuddled and alarmed prisoners. Their lives had been plagued, and Jones realized that most still could not grasp that Jones did not mean them harm. They clutched their parcels to their chests and looked as though they expected to be shot or worse. Perhaps they'd come to believe they'd been rounded up on this stormy night for some sort of mass slaughter.

He ordered them to follow him through the sally port. They did as instructed, seemingly resigned to their fate. Only a few looked as if they understood why a steamboat waited near the shore.

"You are free to go!" Jones bellowed.

Though a few ran for the boat instantly, most hesitated.

"Go," he ordered.

Several more dashed out into the water, assisted aboard by the crew Jones had hired. Still, some remained on the banks, and Jones had to urge them to wade out with the others.

Soon, all were aboard, and the steamboat smoked and began drifting down the Colorado, which was raging faster than ever after the sudden rain. Jones breathed heavily. Their journey might be arduous. They would certainly encounter danger. Some might die. But they were free.

Jones watched as a few grateful hands reached out and waved before he turned toward the livery stables, where his horse was already saddled and his bags packed. He'd leave for now, but, for what he'd just done, he was sure to be back. Only next time, he'd be living on the wrong side of the iron gates.

215

The Sand Castle

for a last hurrah or a dance. Flowers were in her basket. Only now, there'd be living on the wrong side of the iron grates.

CHAPTER TWENTY-THREE

The travel, off the main roads and paths, was hard on the horses and even harder on Flossie. Her back and legs ached, and, by morning, after a full night of riding in the rain, she winced with each step her horse took. Near sunrise, the rain stopped, and the sky cleared. She and Breen stopped at an outcrop of cotton-woods and sycamores along the banks of the Gila, which would provide shelter from any who might be searching for them. After a shadowy wilderness of saguaros and smaller cacti, the lush little grove offered more in the way of protection than she'd seen all night.

Relishing the idea of sleep, she numbly assisted Breen in assembling their small canvas tent and spreading a few blankets on the hard earth for a semblance of comfort. While he remained outside to water and tether the horses, she nearly collapsed inside.

Earlier, she'd presumed that she would sleep with ease. In truth, for the last few miles the only thing keeping her from toppling from her saddle was the very idea of sleep. Now, given the chance, she found herself staring at the side of the gray-green canvas with the sudden realization that she was a wanted woman. Unless she found a way toward a pardon, hiding would be the core of her existence. From now until forever, she would take back roads, avoid people and towns, and plan her days around not being noticed or seen. Singing or acting was out of the question. Broadsides would be replaced with wanted post-

216

ers. She'd be seeking the opposite of fame—its shy sister, anonymity.

The side of the tent blurred as Flossie's eyes began to salt and water.

"You should be sleeping." Breen climbed into the tent after taking off his boots.

"My body heartily agrees," she whispered, "but my thoughts still indulge themselves."

He stretched out next to her and draped a long arm over her new cotton frock, one of the few pieces of women's clothing he'd provided her. All her outerwear was meant for a man.

"You like it?" He ran his hand over the lamb-soft fabric. "Ordered it from a catalogue, hoping it would fit."

"How long ago?" She was still whispering despite his assurance that they were safe.

"Months ago. All of it. Your coat, hat, this tent, all our supplies. Ordered them the first week I signed on."

"I don't understand."

He pulled her close to him. "It's rough travel, even rougher without sleep."

"Tell me why you're doing this, why you planned this," she said. "I want to know."

'Go ahead and shut your eyes. I won't let anything happen to you."

"I've told you my secrets. Your turn to tell me yours."

"We've got hours in the saddle for telling secrets. Right now you need shut-eye. I'll stay up most of the night keeping an eye on things, but, after you wake up, you're going to have to let me sleep for a few before we head out again."

"Back before Gila, I could sleep the morning away. Nothing, not the noise below my window or the people in the halls, could rouse me. Out here, the silence seems like a clamor."

"Silence means we're alone. And that's exactly what we're

217

wanting. What we've wanted for a while."

Alone, she thought. Such a novelty. A treasure. No guards pacing outside her cell. No other inmates to feed or fear. "You know what I wish?"

"Likely the same thing I do."

"I wish everyone would go and find another world to live on. I wish it were just you and me, and that we could come and go as we pleased and no one would ever bother us again."

He brushed her mouth with his own.

"Is that what you were wishing?" she asked.

"Something like that."

"Good."

"You get to sleep. We've got a long ride tonight. And the night after that, as well."

Laying her head on his chest, she listened to his heart pound. It sounded like soldiers marching over a bridge.

"You know why I never told the jury what he did to me? The beatings? The threats?"

"You didn't think they'd believe you?"

"That was part of it. But there was something else. One day, while he sat outside my cell, he threatened that he'd send me to an asylum if I started making up stories about him. That's the way he put it . . . *making up stories.*"

His heartbeat quickened.

"He said that in there I'd be driven insane, if I wasn't already. I was terrified. I'd seen the inside of an asylum, once. It made the Sand Castle look like Elysium."

"Could he have done that?"

"The more I thought it over, the more I believed he could. And I wouldn't have survived it. I couldn't survive in a place like that. I made a pact with myself. I would suffer the indignities of the trial in complete, maddening silence. The prosecutor made it sound as if Matty and I had set Judson up, that we had planned on murdering him, not the other way around."

"We'll remedy it."

"I don't know how."

His hand was resting between her hip and waist. "Stop all that thinking and talking and shut your pretty eyes."

"Would you be offended if I removed this?" She slipped off her frock.

"You making another move for my rifle?"

She smiled in the dark. "Perhaps you should remove your clothes, too. Likely to warm up after the sun rises." She felt him shudder with pleasure when she pressed her bare breasts against his chest.

"Sure?" His skin heated under her warm hands.

Instead of answering him, she started on his buttons. Soon, his shirt was off, and her hands trailed downwards.

"This isn't why I'm helping you."

"You want me to stop?"

Flossie had spent the last grueling months trying to forget her body, trying to rise from it, abandon it, project herself into a place without locks and guards on catwalks with their rifles at the ready and the heat so pervasive, the skin on her back and shoulders bubbled with sunburn after sunburn.

But in this tent, with Breen Dwyer, she felt herself returning. She felt herself. And she felt pleasure—simple, physical pleasure—coming in waves. So she clung to him, as he did her, and the burdens of the world fell.

They'd managed to leave the buckboard behind, but that hadn't fooled Kane. They were easier to track than most; he'd stayed close and had followed the trail of their horses' manure, as he'd always done in these situations.

He'd wait until they were a few miles from Ocotillo before shooting them both. Though he'd fantasized about keeping her around and grazing over the guard's death, he figured fast was best. And then he could get on with collecting his pay, as well as the rest of his life. He'd grown tired of living like a wild animal, and he needed to see a doc, as the flesh around his eye felt like a knotted rope. Too, he craved a good straw bed and a swallow of whiskey.

He'd been following them for only twenty minutes or so when he'd been burdened by the sight of another man, a white-haired fellow on a horse that had to be at least seventeen hands high. Stuffing down his instincts, Kane decided to wait on the killings, as the man seemed to be following the Flame, too. The man was likely the law, and Kane had suffered too many days to be taken back to Gila now.

Kane watched the pair's tent from afar. With his good eye, he saw that the white-haired man was camped nearby. Kane would stay put and observe the goings on. If the old man moved in on the pair, Kane would kill him quick. And then he'd set upon the guard swiftly. The Flame he'd save for last. And after he killed her, he'd carve off something to show Horner that the deed was done. Maybe one of her fingers. Maybe something else.

CHAPTER TWENTY-FOUR

The telegram lay open on Dobbs's desk. The sheriff merely stared at it, baffled by its contents.

Over the crank phone, the day after Thaddeus Samuels's suicide, Governor Zulick had politely informed Dobbs that he would promptly send a new superintendent. When Harper Jones arrived, papers in hand, Dobbs had been delighted with the governor's efficiency. Jones seemed stalwart enough, and Dobbs had headed back home to Ocotillo without a care.

Now, with this letter folded open in front of him, Dobbs rummaged his mind for someone else to blame other than himself. But he couldn't think of a soul. He painfully recalled the audacity of Jones insisting his papers be inspected. So happy to be leaving the confines of the penitentiary, however, Dobbs had barely glanced at them. In truth, even if he had, he wouldn't have been able to discern their legitimacy.

This letter was different. And its contents had prevented Dobbs from sleeping. He'd read it five times already, memorizing certain sections. The new superintendent would be arriving at the end of the month, the letter read, so please be kind enough to introduce him to the guards and instruct him on the layout of the prison.

The end of the month.

It didn't take Dobbs but a moment to realize that Jones was a fraud, and that Dobbs was solely responsible for tendering the care and operation of Gila Territorial, an institution swarming with undesirables, to a complete stranger. In addition, Dobbs was now quite certain that Jones had his own motives for arriving when he did, and those motives were clearly disreputable.

Unaware of the terrible crisis, his wife waddled in with a snack of small butter sandwiches and tea. She didn't seem to mind when he didn't thank her. He never thanked her. However, in his current state, he didn't deliberately ignore her, as was his usual manner. He rarely offered a kind word to his wife. His father had handed down this wisdom on their wedding day, insisting it was the most effective method for ensuring proper devotion.

Dobbs nibbled on the sandwiches and sipped his tea. He knew he should be calling Zulick straight away. Yes, that was certainly the proper course of action. On the other hand, Dobbs believed himself a formidable man. He could handle this charlatan Jones with alacrity and intimidation. So be it, he thought. *I shall go to the prison and extract the fraud myself! He shall be interned in a cell! I will remain at the prison until the new superintendent arrives!*

Tossing the delicate sandwich aside and swaggering with confidence, he strode into the sitting room and informed his wife that he would be leaving for several days.

She offered no resistance. In fact, he thought he saw the slightest glint of joy in her eyes.

CHAPTER TWENTY-FIVE

On their third night, as they traversed slowly and tediously along the river banks, Dwyer was awed by the details he could make out in the moonlight—the honeycomb of granite hills to their left, a jack rabbit bursting from behind a brittlebush, the bats and owls, and the outline of barrel cacti and saguaro.

His route along the river seemed logical. When they made it to the Gila bend, they'd break south and head toward Tucson. Having the luck of a nearly full moon gave him confidence that they'd reach Tucson safely, just as Jones had instructed. If it weren't for the moonlight, they'd be riding twice as slow to avoid injuring their mounts.

He figured Flossie was as anxious as he to reach Tucson, where'd they'd be able to bathe and eat a hot meal. Least that's what Jones had promised. Dwyer had to trust the man. Still, he was glad he had all the cash Harper Jones had paid him stashed in his saddlebag.

So far, Flossie hadn't argued with him about his decision to travel at night, avoiding the towns by forging their own trail. Bushwhacking had helped them avoid people altogether. The few they had seen, they'd hidden from.

But the riding was taxing, more on Flossie than on himself. She didn't complain much, though she surely had the same backache, and he'd noticed how raw her legs had become. She kept at it, same as he. Some hours spent chatting. Others spent brooding. A few hours before sunrise, they'd come upon a patch of large palo verdes. His stomach growling, and his body aching, he decided they could settle here for a rest. If they'd kept going, they'd reach a canyon, one that would surely be better protection than the skinny trees, but he was too hungry and worn out to veer that far from the river in the dark.

Once dismounted, he removed some jerky and hard tack from a pouch in his saddlebag. Flossie was already gulping from the canteen he'd handed her. He passed over the meager food, and she thanked him. Famished and worn through, she still looked beautiful, her red hair, tangled and tousled, falling down around her shoulders.

After taking a long pull of water, she looked up. "Knowing how small we are compared to this big sky of stars, it's hard to believe we're important enough to hunt for."

"We've been lucky," he warned. "They're looking for us by now. I'm sure of it."

A nearby rustling startled them both. Flossie drew in her breath. Gripping his rifle, Dwyer searched around for the source of the noise. Holding his lantern high, he spotted a chuckwalla that was squeezing itself under a rock. The lizard had the ability to shrink at will when it wanted to hide. He wished they could do the same.

"Just a lizard," he said.

She handed him the canteen. Before he could drink, he heard a horse. The hooves in the sand. The heavy *chug chug* of horse breath.

"Someone's coming," he whispered, as sound carried far in the desert.

Flossie stood and brushed herself off. "We'll have to head for the canyon before they reach us."

"Get back down." He tugged at her.

"But our horses. They'll be seen."

He raised a finger to his lips and pulled her behind a palo

verde. It was too late and too far to reach the canyon. And the skinny tree wasn't much of a cover. He just hoped the stranger or strangers would pass without noticing their horses. If their horses were spotted, Dwyer was prepared to step out and mollify whoever it was, likely just another traveler and not someone who posed a threat.

From their view, Dwyer at first couldn't make out the features of the man approaching, only that it was one man on a horse. As the fella neared, Dwyer's eyes narrowed and focused. The moon now exposed the man's pale, puffy features.

Even with Kane's makeshift eye patch and the other eye nearly swollen shut, Dwyer recognized him immediately.

"I need you to run now." He handed Flossie the pouch.

She clearly hadn't recognized Kane yet. "What's wrong?"

"Go! Run. Run, now!"

"Come with me," she urged.

"Run," he growled.

She broke away and began to descend toward the canyon. When with relief he saw that she'd broken into a sprint, he turned and cocked his rifle.

But Kane was already upon him, knocking his rifle into the rocks. The jolt triggered the gun, the bullet meant for Kane skidding into the dust like a spur into a horse hide.

Kane then bashed him in the side of the head with his elbow. "I intend on killing you for good this time." He kicked the downed Dwyer in the ribs.

Flinching though struggling to regain his footing, Dwyer lurched for Kane's boot, hoping to yank the man down to the gritty soil. But Kane spat and snarled, shaking off Dwyer's hand before slamming his foot down on Dwyer's fingers. With maniacal sounds coming from his throat, Kane ground his sharp heel into the dirt and into Dwyer's flesh.

Dwyer resisted screaming from the pain. With his free arm,

Dwyer swung it up to Kane's dirt-caked trousers, wildly slamming it into the back of the man's knee, which awkwardly extended under the pressure. Kane fell hard onto a fishtail cactus.

With the upper hand, Dwyer rushed him, shoving Kane's fleshy face into the vicious plant. But Kane, stronger than Dwyer imagined, wrenched his head off the backward barbs of the cactus, his skin coming off in the process, and whipped around with a high-pitched scream, before solidly striking Dwyer in the gut, launching him backward. With the wind knocked out of him, Dwyer struggled up to his hands and knees. Feeling around for his rifle, he squinted and scanned the soil. There it was. Four or five feet to his right. Near a large granite boulder.

Kane stepped closer.

Dwyer attempted to rise. Finally, he righted himself.

"My whole purpose just ran off into that canyon," Kane said in a rush of hot, foul breath.

Had the man read his mind? Dwyer didn't understand and shuddered, the landscape around him now a wicked graveyard of spiny and needle-glutted plants.

"You're thinking on your gun, aren't you?" Kane said.

Dwyer peered at the shadowy man whose one dark eye disappeared into the pasty recesses of his face.

"I'd like to see you try and reach it. Be fun to shoot off your arm."

Kane stood a few feet away and trained his rifle on Dwyer.

He'd never be able to reach his own gun. But he couldn't lose. Couldn't be killed by this convict. If Kane killed him, then he'd kill her next.

Dwyer leapt over the boulder, plunging across the desert toward the canyon. While running, he turned and saw that Kane was headed after him.

Only a few more yards, Dwyer considered between breaths. *A few more, and I'll be out of the rifle's range.* Propelling himself forward, he urged his long legs into a powerful stride. He was faster than the squat Kane but slower than the bullet coming for him. The explosion echoed, sounding as if more than one man shot a chorus of fire behind him. Diving into the dirt, he lay face first on the pebbly soil, the small rocks embedding in his chin and cheeks.

The bullet missed. Dwyer scrambled to his feet, turned, and saw Kane approaching, steadily, almost jauntily. He was whistling. Dwyer stopped running and let the bastard come. He wouldn't be shot in the back by this creature. He refused to die like that. Worse, he was leading Kane straight to Flossie.

He prayed she hadn't stopped in the canyon. That she'd kept running. At least she'd live, even if she was thrown back in prison.

Dwyer grappled for Kane's rifle. Better to die quick. But Kane yanked the rifle upwards and slammed it against Dwyer's left temple. Dwyer collapsed to his knees.

As he fell, he pictured Flossie safe in a forest somewhere, where the trees were thick and the ground spongy with constant rain. That's where they'd live someday. A land like that. Not this hard desert earth that didn't give an inch.

Flossie had rooted herself behind an outcropping of stones, jagged as a mouthful of sugar-eaten teeth. Squinting at the moonlit landscape, she watched Breen rush, panic stricken, toward her. *Run faster. Please. Please come to me.*

She wanted to scream his name. She felt the scream inside her, as if it were a stone of energy, of fear, bulging in her throat. But she pushed the stone down, swallowed it whole.

Why had Kane come for them? It was not happenstance. She stared at Breen's face, stunned that he was the light and love and breath of her life. And that she would now lose him. She watched him go down on his knees. She watched the only good left in her life fall lifeless.

Her arm began to sting as the raised, ruby strip of skin on her forearm remembered her last encounter with Kane.

She willed Breen to get up, to fight on, but understood he would likely never rise again. Her body began to shake with rage and grief. She should continue toward the canyon. Should run for her life. Should hide. Should save herself.

I must run!

She couldn't move. She was part of Breen, and his pain rushed into her like a dust storm. The comfort of his arms as they slept, his voice, the shape of his mouth. His laugh. The way his touch felt.

She watched Kane flip him over. Watched as Kane raised a long knife. The sharp blade glinted.

The monster, with his free hand, tore open Breen's shirt. And she could bear no more. Her scream burst into the night, setting off nearby coyote howls. Rushing out from behind the rocks, she tore wildly toward Kane. She screamed and sprinted madly, while Kane looked through her as if she were made from glass.

He raised the rifle. She was certain to be shot, and this seemed a relief. If Breen was gone, she wanted the same fate, so she kept on, screaming and running toward her own death, hearing herself and the coyotes. Swallowing the darkness, she took her last breaths.

She heard a gunshot from a distance. The blade dropped from Kane's hand, landing flatly on Breen's chest. She didn't understand, could only think of stopping Kane.

Who suddenly stiffened and fell. His body lay over Breen's, the two men forming a most unholy cross.

As if death were contagious, Flossie shoved Kane's thick, breathless body off Breen. The side of Breen's hair was sticky and damp with blood. She called to him, as if he weren't unconscious but, instead, somewhere in the distance, somewhere she couldn't see. Supporting his head in her lap, sobbing between words, she began to sing, "Oh my darling, oh my darling, oh my darling . . ."

The man who'd shot Kane approached. Perhaps he'd kill her, too. She didn't know why he was here, why any of them were here. Yet, be it life or death, she willed her fate to be the same as Breen's.

So she kept singing and didn't look up. It was only when she saw his fingers on Breen's neck that she glanced up. A silver-haired man stood above her.

"Heart's beating," the man said.

The song caught in her throat. The man held a lantern in one hand and examined Breen's wound with the other, checking his eyes and pupils. The man's face was sharp as the rocks behind them. Flossie decided he was a bounty hunter. Now he'd found her. The prize. Any in his occupation would desire the fame that came with bringing "the Flame" back to prison.

None of that mattered. Only Breen mattered. Again, she started singing.

"Should've stopped it sooner," the tall man said to no one in particular. "I let this go on too long. Got lucky, though. Seems like Kane here might have been out of bullets."

Flossie shivered and embraced Breen, who'd begun to stir.

"Still, it's a shame he's dead," the man said.

Flossie would kill Kane again if she could. "There is no shame in that man being dead."

The man nodded before lifting up the corpse by its heels and dragging it away. "I would've liked to speak with him first. Find out what he knows."

Flossie started to cough. After screwing off his canteen's lid, the man offered it to her. She drank the water, then told the man how much Kane deserved to die. "You don't know what he did."

"Oh, rest assured," the man said. "I would have killed him after our conversation. Maybe slower, though."

"Sing that pretty song again, will you?" Breen mumbled.

Relieved to hear his voice, Flossie again sang, and he opened his eyes slowly, as if he didn't know whether he was in heaven or on earth. While she sang, her soprano echoing off the canyon, the man offered his canteen to Breen, who gratefully raised it to his dried lips.

"Recognize my face?" the man asked him.

Breen wiped the water from his chin and nodded.

"Do you see one or two of me?"

"Just the one. One's enough."

"Who are you?" Flossie asked.

"Harper Jones," he said.

"He replaced Samuels," Breen said.

"You're not a bounty hunter?" she asked. "You replaced the superintendent?"

"We'll camp in this canyon for a few nights until Dwyer's steady on his feet," Jones said.

"We will not be returning to Gila Territorial," she said. "I don't care who you are."

"Glad you've got your pluck back, Miss Abbot. You'll need it. We've a long ride to Tucson." Without an explanation, Jones walked off into the night.

Jones built a campfire big and strong enough to lick at the stars and crackle the meat of the two hares he'd hunted down for supper.

"Who are you, really?" Flossie asked.

"I'm not the law."

"Then why are you here?"

He watched the hares bubble in their own fat. "Kane came to the prison to kill you. And if it weren't for Mr. Breen Dwyer, you'd be dead."

She tucked the blanket around Breen without responding. Without thinking, she kissed him lightly on his head, which was in her lap.

With the sun starting to rise, Harper Jones rose to check on the hare. Seeing it was almost cooked through, he slid the meat off the stick and dished it out. She took it and ate.

He could tell she wanted to trust him, but perhaps, for her, truth had become a song in the dark. "I should have warned you years before about Judson Horner. You see, he killed my sister."

She stared at him, rubbing her lips together, as the fat from the hare likely felt like a balm after the wind and sun's chapping.

After all these years, the story of Helen's death was still difficult for him to tell. Like the balls and chains the prisoners at Gila lugged around, guilt and helplessness over what Judson Horner had done to Helen, his only family, and the sister he'd vowed to his father to protect, weighed him down and stuck to him like a bitter sap. His mother had died giving birth to Helen, but his father, a small, determined man, dedicated his life to his two children. When Sutter and Marshall found gold in California, his family had already been living there, his father working for Sutter on his cattle ranch. It took only a year for his father to go from ranch hand to wealthy mine owner. He'd amassed hundreds of thousands of dollars in gold nuggets before many had even traversed to the state with dreams of their own. For those men, who had "California or Bust" as a slogan, most went home, if they weren't first killed by disease or other angry miners, saying they'd been "Busted by God." Not his father. His father had been one of the few who'd already made money from the gold itself and then from his own mine. Others, like Sam Brannon, made money as merchants, raising the price of not just the pick axes and shovels but of food and rope. But his father found the gold and cashed in on it. Ultimately, he died of tuberculosis but not before he ensured that his children would have easy and worry-free lives and that his son be educated at Oxford.

Harper attended Oxford after the War between the States ended. He and Helen moved to England together. Two years younger than he, she read, kept the household, and socialized while he studied Latin, Greek, and theology. When she met Judson Horner, the British suitor catered to her every need. Judson doted on Harper's sister, and even as protective as he was of Helen, Harper was accepting of Horner and his devotion. Judson was never late, always showed respect, and seemed honest and forthright.

When he proposed, the wedding was large, and his sister seemed happier than she'd ever been. She delighted in the idea of having a family of her own.

Harper completed his studies and was offered a position at the California Wesleyan College. Judson was keen on the idea of living in the United States, so he and Helen followed. Harper took this as another sign of Judson's fidelity and devotion to his sister, knowing how close she was to her brother and how difficult it would have been to be separated by an entire ocean.

Harper lived near the college in Stockton, and his sister and her new husband moved to nearby Sacramento.

At first, the newlyweds often traveled back and forth between his house and theirs. Then, as time wore on, he saw less and less of his sister. At first, he wasn't suspicious of this, as he knew she had responsibilities to her home and husband.

One Sunday, however, he decided to travel to Sacramento to surprise her. When he came to the door, her servant informed him that she couldn't come downstairs. He asked if she was ill and was told yes.

He brushed past the servant and headed for the staircase. When he reached it, he was blocked by Judson, who told him clearly that he was unwelcome in their household, and that he was never to return, that his sister no longer wanted to speak with him. That she never wanted to speak with him again. This baffled Harper, and forever he would remember and regret that day. He should have insisted on seeing his sister.

Suddenly, however, papers were drawn up demanding that his and Helen's shared wealth be divided. They had never concerned themselves with such legalities, as he never would have left her wanting for anything, and he believed their inheritance to already be theirs. Still, he did as he believed she wished, though confused and grief stricken that his sister had somehow grown angry and distrustful of her only blood relative and friend. Yes, they were friends. Confidants. She was the only person in the world who understood him.

She died a year later.

She'd fallen down those same stairs he should have climbed to save her. He understood completely and suddenly that Judson had pushed her. Ignored and disbelieved by authorities, he went to Judson and accused him of murdering his sister. That he had been able to take all his sister's inheritance infuriated Harper. Still, he would have given the man all his own money for one last conversation with Helen, one moment in which they both reminisced and laughed about something from their childhood.

Judson denied the accusations. And then the Brit got the authorities involved, and Harper was not even allowed at Helen's funeral. He found out later that she'd been pregnant when she died, and this brought on a consumptive, murderous rage.

He could no longer eat or sleep. It felt as though a vicious animal were loose inside him or sitting on his chest at night. It wasn't long before he left his position at the university.

From this point forward, he read, traveled, and wrote, living the life of a stranger to everyone, even to himself. He decided life itself was an adversary. Grief infected him. It was black tipped and suffocating. Drinking himself to death seemed the only cure. One night in Denver, he was on his fourth bottle of rye whiskey when Breen Dwyer's father, Duncan Dwyer, took the glass from his hand and ushered Harper to his home, where he could sleep off the poison. For a week, Harper had stayed with the cowboy, who seemed to him the most straight-talking man he'd ever met.

When he'd spoken about what had happened to his sister, Duncan Dwyer was adamant that neither liquor nor death could cure him. The only real cure was an eye for an eye. "Some ramble on about forgiving and forgetting," the cowboy had said. "I say make your enemies regret, and then make them regret some more."

So, when Harper learned what had happened to Judson Horner's second wife, Flossie Abbot, he traveled to California, followed the trial, and then became determined to not only save her but finally extract justice for the murder of his sister.

"Helen," Flossie said, staring into the fire. "Judson told me about her. He said she was a drinker. Fell down the stairs and killed his child. Made me feel sorry for *him*."

Harper rose and turned his back to her. "My sister did not imbibe spirits." It was all he could think of to say.

"I'm sure she didn't. But, if she did, I would not blame her. Judson Horner is not only diabolical, his blood running on pure greed, he is tedious in nature. When he walked into a room, the hairs on my skin would raise from the mere sound of his voice."

"I found a flask that belonged to Horner in Kane's belongings. I then had a conversation with his cellmate, Pike, the convict you had in the Hole upon my arrival to Gila after his partner, Quanto, attacked a guard in the quarries and was killed for it. Kane had confessed to both that Horner had paid him two thousand five hundred dollars in advance to kill you and was to pay him another two thousand five hundred after the deed was done. That's why Kane didn't stray far from Gila Territorial and tracked you here. With your money and my sister's money, five thousand isn't a lot to Judson Horner. It's merely an investment."

Flossie looked as if she couldn't breathe. "Why would he want me dead? Wasn't the idea of me penniless and rotting in prison enough?"

"Men like Judson Horner want complete destruction of women who don't return their affections. I'm confident this is what happened to my sister. And what nearly happened to you."

He expected she might cry, but her face hardened. The only reaction he saw was her fingers trembling.

"So, we will travel to Tucson," he said. "And you will turn yourself in."

She paused and looked into the fire. "I will do no such thing."

"You will also tell the authorities the truth. That he beat you. He did beat you, yes?"

She nodded. "But men have that right."

"They don't have the right to then kill you, which is what that man did to my sister and what he planned to do to you. The law doesn't allow for that. And decency doesn't allow for the other."

"It should not."

"A good man would not beat on his beloved," Harper said. "What really happened to your piano player?"

"Judson shot him in the neck, as the trial revealed. What the jury didn't know is that Matty was trying to protect us. Still, the courts believed that Matty had been shot in self-defense."

"What they saw was a rich socialite who became an entertainer having sexual affairs. And Horner knew the public would find this disdainful. He understood he could get away with anything. And that is what he's done. To you. And to my sister. And it will end now. I have clear proof he hired Kane."

"Quanto's dead," she said. "No one will believe Pike. And Kane could have stolen the flask."

"I have clear proof," he repeated.

"Something other than Pike's paltry word and the flask?"

His jaw hardened as he nodded. "You must understand, I've had Judson Horner followed for a while now. This is why I paid Breen Dwyer to protect you and break you out of there."

CHAPTER TWENTY-SIX

His time at the prison now seemed endless. Accustomed to nights on the town, gambling and then spending his winnings on the youngest whore available, Dobbs felt he would go insane if forced to spend another night in the sickening stench of Agnes and Samuels's dull cottage.

Despite his dalliances with the remaining female prisoners, Wilhelmina and Jesus-Marie, who easily complied with his wishes in exchange for a bath, he was both restless and bored. The prison was in shambles. Half the guards had quit, and nearly fifty prisoners had vanished, along with Flossie Abbot and the incompetent Breen Dwyer. Dobbs couldn't spare his own deputies to search for any of the lot, because they had been pulled from their duties in town to serve as temporary guards over the remaining incorrigible prisoners. They had already experienced one riot, during which the gallows burned to ashes, and two more escape attempts were made. His only moments of pleasure were his lusty encounters with the two women and being able to man the giant Gatling while sipping on Samuels's stash of bourbon. Known in the county as a teetotaler, he always relished time alone to imbibe.

Other than that, it had all been dreadful. And he was counting down the days until the new superintendent would arrive.

He was sitting down for a cup of well-earned tea when Corn rushed in with more news. Evidently, the puddle-brained guard Muldoon had a mishap while attempting to pull someone up

237

from the Snake Den. Prisoners had been rotating in and out of the Hole on a steady basis. Now, it seemed one particularly nasty prisoner had yanked Muldoon down inside with him. As the guard fell, he bashed his head on the trapdoor.

"Muldoon's got a bigger fear than most of the Hole, and he's screaming for his mama down there. The blow to his noggin must've knocked his sense loose because I can't get him to come out. He's curled up in a corner mumbling to himself and bleeding from the gash on his head.

"Where's the prisoner who pulled him in?" Dobbs asked.

"He scrambled out and ran off into the yard. We've been trying to catch him."

"Did you not chain him?"

Corn gave Dobbs a look that entertained insubordination. "Can't chain them, what with so many coming and going. Takes too long. I say we shut the durn thing down until we got the herd under control. Right now, it's getting hard to spare a guard. And now I got Muldoon down there."

"Muldoon's a lunatic." Dobbs thought all the guards were lunatics, but Muldoon seemed dafter than most.

"Well, he's an awfully loyal guard. Didn't quit on me like the rest of them. About the only one I trust. I can't say that about many who work here, especially them new ones."

"Leave him be," Dobbs said. "He'll come out when he's ready."

Corn shook his wide head. "I'm afraid he might end up on the little end of the horn if we let him be."

"Little end or big, I will not risk a single guard going inside after him. He will either emerge on his own or die down there. It is his choice, is it not?"

"I dunno. Muldoon, well, he's a young fella. We should probably fish him out."

"Leave him be, goddamnit!" Dobbs clutched the nearest

item, one of Agnes's fragile vases, and chucked it at the wall.

Christ H. hobbled into the parlor with the hounds at his heels as the shards tinkled to the floor. "Apologize for disturbing you, sir, but I got news."

Dobbs spun toward him, his fists clenched. "What the hell's happened now? And get those filthy dogs out of here!"

"One of your men is coming in the sally port . . . got himself an escapee. Found her on the side of the road, walking this way."

"What is your meaning!?" Dobbs nearly shrieked. "Someone who managed to rid themselves of this hell hole is actually returning?"

"Why, yes, sir. I believe that's it," Christ H. said. "Sure looks that way."

Flossie stared into the brass-framed, cloudy mirror of her room in the Congress Hall Saloon. Her face was sunburned to the point of blistering. She had lost so much weight, her eyes had retreated, and her cheekbones were as sharp as beaks.

When Dwyer walked in without knocking, she didn't turn. She hadn't spoken to him since discovering what his real job had been at Gila and hadn't planned on speaking with him ever again.

"Harper Jones has arranged a meeting tomorrow. He's turning himself over to authorities, same as you."

She didn't answer.

"I should have told you sooner. I wanted to. My father always said it was best to lay the food out and let people pick and choose what they might eat rather than hide it in the kitchen. I didn't follow his advice and should have."

She wished he would leave. Every time he was near her, she felt as if she would dissolve like a dead wasp's wing.

"I had a job to do. Was hired on to watch over you. Was only there for you. That's true. And it wasn't love at first sight, believe you me, though you might be the prettiest woman I ever saw. I don't know what you thought of me. But I was watching over you and waiting on Harper's word to break you out. As it turned out, all the money in the world couldn't—"

"All the misery I felt involving you, and you were simply doing it for money."

"No, didn't go like that," he said. "You know that. It didn't turn out the way I'd planned."

She stared at her hands and concentrated on keeping her voice steady. "Not how it turned out? You helped me escape for money. For a wage."

"It wasn't for the money. You got to trust my word."

"Oh, I'm certain it wasn't. I'm certain our little mornings in the tent encouraged you as well."

"You listen here!" he shouted. "I did it for more than money. Whatever else happened between us is separate."

Flossie turned back to the mirror.

"You're making this harder than it ought to be. You make everything tough. You made this whole job near impossible with all your tongue lashings. I've known bulls easier to handle."

"Now I'm livestock. I am simply a cow in a herd. Is that correct?"

"It's not like that," he said. "No, it ain't like that at all."

"I thought you were my knight in shining armor, but you were simply a hired hand."

"You're an impossible woman and a cussed, sharp tongued shrew. I risked my life a dozen and a half times, trying to save your hide, and not for the money, no ma'am."

"A shrew? My hide? You and Harper Jones are dragging me back to prison or to some asylum if Judson Horner has his way. I do not deserve your insults. I see it all very clearly. You are Harper's henchman, someone to carry out his secret agenda.

And I am merely a pawn." She spun toward the window and watched the women in their beautiful dresses and flowered hats walk down the wide dirt street. He caught her arm, and she shook him off and glared.

"Flossie." His voice was calmer. Lower. "Harper Jones isn't the enemy, and I'm not either. Hell, he'll likely end up back at the Sand Castle for releasing all those prisoners. He's got more to lose than you."

"Doesn't mean I won't be there with him."

"I'll never let you go, not to the prison or anywhere, without me by your side."

"You'll be there, too! We'll all be there."

He looked unsure for a moment. "I'm not going to let that happen."

"I wish I could go home," she said. "I want more than anything to be back in San Francisco."

"We don't have much choice but to go forward. Could lead to a pardon. So we can't head to the city yet."

"Not we. *I.* I want to go home. Just me. Alone. With none of you to remind me of that dreadful prison, this dreadful life, this dreadful me."

Dobbs's deputy, a rather inept dolt by Corn's standards, brought Jo into the parlor. She looked as though she'd been rolled in mud and was skinny as a weed. But she planted her tiny government-issued shoes across from the sheriff and looked him straight in the eyes.

"You gonna toss me in the Snake Den?" Jo asked. "Wouldn't mind a bit. Need some rest."

"The Snake Den's occupied," Dobbs said. "But, of course, most certainly, you will be spending quite a number of days down there, I imagine."

Corn had already fetched a broom from the kitchen and was

busy cleaning up the glass. Jo moved her feet, so he could sweep the shards from that part of the floor.

"Where are the others?" Dobbs asked the deputy.

"Weren't no others, sir. She's the only one I found."

"Where are the others?" the sheriff repeated.

"Don't know. Only got the one. She was headed on back this way, anyhow. Told me she needed a ride. I didn't even cotton to the fact she was one of the escapees until we rode on through the sally port. I had it in my mind she was set on visiting her son or something of that nature."

"You're a fool to return to this hell hole," Dobbs said to Jo.

"I don't like living a life that's not my own or having to look over my shoulder with every dang noise. Don't like traveling about either. I like living in one place and knowing what I can expect from a day, good or bad. I also got folks here that are more like kin to me than any kin I had before. Didn't like the idea of never seeing them again. And, when I die, even if it's by hanging, the last thing I want to see are their faces," Jo stated firmly. "And if you are all done here, I'd like to have a word with the man in charge, since your deputy told me old Samuels is buried in the bone yard."

"I'm in charge," Dobbs said.

Jo looked to Christ H. and Corn, who both nodded.

"The good Lord wouldn't put a varmint like you in charge of my prison. No, sir. Where's the new superintendent? It's my right."

Christ H. stifled a giggle as the sheriff's already plum complexion deepened a shade. "I am in charge," he said. "Ask the guards, old lady, if you don't believe me."

Again, she looked to Corn.

"Yep. Afraid so," he said. "But a new one's arriving at the end of the month. That's the word."

"Well, then, suppose I best start working. I'm sure everyone here needs a good hot meal. My guess is that you all have let my kitchen go to the dogs. It'll need a harsh scrubbing."

Both Corn and Christ H. smiled with relief. They hadn't eaten well, nor had any of the prisoners, since Jo had left.

"What in Sam Hill are you two oafs grinning for?" Dobbs asked. "Do you honestly believe I would allow this escaped convict to automatically resume her privileged post in the kitchen? What do you take me for?"

Corn dropped the remains of the vase into the trash.

"First, she will tell me the whereabouts of her co-conspirators. I would like to have everyone home again. That would be a fine welcome for the new superintendent. A proper reception would be proper information regarding those who left these walls with you."

Jo stuck out her chin. "Sheriff Dobbs, I ain't gonna utter a word about my fellow travelers. Nope, not one word. You can toss me on down in the Dark Hole from now until eternity, and I still won't be speaking on those matters."

"I'm interested in more than your fellow travelers. I also insist upon knowing where Flossie Abbot got off to, and I need to know now!" With this, he slapped Jo's lined face with the palm of his hand.

Jo recoiled but didn't speak in her defense.

Corn had taken all the sass he could handle from Dobbs, who was nothing but a leaky-mouthed dandy in his opinion. One quick yet powerful jab to the sheriff's temple, and Dobbs was sprawled on the floor. With Dobbs unconscious, and the deputy riding off on his horse as fast as the pony could take him, Christ H. and Corn gently escorted Jo to the Dark Hole.

The night before, Dwyer had dreamed of crows falling out of the sky, landing on Flossie's body, and, when they lifted off, nothing was left of her. He didn't know why he dreamed of crows, but he didn't like them much on earth, and the dream variety were twice as bad.

He'd already knocked twice on her door. He'd brought a breakfast up: eggs, toast, some thick bacon, and a large glass of cold milk. Today was the day she would be turning herself in and the day Harper Jones would present the evidence against Judson Horner. Dwyer would stay by her side no matter how much she disliked him. He knew that much.

If he doubted at all that she would be fully pardoned, he wouldn't have taken the risk. He would have led her out of the hotel and fled to Nogales, where they'd both be fugitives for the rest of their days. But he was sure. Jones had enough concrete evidence to send Horner to the gallows. And, fortunately, Jones had enough money to keep the owner of the Congress quiet about who their lodgers really were.

Dwyer knocked again, and she answered. Her hair wet from a bath and freshly combed, she was dressed in the undergarments he'd bought her for the trip. "I know you're not much for speaking to me these days," he said, "and I've run out of things to say or do to get you to, so I'll just talk at you like I'm thinking out loud."

He set the food down on the room's table and watched as she embraced her own body, as if guarding herself from a chill.

"Oh Jesus, Floss. I'm sorry for those things I said. Sorry for it all." He gathered her up. Couldn't help himself. She didn't wrench away. Just wept. "I know you've been through it. But you got to know me and Jones are working to help you." Pulling her down on the bed, she didn't resist. Now side by side, he faced her and with all his might tried to convince her into believing in him. It was only after he told her about the crow dream did it seem she was coming around.

He kept talking after that, as if he'd been saving up all his thoughts and words and had to get them out before she stopped him.

Then she touched his face, and he ran his finger down the scar on her arm.

"Have you read *The Count of Monte Cristo*?" she asked.

It was a strange question after he'd spilled his heart out to her. "Afraid I haven't read very many books. I'm not as smart as you, as you already guessed."

"I hadn't guessed any such thing."

He slipped the cotton off her freckled shoulder, then pulled her toward him, burying his head in her hair, which smelled of lemons. They didn't have long, but he didn't want to talk about books. He figured the mattress might serve them better than their tent's dirt floor, and he guessed by the way she was looking at him, she felt the same.

"He won't come out," Corn said. "Nothing we tried has worked."

"He crawled into a corner and won't move," Christ H. added, sucking on one of his hand-rolled cigarettes.

Jo got down on her hands and knees and stuck her head inside. "Muldoon!"

Silence met her call.

"Muldoon, it's me, old Jo. Come back to cook for you. Gonna head over and fix up chicken and dumplings with peas."

She was hoping all the ingredients would be there for the guard's favorite meal; but if they weren't, she'd make something else sure to please him.

"Don't that sound tasty, Corn?" she loudly asked.

"Mighty tasty," Corn answered, just as loud.

"Come on out, Muldoon. I need someone to fetch my wood, and I ain't gonna have no one do it but you. Hell nearly broke out last time I set one of these convicts to the task."

"Jo?" a voice croaked from the black space below.

"That'd be me," she said. "Now come on out of there and greet me proper, you dang fool."

"They caught you?" he hollered up, his voice stronger.

"No, I came back for you boys. Came on home to cook you up those chicken and dumplings you love so much. Come on out of there, Muldoon. The good Lord won't stand your foolishness for too much longer."

She and the others stood at the trap door and listened as Muldoon crawled toward the light. "That's a good boy," Jo said. "Come on up here and give me something to smile on."

"I just need the rope ladder, is all."

Corn and Christ H. rolled down the ladder and yanked Muldoon out, his hair disheveled, his uniform creased with dirt and sweat.

"Land sakes," Jo said. "You look like death, and you smell like a tomb, but I am sure glad to see you. I sure am."

Muldoon wrapped her up in his arms and rested his head on her shoulder.

"Look what you gone and done, son. You made an old woman cry. But I always did enjoy a few tears of joy. I always did."

Jo didn't let the moment last for long. Wouldn't look good for Muldoon to be carrying on like this. She headed toward her kitchen with Muldoon following. When he went to fetch her wood, she began to search for what she'd need to prepare a meal. There wasn't much to work with, but she'd settle on some bacon potato soup and biscuits. She searched through the drawers for her best knife in order to slice some onions and potatoes but couldn't find it anywhere.

Dobbs hadn't decided whether or not to fire Corn. Resting in the cottage, nursing on bourbon, he dwelled on the idea. He needed the head guard to run the prison. And he was certain if he let Corn go, many guards would quit in protest, and he'd be left with a bigger calamity than he currently had. Still, a man cannot be allowed to strike the town's sheriff. For that matter, he was Corn's supervisor. He was the interim superintendent, after all. Corn had to be summarily discharged. Dobbs had no choice. He would carry out the termination in the morning.

For now, he needed to enjoy himself. He'd head over to the women's cellblock and try out some positions with Wilhelmina. Her body was supple, and he liked the size of her breasts. Her nipples were the color of peaches, and they tasted fine in his mouth. Tucking a flask of bourbon in his pocket, along with the ring of prison master keys, he grabbed a lantern and headed out into the dark. Only one guard was posted on the catwalk and hadn't seemed to notice him walking toward the women's cellblock. Even if the guard had noticed, what could he have said? Dobbs was in charge. He could do whatever he pleased.

And he would be very pleased to see Wilhelmina nude while he fondled her and found other new and painful ways to pleasure himself inside of her.

When he reached her cell, he saw that she was asleep. He whispered her name, but she didn't move, and her back was to him. Though the night was warm, she was curled up on the cot like a dog. He let himself into her cell quietly. He would surprise her. He would undress and ready himself before waking her.

With all his clothes off, he stood nude over her in the dark. He bent over to touch her shoulder and let his hand slide to her young breast.

When she swung around with the butcher knife in her hand, her teeth gritted, he stepped back quickly. He had the urge to run but couldn't run through the prison naked. How could he fight her off and put on his trousers at the same time? This ridiculous thought blended with excruciating pain when she rushed forward, stabbing him in the heart. He didn't die with the first stab. So he tried to crawl away, but she knocked him on his back, straddled him, and laughed hysterically as she stabbed him over and over in the chest, and the world simply came to a stop, as if someone had buttoned up the sky and set a glass jar over all the sounds he had ever heard.

CHAPTER TWENTY-SEVEN

The world was bigger than she remembered, or she, smaller. Maybe the tall men, one on either side of her, were causing this sensation of smallness. She caught a scent of rich beans and chile, then side-stepped a pile of fresh manure left by the carriage that had passed them a block before. She listened to the sounds of merchants and neighbors and children, their voices together seeming like a melody. She noticed how warm it was. Not as warm as Gila, though. The sun here hovered gently rather than bearing down like a fire-dipped sword. Now she heard two women chatting about seeds. She heard another calling out in Spanish to her young daughter, who'd run too far ahead.

She wished she had the child's confidence. Or even some of Breen's. She wondered if the crows in his dream really would take her away. Away from him. Away from freedom. Take her back to the Sand Castle, a place that felt like nowhere. By going to prison, she'd left the world and entered herself. Her memories. Thoughts. Nightmares and dreams.

Outside the prison and outside herself, the world had its own surprising stories and corners. She didn't know what would happen when they reached the sheriff's office. Or what might happen in the short walk there. Anything could occur at any time. The world outside herself she could never own or control. That's what made it terrible and wonderful. That's where she decidedly wanted to live.

249

Meyer Street soon turned into Main. Harper Jones stopped on the corner, in front of what looked like an open-air chapel. Adobe bricks formed a church wall, and at least a hundred half-melted candles of many colors were positioned in the cove the half wall created. Looking closer, she saw small, rolled-up notes wedged into crevices between the bricks, and a red and turquoise festoon draped an iron candle holder in the corner.

"The Wishing Shrine. *El Tiradito*," Jones explained.

Breen hung back, as if he wanted nothing to do with the large shrine. But Flossie wondered about it.

"It's a shrine to a sinner who was buried on unconsecrated ground," Jones told her. "An adulterer, slain by his lover's husband. If you make a wish, light a candle, and it burns all night, your wish will come true, or so I've been told."

She didn't have any candles. "I'll have to rely on more than wishing."

He nodded. Paused to light a candle of his own that he pulled from his overcoat pocket. Then began heading south. She and Breen followed.

On the walk, Flossie started thinking again about *The Count of Monte Cristo,* how Edmond Dantès, like herself, was wrongfully imprisoned. She couldn't recall for how many years, but he did finally escape. After being sewn into a burial shroud, he was cast into the sea. He nearly suffocated before he was able to tear out of it. His character had to die before he could be set free. She wondered if this would be true for her, too. After she died, she wondered if anyone would light candles for her or leave her notes.

They'd stopped in front of a building with thick adobe walls and iron bars on several of the windows. The narrow porch she stepped up onto seemed too delicate a timber for the building's solid walls.

She paused and looked at Breen, who nodded quickly. He

didn't show any fear, but she knew he'd hide that from her, despite what he might be actually feeling.

Without hesitation, Harper Jones urged them inside. Perhaps she should have found a candle to light or at least left a note at that shrine. But what would her note say? *Please bring me justice. Don't send me back to prison. Don't let the crows take me.*

Breen held her close to him while Harper Jones spoke with the sheriff. She was staring at a "Wanted" poster of Geronimo—the reward set at one thousand dollars—when he whispered: *I won't be letting you go. Ever.*

Perhaps she could count on this man. She should, at the very least, try.

EPILOGUE

Under the spotlight, wound tightly in a long, ruby-encrusted gown with a marvelous ribbon-adorned hat framing her heart-shaped visage, Mrs. Flossie Dwyer, once renowned as the Flame, stole the very hearts of San Francisco with her meadowlark's voice and sultry dance. After she twirled the chiffon cane, as is her custom, a roar louder than an avalanche was the audience's applause.

Fully pardoned, the Flame is back amongst us and has not lost the flair and personal attraction that drew thousands to see her perform in years past. An opera glass fixed on her may perhaps reveal minute traces of her years and ordeal with convicted murderer Judson Horner, but the hair is still glorious, flouncing down the snowy-white shoulders like a festoon of tangerine-hued daylilies. She remains poised, and one cannot call her matronly yet, despite her married state.

This writer had the pleasure of speaking with this intriguing woman backstage, and she met me, a stranger, as an equal. Her beauty was blinding, but she acted as if she were as plain as a harvested field. The Flame warms your heart with her generous nature. In her own words, Mrs. Dwyer remarked on the injustice she had so willfully survived.

"Injustice strikes those less deserving than I," she said.

When Mr. Breen Dwyer arrived backstage, the affection bridging the newlyweds incited a blush from this writer, as did the genuine sentiments exchanged.

In short, never have we seen such enthusiasm more fervid and

252

absolute than what Mrs. Dwyer has stirred. Show after show, her houses have not only been filled to capacity, but those ardent thousands of fans seem to have been aroused by a feeling of vested interest in her welfare.

The incomparable Flame has no peer. This writer will not soon forget her.

—The California Tribune, 1888

ABOUT THE AUTHOR

K. S. Hollenbeck is a native of the West. Growing up in the Sierra Nevadas, she went on to study English literature at Chico State, where she served as a judge for the Flume Press Chapbook Contest. She earned her MFA at University of California, Riverside, and has worked as a professor of English literature, history of the West, theatre, Shakespeare, and creative writing. She's the author of *Closet Drama* (Bear Star Press, 2001) and has published work in more than thirty literary magazines, including *The Sonora Review, Puerto del Sol,* and *Willow Springs.* She currently lives with her husband—whose family have been ranchers in southern Arizona for nearly a century—a mile from Joshua Tree National Park.

The employees of Five Star Publishing hope you have enjoyed this book.

Our Five Star novels explore little-known chapters from America's history, stories told from unique perspectives that will entertain a broad range of readers.

Other Five Star books are available at your local library, bookstore, all major book distributors, and directly from Five Star/Gale.

Connect with Five Star Publishing

Visit us on Facebook:
  https://www.facebook.com/FiveStarCengage

Email:
  FiveStar@cengage.com

For information about titles and placing orders:
  (800) 223-1244
  gale.orders@cengage.com

To share your comments, write to us:
  Five Star Publishing
  Attn: Publisher
  10 Water St., Suite 310
  Waterville, ME 04901